MAXIMUM DEEVOR

McKENZIE FILES
BOOK 4

MAXIMUM DEEVOR

McKENZIE FILES
BOOK 4

BARRY K. NELSON

Maximum Deevor
The McKenzie Files Book 4
Copyright © 2020 Barry K. Nelson

Content Editor: Chance Settlemire
Copy Editor: Anita Gipson
Cover Art: Barry Nelson
Cover Design: Kristi King-Morgan and Macario Hernandez
Editor-in-Chief: Kristi King-Morgan
Formatting: Kristi King-Morgan

ISBN- 978-1-947381-28-5

Dreaming Big Publications
www.dreamingbigpublications.com

CHAPTER ONE

Deevor's mind was concentrating on only one thought as she was sitting on her black, metal chair among the long rods protruding from the top and bottom sections of the fusion reactor that she was within. Each rod glowing bright red as they bathed her with an energy that would be lethal to any lesser being. Even the dark, oval shaped helmet that she wore was feeding her power. The continuous, faint hum from the machine was filling her ears. The reactor's energy was radiating through her black breastplate armor of over-lapping scales and her blue leggings tucked into her black, knee-high boots. Her normally dark skin took on a red glow from the energy. Strands of her long, black hair were draped over her face, obscuring her glowing, yellow eyes. She parted her yellow lips, exposing her gnashing teeth. The reactor's energy was healing and strengthening her, giving her the power to carry out the sole mission that was on her mind: Destruction.

Deevor had lost all track of time while she was sitting here. Her mind focused on

the task of finding and destroying the three aliens

that she had fought just a few days ago. The ones that appeared to be human but were far more than what they seemed to be. The ones named Colin McKenzie, Kelly Lytton, and Diane Christy. Deevor was still finding it difficult to swallow her defeat at their hands. Ever since, she was seething with rage, her mind was driven by her hunger for revenge. She noticed that the hum from the reactor suddenly stopped. An indication that it's charging cycle was now over. She removed the helmet, leaving it hanging from its thick cable. She saw that the top section of the reactor began to rise while the bottom section was spreading apart. She rose from her seat and stepped out of the black, cube shaped device which was sitting in the middle of a large, circular room with a blue metallic floor and walls. She was greeted by a young man with long, blond hair, dressed in a hooded white rode. He was Halford Crayden of the mysterious organization known as the Gatherers. Like herself, Crayden and the Gatherers centered their lives around one prime goal: To free their lord and master, Kimdrack, from his exile in the dimension beyond mirrors and help him wage war against his fellow beings, the Dark Masters.

"We've arrived at the destination," Crayden informed Deevor.

Deevor responded with a nod. "Any signs of resistance activity here?"

"So far we have no indication that these outlaws are hiding among the populace," Crayden responded. "We'll begin monitoring all transmissions to see if we can pick up any resistance chatter. These people always manage to eventually give themselves away. And we'll also order the local authorities to turn over any resistance suspects for questioning."

Deevor scoffed at Crayden's proposal. "We have no time to be subtle. My own methods will be much more effective and will send a greater message to these people."

Deevor walked abreast with Crayden to a pair of metal doors. Both doors slid apart upon their approach and they stepped out into a circular corridor. They walked down the corridor until they approached a large, metal door with a small, glowing red keypad mounted to the right of the wall. Crayden pressed a key on the keypad and the left and right sections of the door slid apart with a low hum, exposing a view to the outside. Deevor stepped through the open doorway and leaped out from the huge, silvery, disk-shaped craft which was hovering several feet above a tall building. She rapidly fell and landed on her feet in a crouched position on the concrete surface of the building's roof. Her steely muscles easily absorbing the impact of her landing. Deevor stood and looked down at the hard surface beneath her feet. It was certain that, within this building, there were scores of humans dwelling below. In her current state of mind, it did not matter if they were collaborating with the resistance or not. The only fact that mattered was that they were all going to die.

Deevor's hands emitted a bright red glow. She aimed both hands down to the roof. A powerful burst of fiery energy blazed from her hands and burned into the concrete surface of the roof. The next second, there was a massive explosion. Deevor was enveloped by a cloud of flames and concrete debris but stood unharmed. She again aimed her hands to the roof and released a second blast of energy. She listened as the energy burned its way into the building, creating a series of loud explosions as it traveled down. Deevor disengaged her assault and stepped back from the flaming hole that she blasted into the building. From beneath her feet, she was able to hear the agonized screams of men and women on the floor below. The sounds of the humans screaming pleased her. She would be pleased to hear more of them before she was done here.

Deevor ran over to the edge of the roof. Without breaking her stride, she leaped off the roof and made a rapid fall, feet first, down to the street. With her super-human strength, she was able to dive from the top of the five-story building and land safely on her feet. She now had the perfect opportunity to inspect her handiwork. Huge billows of black smoke were rising from the broken windows of the red brick building's top floors. Her ears were still picking up the screams of the humans inside. Dozens of humans were now starting to rush out from the building's twin glass doors. A smirk appeared on Deevor's face. She raised her glowing hands and fired a blast of energy towards the doors. The attack incinerated the fleeing humans on contact and caused a powerful explosion when it struck the building.

With the building now ablaze, Deevor turned around and faced a small crowd of bewildered humans that had gathered across the street to observe her attack on the building. Deevor grinned, thinking that their curiosity would be costly. She raised her right hand and fired a blast of energy that engulfed the humans in a fireball. Deevor noticed that the other humans were now scattering and fleeing from the area, obviously comprehending the seriousness of the threat among them. Deevor laughed, knowing that their attempt to escape will be futile. She sent an energy blast at a group of humans that were running down the street. The blast incinerated the humans and continued traveling towards a tall, grey brick building. The destructive energy caused the building's entire bottom section to explode. The next moment, the entire building collapsed in on itself with a loud rumble of falling masonry, metal, and a rising cloud of thick grey dust.

Deevor did not end her assault there. From both

hands, she discharged a wide stream of energy down along six other buildings at the left sides of the street. Each one of them, demolished in a ball of fire. She let out a laugh of sinister glee and aimed her right hand at the automobiles that were parked at this side of the street. Her energy blast exploded eight of the vehicles in a swift motion. Deevor began to walk down the street. She aimed her hand at the line of vehicles that were parked on the left. She discharged a stream of firepower that exploded six of them on contact. She continued firing destructive streams of energy at more cars, buildings, and fleeing humans in sight as she began to casually walk down the street. She began to laugh at the carnage she was creating around her.

She then heard running footsteps approaching her from behind. Seconds later, the loud cracks of gunfire rang through her ears. She felt several projectiles striking against the back of her head. She spun around to see three men in green camouflage military uniforms firing at her with machine guns. She recognized them as members of the militia charged with protecting this region. She laughed at their paltry efforts to do her harm. The bullets from their weapons were a mere annoyance to her, but hardly a threat. To deal with them, she simply raised her right hand and discharged a burst of energy that blew all three men back several feet through the air while at the same time setting their bodies ablaze. As their bodies landed on the ground and rolled to a stop, she paused to watch them struggle to their feet, screaming in agony while burning to death.

Deevor had little time to continue observing the gruesome spectacle as three more armed militia men came rushing upon her from the left. More running footsteps and gunfire from behind. She spun to the left. A blast of energy from her hand engulfed the humans in a fiery explosion. She spun around again. The militia men behind her halted in their tracks and stopped shooting when they saw her raise her arm. A huge ball of energy, glowing red with an arcane fire, grew in front of her hand. Deevor waited until the energy ball grew to a length of three feet. Then she launched it forward. The flaming ball continued to rapidly increase its size as it soared forward. Within seconds, it reached the length of an automobile and continued growing. The militia men were unable to move fast enough to avoid it and were all incinerated on contact. The flaming ball burned its way through a car and a building before it detonated a block away. She watched from the distance as the resulting explosion, with a deafening boom, shattered an entire row of six tall buildings along that street. A giant ball of fire emerged from the area, growing into a towering mushroom cloud of flame and debris.

Deevor laughed with an evil joy at the destruction that she created. From the fires that were rising from the buildings in the distance she was imagining the faces of McKenzie, Christy, and Lytton. She was looking forward to seeing them all die slowly. Much more slowly than this city. From the corner of her right eye, she noticed several humans in the distance fleeing down the street. "Little insects," she hissed. None of them would escape her wrath. She strode over to a blue car and kneeled, placing her hands underneath the vehicle, then lifting it up over her head. With little effort, she hurled the car into the air towards the humans. The car flew down the street, traveling several yards before it bounced off the pavement and rolled over a fleeing man and woman. Their screams were brief as they were crushed to the ground and remained still. The car continued rolling down the street, striking a black pickup truck, then crashing into a building.

Deevor picked up another car and threw it at a third-floor window of a building across the street. It crashed through the brick wall, leaving a gaping hole in the side of the building. She jumped onto the roof of a white pickup truck, reared her head back, and let out a loud scream of rage. In her mind's eye, she could still see the faces of McKenzie, Christy, and Lytton. Her memories went back to their past battle. These aliens had beaten her. They humiliated her in the face of her great lord Kimdrack, and their interference prevented him from gaining his freedom from the dimension beyond mirrors. For those transgressions, she was determined to hunt all three of them down and make them suffer.

Deevor decided to deliver the endgame to this section of the city. She spread her hands out in front of her and released two separate orbs of glowing energy. From her right hand, yellow. From her left hand, red. She spread her hands further apart as the orbs continued to grow, from a basketball size to three feet in diameter. Deevor grinned as she gazed into the burning glow of both orbs. This was her most devastating weapon. Two opposing charges of energy that, when brought together, will produce a massive explosion and shockwave obliterating anything over the radius of a mile. She will survive the devastation. It was what she was designed for. But the lesser things, the buildings, the vehicles, and the people will all be consumed. Just as she will use this same power to consume McKenzie, Christy, and Lytton. Not delaying any further, Deevor brought her hands and the two charges of energy together.

CHAPTER TWO

Colin felt at ease as he sat upon the soft grass near the riverbank and watched the small group of young children fishing. After what he, Diane, and Kelly went through these past few days, he was appreciating the chance to enjoy a little peace and quiet. As well as the pleasant weather. The warm climate allowed him to wear a bright blue, short sleeved shirt along with his blue jeans and white sneakers. For the moment, Colin's mind wandered back to the titanic struggle that they went through with the powerful alien menace Deevor. She proved to be, by far, the most powerful enemy they have ever faced. If it were not for the help of Silas' wife, Ava, the task of defeating Deevor would have been much harder, if not impossible. After that struggle, they fled here to the resistance base located in the southern continent of Zalakar, where they could take the opportunity to rest and plan their next move.

The high-pitched sounds of laughter brought Colin's wandering mind back to the real world. One of the children, a blond girl wearing a bright green dress, ran over to Colin. She was beaming with a bright smile on her face, holding a fishing rod in one hand. In the other, she was holding up a blue, foot-long fish.

"Look McKenzie. Look what I caught," the girl told Colin.

Colin returned a smile to the girl. "Wow. Look at that. That thing is a monster."

"I'm going to take it home and get my mom to cook it for me," said the girl. "Fishing is fun. You should try it."

"I just might do that," Colin told the girl.

"Can you do a magic trick for me, Mr. McKenzie?" asked the girl.

"A magic trick?" said Colin, rubbing his chin. "I don't know."

"Please," the girl pleaded.

"Ok. Just a little one."

"Yay!" the girl shouted with glee. She turned to the other children at the riverbank and cried out, "Hey everybody! Mr. McKenzie is going to do a magic trick!"

The other children instantly dropped their fishing rods and ran over to Colin. Their loud cheers filled the air.

"Before I start, I'm going to need some water," said Colin, then looked at one of the children, "Would you please bring me some?"

A small, black boy wearing a blue shirt and pants ran over to the river and picked up a white, plastic bucket. He carefully leaned down to the riverbank and scooped the bucket into the river to fill it halfway with water. Holding both hands onto the bucket's metal handle, he ran over to Colin. The boy sat the bucket down before him. Colin stood up. He had a trick in mind he wanted to show the children. A feat they have not seen before.

"Now, this isn't exactly magic. This is just another way that my powers work," Colin explained to the children. "I create and control electrical energy. And that means I can also control any material that conducts electrical energy. That includes metals and liquids. Allow me to demonstrate."

Colin raised his right hand over the bucket. A few short arcs of electrical energy sprang out from his palm. In Colin's mind, he could feel his power coursing through the water. With his mental link to it easily established, all he had to do was issue a command. *Rise.* Colin watched as a two-foot-tall column of water began to rise out of the bucket. Colin issued another mental command. *Spin.* The column of water began to spin. Its tip forming into a point. Colin repeated the rise command. The spinning column of water continued to rise until it was hovering in the air above a now empty bucket. In Colin's mind, he visualized the shape of a sphere. In that instant, the liquid column took on a round shape. Colin's concentration was not broken by the children's chorus of "oohs" and "aahs." He visualized another shape in his mind. This time a cube. The ball of water reformed itself into a cube shape.

Colin heard footsteps coming from behind. He turned to see Diane approaching him. She was suitably dressed for this warm climate in her blue tank top, cut off blue denim shorts, and no socks with her blue sneakers. Her gun belt with her large laser pistol strapped to her side was standing out prominently.

Diane stopped close to Colin's right side and watched as he continued his demonstration to the children. "Watch this," Colin told them. The shape of a ring came to his mind. The liquid cube now changed into a swirling ring. The children all laughed as they watched small balls of water spring out from the ring and then float through it like mice jumping through a hoop. Colin was happy to hear the cheers and applause from the children, but now he felt that he had entertained them enough. He lowered his hand and the watery shapes dropped back into the bucket.

"That was great, Mr. McKenzie," exclaimed a smiling girl. "Can you do another one?"

Colin grinned. "Maybe later. Right now, Miss Christy and I have some business to take care of."

Colin watched as the children returned to the riverbank to resume their fishing. Their smiling faces reminded him of the abducted children from the town of Willoby. A dire fate waited for them if they were not soon rescued from the clutches of the Tritians.

"These kids love you," Diane told Colin.

"I think they love all three of us," said Colin. "We're different. They see something magical about us."

"It's not just the kids. It's the adults too," Diane pointed out. "They're looking at us as if we're some kind of heroes."

Heroes, Colin liked the sound of that. "We are heroes. I just hope that we can measure up to their expectations. We've got a rough road ahead of us."

"Speaking of rough road, Kelly thinks that he's finally got Val fixed."

Val, Colin thought. Their ship's robotic pilot that came with them to this distant quadrant of space. "Finally. We could certainly use Val's help."

Colin and Diane walked away from the river and headed towards the huge airbase where scores of resistance ships were parked in hangars. Including their own spacecraft, The Black Raven. They followed a paved road until they came to a tall, chain link fence with two black uniformed resistance soldiers standing at the left and right sides of the gate. The soldier on the left took out a small, black remote box from his pants pocket and aimed it towards the gate. With the press of a button, the automated gate began to slide open to admit Colin and Diane. Advancing further into the base, they passed by dozens of jet styled resistance ships, parked in long rows on the pavement. Inside the huge, olive-grey hangars were parked the larger fighter bombers. Colin and Diane passed by two hangars to reach the one where the Black Raven was housed. They entered the hangar through its wide entrance and came upon the black oblong vessel resting on its four thick metal legs. At the rear section of the ship, its two broad wings with their vertical fins left only ten feet of space between the left and right hangar walls. Underneath the ship was a lowered metal ramp.

The Black Raven sustained damage from a Tritian missile attack. The situation became worse when the ship was captured by the hostile humans of the Guydrun Unified Star Reich. Their technicians partially dismantled the ship's main engines, along with the robot Val. Colin was fortunate that Kelly had the technical knowledge to reassemble Val and the engines. It was also fortunate that Colin was able to use his power over electrically conductive material, in this case metal, to effortlessly restore the damage to the ship's hull.

Colin and Diane approached Kelly, who was working at a long white plastic table at the right side of the ship. Kelly was wearing nothing more than his black shorts and blue flip flop sandals. Beads of sweat had formed on his brow. He was standing next to the five-foot-tall, shiny, cylindrical form of the robot Val. Standing on its two, thick legs with large, round feet. It's four thin, metallic arms were hanging limp at the sides of its body. The three long fingers on each hand were immobile. There was a glowing red eye in the middle of its sphere-shaped head. Scattered across the table was a large collection of tools and electronic components.

Colin smiled when he saw the robot standing.

"Val. You got it standing. Please tell me that you've got good news, Kelly."

"Not just yet," said Kelly. "I'm just finishing up now. Putting Val back together wasn't easy. The Guydruns had it completely torn apart. And they even took some vital components."

Colin shuddered at the sound of that news. "How vital?"

"Watch," said Kelly.

Kelly picked up a dark, rectangular component from the table and inserted it into a slot on Val's back. He stepped back and then addressed the robot. "Hello Val. How are you feeling?"

Val's sphere head with its single red eye swiveled around to face Kelly. The robot responded to Kelly in its soft female voice. "I'm feeling fine. And you?"

"That all depends," replied Kelly. "Do you know me Val?"

"Yes. You are Kelly Lytton."

Kelly smiled. "Great. How about my two friends here?"

Val swiveled its head around to face Colin and Diane. "Yes. I know them. The male is Sergeant Colin McKenzie. The female is Captain Diane Christy."

Kelly nodded. "Great."

"Would you like some coffee?" Val asked.

"No thanks," said Kelly. "So, Val. How is your flight capability?"

"Flight capability? I have not been programmed to operate any aircraft. Would you like some tea? Did everyone have breakfast yet?"

"What's up with it?" Diane asked Kelly.

Kelly explained, "It's what I told you. The Guydruns took several vital components. Some of them were its memory chips. A lot of what it knew is gone."

The red light of Val's single eye began to fade. The robot leaned forward and then collapsed to the floor with a loud metallic clang.

Kelly explained further. "They also took it's fusion energy cell. So, I had to jury-rig a crude battery pack to keep Val working. I just need to fine tune it a bit more."

Colin heaved a sigh. "So basically, the Guydruns took all of Val's important parts and left us with a toaster. Those parts could be anywhere on this planet. That is, if they're even still on the planet. And we don't have time to look for them."

"Well then. I guess we can pretty much write Val off," Diane assessed. "Unless we need someone to make pancakes."

"So now the job as our full-time pilot is resting on your shoulders," Colin told Diane. "Do you think you can measure up?"

Diane laughed. "I brought us this far. Didn't I?"

The conversation was suddenly interrupted when Gaylie, dressed in her black resistance uniform, came running into the hangar, charging over to them. She stopped, taking a moment to catch her breath. "Guys. You have to come to the meeting hall. You really need to see this."

Colin, Diane, and Kelly accompanied Gaylie as she ran out of the hangar. They followed her across an airstrip and into another hangar where several other people were also heading. Inside the large building, they passed between two rows of long, wooden benches at their left and right to reach a crowd of men and women dressed in resistance uniforms and civilian clothes, all gathered in front of a wooden stage. Suspended just six feet above the stage was a large video monitor hanging by cables from the ceiling. As they were drawing closer to the stage they could see and hear what was on the monitor. The image of a dark-skinned female in black breastplate armor firing a blast of energy from her hands that caused a nearby five story building to explode into a fireball. She spun around and fired another blast, this time at a group of people who were fleeing from the area. The assault instantly incinerated them all in their tracks. She spun to her left and fired a blast of energy at a woman several feet away who was trying to get into a car to make an escape. The blast caused the car to explode, killing the woman in the process.

For Colin, there was no mistaking the identity of the monster that was responsible for this carnage. With a bitter tone, he spat out her name. "Deevor."

Gaylie, standing at Colin's right, gasped and raised her hands to cover her mouth. Colin could sense that the young girl was taking the horrific footage very hard, considering that she watched Deevor murder her sister Zoe. "Maybe you shouldn't be watching this," Colin advised her.

"No. I'm ok," replied Gaylie.

"Where the hell is this?" Diane asked.

A woman standing in front of Diane turned to answer. "This in in the city of Travallian. It's far up north from here."

"Look at those people. They don't stand a chance,' said a male voice from behind Colin.

For the next five minutes, everyone continued watching the footage of Deevor assaulting the city unopposed, slaughtering anyone in her sights as casually as any human would kill an insect. Finally, after hearing enough of the distressed cries from the crowd, Colin decided that he needed to act.

"I've seen enough," Colin said in a stern voice. He turned to Diane. "Get the ship ready. We're taking off."

Diane and Kelly followed Colin as he made his way through the crowd and exited the building. They only got a few feet away from the hangar when a familiar female voice was calling out their names. Colin turned to see Ava, accompanied by Gaylie, running over to them.

"Where are the three of you going?" asked Ava.

"We're going to Travallian to deal with Deevor," Colin told her.

"You can't," said Ava.

Colin could not believe Ava's objection. "What do you mean we can't? We must. Didn't you see what's going on back there? Deevor will destroy that entire city if we don't stop her."

Colin turned and tried to walk away, but Ava darted in front of him and barred his way. Holding her hands out in front of her.

"You can't go. You mustn't," Ava insisted. "There is nothing that the three of you can do. If you go and confront Deevor now, then you will die."

Colin stared at her perplexingly.

"You can't fight Deevor here. On her terms. She's much too powerful, even for the three of you. You can't fight her here."

With the memory of their last encounter still fresh in his mind, Colin knew that there was much truth in what Ava was saying. He also knew that another confrontation with Deevor was inevitable. "Well what are we supposed to do? Just stand around and watch videos of her destroying the planet one city at a time until she finds us?"

"I don't like the situation any more than you," Ava countered. "This is my world. These are my people. I would love to see Deevor and her compatriots all pay for their crimes. Don't forget that she murdered my daughter. But now is not the time. You will know when it comes. It will be tragic, filled with death and chaos, but that will be your chance to strike back at her."

"Is this another one of your predictions?" asked Kelly.

Ava nodded. "Yes. Some things I can see clearly. Others I cannot. But what I can see clearly is your deaths if you leave now. The three of you are valuable friends and allies to us. I can't begin to tell you how much the resistance appreciates all that you have done. We can't afford to lose you. So, I'm asking you not to go. Please."

Colin lowered his head and stared at the ground as he pondered Ava's words. He raised his head and looked over at Diane and Kelly. He could interpret the frowns on their faces as a willingness to stop Deevor's reign of terror, but despite their best intentions, Colin wanted all three of them to survive. Colin turned back to Ava and revealed his decision. "Alright. We'll play it your way. I just hope you're right."

Ava heaved a sigh. "Thank you."

"Besides, we've got a more important mission on our plate to deal with. The missing children," said Colin.

"The Children of Willoby," replied Ava. "I think we might have a lead on them. One of our contacts in a city far up north claims that he knows some people who can track all Tritian activity through this sector. This might be a big help."

This news aroused Colin's interest. "Where are these people?"

"They're in the city of Devarow. It's located on a large continent to the northwest called Potsdam," Ava explained. "It will take us less than an hour to fly there."

Colin was leery about traveling to an unknown location on this war-ravaged planet. "Potsdam? How safe is this place? The Tritians and Guydruns could be there waiting for us."

"We don't have to worry about the invaders. From what our intelligence told us, Potsdam is one of the many areas on this planet that the Gatherers have restricted the enemy's access. They're forbidden from staging any large-scale attacks, but there's still the danger of dealing with enemy spies and assassins. And the Guydruns have a token military presence in several cities there. So, we'll still have to move carefully."

Colin pondered this information, as well as the unanswered questions popping up in his mind. "It's scary knowing that the Gatherers can dictate how the Guydruns and Tritians can move on this planet. It sort of makes me wonder what capabilities they have besides having a monster like Deevor watching their backs."

"We've already seen how technologically advanced the Gatherers are. Much of their technology comes from Kimdrack," Ava explained. "The same technology that they've been using to try and free him from his imprisonment. They will not stop until they've achieved this goal."

"We stopped them once. We can stop them again if need be," Colin's reply. "But in the meantime, our priority is getting those kids back. Ok, then. We'll go meet with these contacts of yours. I just hope this won't be a waste of our time."

Ava smiled. "I'll go get a few things before we leave. We can take your ship if you like."

Colin nodded. "We can all go in the Black Raven."

Ava, joined by Gaylie, turned and walked off.

Colin turned back to Diane and Kelly. Diane, with her hands balled up into fists and resting on her hips, confronted Colin. "Are you nuts? Are we just going to run and hide from that bitch while she tears this planet apart looking for us?"

"I don't like the situation as much as you do," Colin's stern reply, "but Ava is right. Facing Deevor on her terms will be suicide. We were barely able to beat her the first time, and that was under special circumstances. It's different now. She has no weaknesses. We'll just have to wait."

Colin turned and began to walk back to the hangar with the Black Raven. Diane and Kelly followed close behind him.

"So, we're going to rely on Ava's psychic predictions for our intel?" Kelly asked Colin.

"She's been right so far," Colin returned. "We just need to have faith in what she says."

"I do believe in what she says, but I don't like the idea of running from a fight." Diane told Colin.

"I have to remind you that our mission here isn't to get into fights with anybody. Our mission here is to find the missing task force ships," Colin stated. "This isn't our war, but now we're stuck in the middle of it. So our priority right now is getting those kids back from the Tritians."

"I agree," Diane's reply. "So, what do we do after that?"

Colin's mind recalled Captain Melony Carter's words to them on the day they embarked upon this deep space mission. "That's easy. We try not to screw up."

CHAPTER THREE

Sitting in the co-pilot's seat at Diane's right inside the Black Raven, Colin was still feeling apprehensive about meeting with Ava's resistance contact. They were entering a strange city on another continent to possibly face any unknown threat that would pop up without warning. But he was hoping that this effort will pay off for their mission to save the abducted children. Looking out of the cockpit's large, panoramic window, Colin took in the view of the ship flying over the blue waters of this planet's Posiedic Ocean. Diane was silent as she concentrated on her flying. He had to admit his surprise at Diane's proficiency in piloting the ship. So far, she was displaying a level of skill he never expected. If a conflict were to arise, he hoped that Diane had this same level of skill to get them through a battle with their lives. Leaving behind the now impaired Val at the resistance base in Zalakar, Diane would have to carry the full responsibility of their flying needs on her shoulders alone.

Colin turned and looked back at Kelly, seated at the ship's communications console, his eyes glued to its monitor. Sitting at the computer station at his right was Ava. She was giving Diane directions to reach Potsdam. Gaylie, with her machine gun slung over her shoulder, was standing behind Ava.

Colin looked at Ava. "So how much longer do we have to go before we reach Potsdam?"

"Just a few more miles," said Ava. "Just keep heading north. We should be there soon. We'll pass over the docks and reach the Devarow airfield near the coast."

"This airfield, will there be a problem with them allowing us to land?" Colin asked.

"Local air traffic is required to submit a valid flight ID code," Ava explained. "But don't worry. Even though your ship is alien they'll accept the military ID code that I gave Kelly."

The Black Raven continued its flight over the ocean for the next few minutes. Colin could see the shoreline coming into view. As the ship drew closer, the details of the scenery were becoming more defined. A long line of huge ships docked at a harbor. The grey forms of warehouses with large trucks parked in front. The Black Raven flew over the docks and approached a large grassy field. It flew over the field for several more minutes before it came to a tall chain link fence below. In the distance, the sight of a wide, grey runway could be seen.

As Colin continued watching the scene through the window, he heard Ava instruct Kelly to contact the airfield's flight control center with the information she gave him. Kelly's voice was clear and calm as he spoke.

"Devarow flight control, this is militia transport Black Raven. Militia ID Paladin, five, two, two, four, one, two. We are requesting permission to land on runway three. Do you copy? Over."

After a few seconds a female voice gave a response.

"Black Raven. This is Devarow control. Your ID is confirmed. You are cleared to land on runway three. Welcome. Hope you gave the bad guys some hell out there."

"Don't worry. We kicked our share of asses out there," was Kelly's reply.

Diane reduced the Black Raven's speed and brought it to a soft landing on a wide area between two small planes. With the ship now landed, Colin rose from his seat while Diane pressed the touchpads on the instrument panel to power down the ships systems.

"Alright. Where do we go from here?" Colin asked Ava.

"There should be a car waiting for us," Ava revealed. "From there we will ride into the city and wait to meet with our contacts. I must warn you that these people will be a bit suspicious of you three because you're strangers. Aliens. So, let me do most of the talking."

Colin saw nothing wrong with that stipulation. He gave a nod. "OK. We can do that."

"As long as things don't go south on us," Diane added.

"I'm sure you can put a leash on your bad temper until we find out what's going on," Colin told Diane.

They followed Ava and Gaylie out of the ship. After Diane used her data pad to activate a remote signal to close and lock the ship's ramp, they followed Ava across the runway and approached a large parking area where there were several vehicles sitting idle. Ava pointed to a blue car that was parked several feet away. There was a middle-aged, black male wearing a dark blue suit against the side of the car. His arms were folded against his chest. As the group got closer to this person, Colin noticed a smirk on the man's face that instantly aroused his suspicion. But despite this, Colin was willing to wait and see what this man's intentions were.

"Ava. It's been a while. Glad to see that you're

still in one piece," the man's greeting.

"It's good to see you too, Grant," Ava replied. "Everyone, this is Grant Wilson. He will be taking us to our contact in the city."

Grant switched his gaze from Ava to Colin, Diane, and Kelly. "So, who are your friends here?"

"This is Colin McKenzie, Diane Christy, and Kelly Lytton," said Ava. "And you already know my daughter Gaylie."

Grant unfolded his arms and walked closer to the group. "McKenzie, Christy, Lytton. I've heard those names before." Grant reached into his pocket and brought out a square, black device that resembled a data pad. He tapped a finger onto the device and then tapped it three more times. He swiped his finger over the device, then stopped a moment to study it. His eyes glanced over at Colin, Diane, and Kelly. He looked back to the device, then he looked at Ava. "According to this, you and your friends here have been red flagged by the enemy."

"Red flagged? What does that mean?" Colin asked.

Ava answered, "That means there's a high priority bounty on our heads."

"So what?" said Kelly. "I imagine that everybody in the resistance has a bounty on them."

"Yeah. But in this case, the enemy has your full names and individual photos. They know who you are," returned Grant. "And you're not only wanted by the Tritians and Guydruns, but apparently the Gatherers want your asses too."

To prove his point, Grant held out the device in his hand so that the group can see their images, including Ava's, in the temple of mirrors being displayed one by one.

After their recent events with the resistance, Colin was not surprised to hear this news. "No doubt pissed at us big time after we botched their plans in that temple of mirrors."

"The Gatherers usually don't get involved in the war, considering they have their own agenda. But if you've gained their attention, then you must have really done something to piss them off. Their people will be out looking for you. Taking you three into the city could be more dangerous now."

Diane moved towards Grant, bringing her face closer to the device in his hand. "God. That's an awful picture of me. I wish they hadn't used that. My hair looks a mess."

"Your bad hair day is the least of our problems," Kelly told her after rolling his eyes.

"I'm starting to think that taking you into the city is too big of a risk," said Grant to the group. "Since you're all red flagged, you'll practically stand out as if you're on fire. And the city is crawling with Guydrun agents."

"I know the risk. But we've come too far to turn back," Ava told him. "And this is too important. It's vital that we get this information."

Gaylie, clutching the weapon hanging from her shoulder, stepped up to her mother's side. "And we can take care of ourselves. So just let the enemy come and try us," was her bold statement.

The smirk was frozen on Grant's face as he silently stared back at the group. Then he revealed his decision. "Ok. I may catch hell for this, but I'll take you to Markus. But I'm only doing this for you, Ava. I just hope you know what you're doing."

Grant stepped to one side and opened the car's rear passenger door. With a smile, he extended his hand to the vehicle's interior, an invitation for the group to get inside. Colin, Diane, Kelly, and Gaylie all crammed themselves into the back while Ava got into the front seat to ride with Grant. Colin remained apprehensive but held his tongue until any serious problem reared its head. Grant sat down into the driver's seat and started the car. As it pulled off, Colin noticed a black car pulling out, following close behind them. He could see that it was carrying three men, two black and one white.

"There's a car following us," Colin said.

"Don't worry. They're with me," Grant's reply. "They're my back up. You don't think I'd come into a situation like this alone, do you?"

Colin had to agree. "Smart move."

Grant drove the car out of the parking area and past a wide, open metal gate. He steered to the left and headed down a street that was leading to the city of Devarow. Looking through the windshield, Colin could see a view of several tall buildings in the distance. His apprehension was still nagging at him. *Here we are, going blind into an alien city with enemy agents lurking about. Great way to start out our day here.*

The traffic on the street began to increase as the car was drawing closer to the city. The car merged with several other vehicles as they were coming from an intersection. When they entered the city, Colin was amazed as he looked out through the window to his left, noticing the similarities between this city and the ones in the United Protectorate. Even though most of the architecture of many buildings were not as advanced, he still felt as though he were back home. Then he remembered what he had learned during his brief stay on this planet. Everything appears this way because of Kimdrack's manipulation and using humanity as his personal laboratory experiment. The similarities in the language of both worlds, as well as that of the Brelac. And now without his direct influence, both worlds have progressed differently over the years. This world developing at a slower pace than that of the Protectorate. Colin wondered if there are other human worlds out in space and how they have developed in that amount of time.

The car stopped in front of a tall, circular building constructed out of gleaming metal. The black car stopped behind them. "We're here," Grant announced. He got out of the car.

Colin opened the passenger's side door and got out of the car, followed by the rest of the group. He looked up at the shining tower before him. It's multi-story structure reaching up to the sky. "This building certainly stands out. What is this place?"

"This is the Fenwig Building," Grant's answered. "Twenty-three floors of prime office space and the location of The Prime Kitchen on the twenty-first floor. The finest restaurant in town. This is where you will meet with Mr. Haggar."

"Markus Haggar. He owns the place," Ava added. "He's the man we want to see here. Remember, let me do the talking."

Colin looked behind him and saw that the three men from the black car, all wearing black suits, got out and began to follow the group as Grant led them to the wide, glass doors at the building's large circular entrance. Both doors slid open to admit the group. Inside the building's lobby, Colin took note that the flooring was smooth and reflective, much like the surface back at the temple of mirrors. *How can I not get a funny feeling about this?* was his thought.

Grant brought the group over to a circular, blue receptionist desk where three young men in blue suits were sitting. "Can you take care of the cars for me, Jimmy?"

One of the men quickly rose up from his seat. "Sure thing, Mr. Wilson."

As Jimmy was walking away from the desk, one of the other men spoke out. His hands hovering in front of a computer keyboard and flat screen monitor installed on the desktop. "I've logged you in,

Mr, Wilson. And I see Mrs. Johannon is here. I'll log her in. I don't recognize the others."

Grant turned his head to briefly glance back at the other members of the group. "The young lady here is Mrs. Johannon's daughter, Gaylie. The others here are Colin McKenzie, Diane Christy, and Kelly Lytton. Mr. Haggar is expecting them."

The man began to type the information on his keyboard. Then he looked up. "You'll have to check your weapons here before we allow you to go up."

Colin was able to accurately predict Diane's reaction to this demand. A grin appeared on her face and she shook her head. "Yeah. Like that's going to happen."

Even Gaylie shook her head. A sign of refusal. "I'm not giving up my weapon."

"Those are the rules," the man said.

Ava raised her hand as she looked back at Diane and Gaylie. "It's alright. We have to go by their rules if we want to see Markus. You'll get your weapons back when we're done."

Diane looked to Colin, to which he responded, "Just do it."

With a frown on her face, Diane unbuckled her gun belt with its holstered laser pistol from around her waist and handed it to the young man. Gaylie, receiving a nod from her mother, also surrendered her weapon.

Grant led the group past the receptionist's desk and over to a shiny metal wall where there were three wide elevator doors. Grant went to the middle elevator and pressed a button on the panel at its right. The door slid open and the entire group stepped inside. It took the elevator only a few seconds to reach the twenty-first floor. When the door opened, the group stepped out and found themselves in an elegant restaurant with shiny black and red floor tiles and round, glass tables. There were several people seated, eating their meals. A young man wearing a white suit and gloves approached Grant as the group exited the elevator.

"Mr. Wilson. Mr. Haggar is already seated on the balcony and waiting for you."

The group followed the man through the restaurant and out onto the balcony area where several people were also seated at tables there, dining in the open air. They came to a long, oval-shaped table. Sitting at its head was a middle-aged man with short, black hair, wearing a grey suit. He was using a white cloth to clean his glasses. He put them back onto his face and looked up at the group. Standing behind him were two young females wearing white suits, both with long, black hair tied into ponytails.

"Grant. Welcome back. And you've brought our guests. Everyone, please be seated."

The group took their seats at the table. The three black suited men all stepped a few feet away from the table and stood to keep a watchful eye on the others. Ava sat down at the man's left while Grant sat down at his right. Colin, Diane, Kelly, and Gaylie all sat down at the left side of the table with Ava. Colin glanced down at the place setting before him where a transparent plate with silverware rolled up in a light blue cloth napkin at its right laid. In front of the napkin was a glass goblet.

The man at the head of the table smiled and held up his hands. "Good afternoon, everyone. For those of you who don't know me, my name is Markus Haggar. I own this fine establishment, as well as this building. I hope you enjoy your stay here. You will find that the food here is second to none."

Grant turned to the white suited females standing behind him and raised his hand. One of them took a bottle of wine from a serving cart behind her and walked over to the group seated at the table to pour wine into their goblets. The other female took menus from the cart and handed one to each person.

"I highly recommend the scolapendras on the menu. They are most outstanding, cooked in the butter sauce," Markus suggested.

Colin was unfamiliar with the cuisine on this planet. "What are scolapendras?"

"A large insect found way up north," Markus explained. "They burrow into trees to make their nests. They're a bit hard to come by now with this war going on."

"I'll pass on eating bugs right now," replied Colin. "Maybe I'll pick something else."

"Your choice," said Markus. "And keep in mind that the meal is on the house. My treat. But before we do anything, I'd like to offer Ava my condolences for the loss of your daughter, Zoe. I am very sorry."

Ava frowned. "Thank you, Markus. She is in a better place."

"And then we come to your three friends here. Colin McKenzie, Diane Christy, and Kelly Lytton. Three off-worlders who have managed to piss off the Guydruns, Tritians, and the Gatherers all at once. You bringing them here places four red-flagged targets on my doorstep. It's enough that I'm taking a chance letting you come here, Ava, but bringing these three is a hell of a risk. All four of you are hot targets."

"I understand that. But as I've already told you, we have a desperate need for information that only you can provide," Ava told Markus. "We had to take the risk."

"Yes. You need my help to find a bunch of missing kids. A noble effort. And highly dangerous. You can't just waltz into a Tritian detention center and ask them to release their prisoners. Let alone make threats against them. For all you know, you might be committing suicide for a wasted effort."

"But we still have to try," Colin told him.

"I can't stop you. But keep in mind that my main priority is to protect my interests and my operation here," was the stern reply from Markus. "I have too much at stake risking it all for the sake of three off world strangers. I'll cut you loose if I sense that there is even the slightest threat coming to my door. And that includes you too, Ava."

"Fair enough," said Ava. "If it's ok with my friends, I would like to skip the meal and get straight down to business."

"I agree," said Colin. "We're wasting time."

Markus smiled at Colin. "If you wish to skip the meal, then very well. Although enjoying a meal will give us a chance to get to know each other better. And give me the chance to see if I should let you three strangers into my operation or not. Three very strange off-worlders at that. I've heard about you three. Word travels fast in my network. Colin McKenzie, a man who fries people with lightning bolts from his fingertips. Kelly Lytton, a kid that summons fire. And the charming Diane Christy, who can leap fifty feet into the air and tear a man in half with her bare hands."

Kelly raised his hand. "Excuse me. You think that Diane is charming?"

Markus ignored Kelly's question. "I don't know if you three can really do the things that I've heard about, but you must be a threat serious enough to have the Tritians, Guydruns, *and* the Gatherers out for your blood. And having you here could pose a threat to my operation."

"We can handle any threat that pops up," Colin assured Markus. "And it's my understanding that the Gatherers are the ones keeping the Guydruns and Tritians at bay."

"The Gatherers are keeping those two from waging a full-scale war in this city. They may not have swarms of troops marching through the streets, but that doesn't mean that they can't have spies and assassins infesting it."

"But don't forget that unless the Tritians are staging an all-out attack, they're not going to enter a human city just to wander around," Ava pointed out. "So that removes them as a threat."

"I take little comfort in that," said Markus. "At any second, we could still be facing a major threat. Just look at what's happening up north. I'm sure that you heard about the carnage. Whole cities being destroyed."

Colin suspected what Markus was referring to. "Deevor. Yeah. We've seen what's going on with her."

"That bitch is a demon. I shudder to think about what would happen if she were to turn her attention to this city. There would be nothing that anyone can do to stop her."

Colin disagreed. "Deevor isn't invincible. We found that out sure enough."

Markus laughed. "Oh really? I'm glad to hear that you have such courage. Too bad it won't be enough to deal with someone that can destroy an entire city single handed."

"Let us worry about Deevor. But for now, our main concern is to save a bunch of abducted children," Colin returned.

Markus smiled as he gazed back at Colin. "You are indeed persistent. And brave. Perhaps too brave for your own good. Two qualities that could end up getting you killed in this conflict. But if you insist upon this suicide mission, then so be it."

Markus rose from his chair and instructed everyone to follow him. He led the group back through the restaurant and to the elevator. He pressed a button on the panel at its right and the door slid open to admit the group. He took a key out of his pants pocket and inserted it into a small keyhole at the top of the elevator's control panel. There were three columns of glowing white buttons on the control panel. Markus pressed the bottom button on the third column. When the door closed, Colin heard the faint whir of machinery and felt the slight jolt of the elevator moving. Watching the digital display at the top of the control panel, Colin saw that they were descending from the twenty-first floor to a lower level designated B2. The elevator stopped. The door slid open.

"Come with me," Markus told the group.

They followed Markus out into a corridor. A row of small, white globes on the ceiling, spaced six feet apart, provided the corridor with a dim light. They continued walking for several feet, with the multiple clicks of their footsteps echoing off the walls. The corridor made a right turn. The group continued walking for a few more feet before they came upon two men wearing black shirts and pants sitting at a dark wooden desk positioned at the left side of the corridor. There was a small lamp on the desk that provided this area with a greater light. Laying near the lamp were two assault rifles. The men both rose to their feet when Markus and the group approached. Markus instructed the men to remain at ease while he and the others passed. The group continued traveling down the corridor for another few feet before they came upon two more men sitting at a desk. These men had their weapons slung over their shoulders. Behind the desk was a metal door.

Markus pointed to the door. "Open up for me."

One of the men rose up and took a key from his pocket, inserted it into a lock on the door, then pulled it open to allow the group to pass. Beyond the door, they walked down another dimly lit corridor, then entered a large circular room illuminated by the bright glow of the rows of large globe lights on the ceiling. The room's floor had the same shiny, reflective surface as the lobby above. Before them were men and women in black uniforms seated at two rows of tables, working at computer stations. Past the tables were male and female technicians seated at small metal tables in front of five-foot-tall columns protruding from the floor. The columns all had a reflective surface. The technicians were busy typing their fingers onto glowing green and glue holographic displays that were being projected in front of each column. At the far end of the room, three men stood over a technician who was seated at a table in front of a taller column. This one being seven feet tall. Projected in front of it was a row of three large holographic screens displaying images of scenes from the countryside.

Markus stopped in the middle of the room and turned to face the group. "Ava has been here before. But for the benefit of the others, this is my main command center, the nerve center of my operation. From here, we plan our actions against the enemy. Here we can follow their every movement and keep one step ahead of them."

Colin walked over to one of the smaller columns. Then he looked over at the larger one. "This entire set up looks familiar."

"Yeah," said Kelly. "Reminds me of the temple of mirrors." He took his small, blue, handheld sensor pad out from his back pocket and walked over to a column. He tapped his finger on the pad and examined its readings. "I'm picking up some pretty weird energy from these things."

"The columns somehow generate their own power," explained Markus. "We don't know how exactly."

Kelly tapped his finger on the sensor pad. He studied its readings, then tapped it twice. "I adjusted the sensor pad to try to narrow down the energy signature coming from these things. If I'm reading this correctly, the columns are powered by a low level of psionic energy."

"Psionic?" Markus inquired.

"It's a form of mental energy generated by our

brains," explained Kelly. "This is definitely like the temple of mirrors."

With this information, Colin was able to form a fast conclusion about the origin of these columns. "Then that means this is all Gatherer technology."

"That was our very first guess," said Markus. "Or more like technology left behind by Kimdrack or some of the other Dark Masters."

"You know about them?" Colin asked.

"When you have people like the Gatherers running around sticking their noses into our planet's war from time to time, then it's wise to make it your business to know such things. I remember the stories my father used to tell me about the Gatherers. They came here many years ago from beyond our planet, digging around and unearthing these ancient alien ruins. Certain areas they laid claim to and ran everyone off so that they could set up shop. Nobody argued with them because they had advanced weapons and monsters to back themselves up."

"Monsters? asked Diane. "You mean they had other monsters besides Deevor?"

"Yes. There were others like her, but not as powerful. Deevor appears to be their strongest and ruthless weapon yet. I've heard about her doing unspeakable acts. But she also keeps the Guydruns and Tritians in check. So, I suppose that works in our favor."

During the conversation, Kelly was still studying his sensor pad. He tapped his finger on the device and then slowly walked over to a female technician sitting at a table in front of one column. The technician stared at Kelly as he approached her while holding out the sensor pad. He read its findings, then announced it to the others. "Guys. I'm picking up several faint energy streams leading from all of us to these columns. It's like these things have established connections to our minds and are drawing off low levels of our mental energy to power themselves."

"What?" Markus gasped.

"Are you sure?" asked a wide-eyed Ava.

"The data doesn't lie," Kelly told her. "These machines have tapped into everyone in this room. I'm even getting these same energy streams leading to the outside. Several of them. It's like they've also tapped into the minds of the people outside for power."

"How the hell are you able to find this out with that little device?" Markus asked Kelly. "My staff and I would have never caught on to such a thing. And we've examined these things inside and out."

"My God," Ava exclaimed. "They're leeching off our minds. Is this dangerous?"

Kelly glanced at the sensor pad. "I don't think so. I think they're just absorbing residual energy that our brains give off. Sort of like a photocell absorbing light. But I'd have to study this longer to make sure."

"How did your people get a hold of all this?" Colin asked.

Markus explained, "This chamber was first discovered by my grandfather when he was developing the land. Some of his workers unearthed it. I suppose he understood the significance of what they found and thought it best to keep things quiet from the rest of the world. Fortunately, he owned the land, so he had this building constructed over the chamber to keep it hidden. Over the years, this building and this chamber have passed down from him to my father. And now to me. We are in the building across the street from the one that I also own where my restaurant is located. Obviously, we had to travel by a tunnel to reach this chamber. It's a clever security measure."

"I'm surprised that the Gatherers haven't come looking to take this place back," Colin pointed out.

"Who knows?" replied Markus. "Perhaps this place

wasn't important to them. Or perhaps they don't know of its existence yet."

Whatever the reason, Colin knew they had to take advantage of this technology while they could. "Before they ever do come looking for this place, we've got to use this technology to try and find those children taken from Willowby. Can you help us?"

Markus replied with a nod. "Indeed, I can."

Markus lead the group over to the table at the far end of the room sitting in front of the seven-foot-tall column. The men standing near the table stepped aside as he approached. "As I've told you earlier, we are able to monitor the enemy's activities, almost on an individual level. As well as intercepting and monitoring their communications. Let's have a little demonstration."

Markus pointed a finger at the three holographic screens. Upon getting a closer view, Colin saw that the screens were displaying the images of Guydrun soldiers and Tritians roaming through a forest. The technician tapped his fingers on the computer touchpad before him. The image on the center screen changed from the forest scene to a map with several small red dots.

"Here we have a platoon of Guydrun troops from the sixty-third assault division," said Markus. "They are joined by Tritian combat drones from Hive Kymera. They're a mean bunch. This data is coming from the Rosewind Forest in Osgold. That's a small island country about five thousand miles to the northeast. From this station here, we are able to monitor their every action and listen to their radio communications."

Colin studied the map and the small moving red dots. "And you say that you can track people, even down to a single individual? That's similar to our own scanning technology. If you have this capability to keep track of the enemy, then this should make it easier for you to fight this war."

"If only it were that easy," Ava replied. "Keeping tabs on the enemy and staying a step ahead of them is one thing. But it's a different matter when it comes to having the firepower and numbers to do the job."

"We also have recorded data from all enemy transmissions," Markus told Colin. "I'm pretty certain we can search through our past logs and find out where the Tritians took the children."

"Pretty impressive," was Colin's compliment. "I hope you're also able to translate the Tritian transmissions into English."

"Yes, we have that capability. Let me demonstrate."

Markus tapped the technician on his shoulder. The technician began to type his fingers on his touchpad. A moment later, the image on the screen turned snowy, accompanied by sharp, hissing static.

The technician typed on his touchpad again, then looked to Markus. "We're getting one of those strange transmissions again," he reported.

"Try again to see if you can pinpoint it's origin," Markus ordered. "I want to know who and where these people are."

After several seconds the static began to abate, then a male voice could be heard delivering a message fading in and out from clarity to heavy static.

"This is…Hemlock. We… still experiencing power loss…Disabled. We have heavy casualties…They are relentless. To anybody…this message. Please send…"

The message ended.

The name mentioned in the message immediately stuck out in Colin's mind. "Hemlock. That sounds like one of the ships in the missing task force."

"You're right. Destroyer, Hemlock," Kelly told him. "They're sending out a distress call."

"Task force? Hemlock?" Markus inquired. "What the

hell is this all about?"

"We were sent out here to find a task force of missing ships from our home quadrant," Colin explained. "How long have you been getting these messages?"

"They've been coming in for about three weeks now. But hold on. What the hell is this about your home quadrant?"

Ava gave the answer before Colin had the chance. "My friends here come from outside our known quadrant."

Markus smiled. Then laughed. "They're from outside our quadrant? This is a joke. Right? There's nothing outside our quadrant."

"You're wrong about that," said Colin. "We'll explain it all later. Right now, I want to hear more about these messages."

The technician explained further. "At first, we thought that they were part of some ploy by the enemy. Maybe they were trying to set us up for a trap. We heard some terms that we didn't understand. Task force five. United Protectorate. We tried to use this technology to trace the messages back to their source. But according to our readings, they were originating from nowhere."

Colin was confused. "From nowhere? That makes no sense. The signals have to have an origin."

"I know it sounds crazy, but there's no other way to explain it," replied the technician. "Our instruments don't lie. The closest we've come to pinpointing the origin was a week ago. We've traced a transmission to a set of coordinates out in space, but our long-range scanning revealed that there's nothing in that location except empty space."

"A signal coming from empty space…" Colin was still confused. He turned to Kelly who's technical skills could shed some light onto this mystery. "What do you make of that?"

Kelly tapped his finger twice onto his sensor pad. "That's hard to say. I tried to trace the message on my pad, but it's too far out of range."

"I figured that," Colin's reply. "Then I guess the best way of investigating this is to take the Black Raven and go out to this location. And possibly exposing ourselves in enemy occupied space. Is it possible for the resistance to give us an escort?"

Markus grinned. "Oh sure. Just find any commander that has the ships to spare in order to send out into enemy space to search for supposedly lost alien ships and you're all set. You said that you were here for information. Not to request a combat escort."

Colin predicted the sarcastic reply from Markus. "Then we'll have to go it alone. Just give us the coordinates. We'll settle for the information that you have on the Willoby children for now."

Markus gave a nod to the technician, who then began to type onto his touchpad. A moment later a green map appeared with eight large, red circles scattered across its surface. Markus explained the meaning of this map.

"This shows the location of every Tritian detention center on the planet. The Tritians handle their prisoners differently than the Guydruns. It's standard procedure for the Tritians to process their prisoners before they're shipped to their final destination. Prisoners are scanned for any diseases or physical defects. Any prisoners considered to have vital information are kept in solitary confinement for interrogation." Markus pointed to one circle at the far-right side of the map. "This center, called number eight, is the closest one to the vicinity of Willoby. We've noticed that there's been increased activity there. It's possible that this is where the children were taken."

Colin studied the map. "I imagine that the security measures at these places aren't light."

"That's putting it mildly," said Markus. "Each one of these centers has at least a full battalion of combat drones stationed there. In addition to surrounding mine fields, auto defense guns, and twenty-foot-tall stone walls covered by black ivy."

"Black ivy?" asked Colin

"You people must really be from off world," Markus scolded. "It's a species of ivy with thorns containing a toxin that's lethal to humans."

Colin cringed at this information. "So, climbing over the walls is not an option."

"Waiting around too long is not an option either," Markus added. "If the Tritians follow their usual procedure, those kids will be shipped off soon."

"Shipped off?" asked Diane. "Where?"

Markus and Ava both looked at each other. Then Ava spoke to answer. "Then they'll be shipped off to the Tritian's home planet, Osidra. Once there, they will be used as reproduction material. The Tritians consider human children to be prime hosts for their eggs. They implant human hosts with their eggs. The eggs hatch and then the larva slowly consumes their hosts."

Diane let out a gasp and her eyes widened at this horrific detail. Even Colin was shocked. But also, not surprised. "I didn't expect the Tritians to be sweethearts. But no matter what, we've got to save those kids." Colin took another moment to study the map. "Heavy security surrounding these detention centers."

"Heavy bordering on suicide," Markus told him. "You'd need an army to go anywhere near these centers."

"I'd have to agree with Markus," said Ava. "The Tritian security is far too heavy. Even for the three of you."

"Don't tell me that these three are insane enough to think about breaking prisoners out of a Tritian detention center by themselves?" Markus asked Ava. A grin appearing on his face.

"We might not have to," replied Colin. His mind began to form a plan. "What about when the prisoners are being transported?"

"The prisoners are loaded into a shuttle pod and transported through space with a fighter escort," Ava explained.

"How many fighters?" asked Colin.

"Typically, a squadron of about twelve or more."

Colin turned to Diane. "Think you can take on a few Tritian fighters?"

Colin could understand Diane's reason for giving a brief pause before she answered his question. It was a huge job to suddenly find herself thrust into.

Diane looked into Colin's eyes. "If it comes to a fight, I can handle it. And besides, the Black Raven is more advanced than anything those bugs have. So, it will be a breeze."

"It wasn't much of a breeze when they almost shot us out of space," Kelly grumbled.

"Then we're set," said Colin.

Markus turned his gaze to Ava, then back to Colin. "I don't know what the three of you think that you're going to accomplish by yourselves, but the resistance has limited ships and personnel to give you any help. If we had the power, we'd free the prisoners ourselves. But at this time, we can't."

There was a sudden chiming sound coming from the holographic screen. "I think we've got company," the Technician announced. He tapped his touchpad and the map changed to a top down image of the city with six red circles moving over it.

"What's going on?" Colin asked.

"It's a Guydrun special forces team doing a fly by,"

the Technician explained. "They're very rough customers."

"We've got experience in dealing with rough people," Colin replied.

Markus frowned. "This could be trouble. The Guydruns usually don't bring out their special forces team this far over the city unless it's to deal with a high priority situation."

Diane stepped forward. "Ok. So, we'll just have to go out there and see how special these guys really are."

"Stand down," said Markus, raising his hands. "Let's just wait and see what they're doing. If we wait them out, they might leave without any trouble."

Ava agreed. "Markus is right. We have to keep a low profile and avoid any violence unless we don't have a choice."

I hope you're right, was Colin's thought. He was in no mood to get into a firefight this soon, but would not walk away from one if it was unavoidable. He continued watching the circles for several minutes as they remained in a stationary position over the city. Then they slowly moved to the right edge of the map.

"They're leaving," said Markus.

"Lucky for them," was Diane's dour comment.

With the threat of the Guydruns seemingly passed, Colin turned his attention back to the abducted children. "How soon before the kids are shipped off?"

"We have no idea. The Tritians don't have a set time for prisoner transportation," Markus explained. "We only have the ability to detect and watch them as they leave."

"And when they do that's when we make our strike," Colin revealed. "I figure that instead of fighting our way in and out of the Tritian's security, the job will be easier if we intercept the kids as they're being transported off world. All we have to do is wait for them. But while that's happening, maybe it will be a good idea to head out to this location in space and investigate these messages."

The Technician recited the coordinates of the mysterious messages to Kelly, who entered the information into his sensor pad. After their business was concluded, Markus escorted the group out of the command center and back down the corridor to reach the other building. A quick elevator ride brought the group back up to the lobby. As they approached the receptionist's desk, Markus raised a hand to the men seated there.

"My friends here are leaving. Please return their belongings."

One of the men brought out Diane's gun belt and Gaylie's machine gun, which both females quickly retrieved.

"I'll have the cars brought back to return you to the airfield," Markus told the group.

Grant approached Markus. His finger was pressed onto a small, round device that was inserted into his right ear. He raised his head and looked about at the people passing by on the sidewalk. He then approached Markus. "Sir, surveillance has just called in an alert. We've got company."

Colin winced at Grant's warning. *So much for us just walking out of here without any problems,* he thought.

"What the hell is it?" asked Markus.

Grant pointed to a café at his right across the street. Among the other patrons sitting at their tables was a young man with short red hair, dressed in a brown suit. He was sitting alone at his table while sipping from a white cup.

"What's going on?" Colin asked Markus.

Markus pointed to the café across the street. "It's

one of the Guydrun officers from their military investigations division. Lieutenant Drake. He's well known by the resistance. He's one of the worst. If he's here, then he must be onto something."

"Or someone. So, what should we do?" asked Kelly.

"Nothing. Just stay calm," Ava's advice. "This is the wrong time and place to get into a fight. There are too many innocent civilians on the street."

Grant pressed his finger back onto the device in his ear. Then he made a report to Markus. "Sir, surveillance has picked up the Guydrun special forces unit. They've turned around and are heading back to the city."

"What?" Markus spat out. "I thought they were just making another fly by."

"Maybe they forgot something," Colin's cheerless quip.

"Enemy units coming in fast," came Grant's warning.

"Tell the command center to issue a full alert," Markus ordered to Grant.

"Maybe we should get to the cars and try to leave before they arrive," said Ava.

Colin did not respond to her suggestion. Looking across the street to the café he noticed that Lieutenant Drake had left his table and was nowhere to be seen. *Where the hell did this guy go? I've got a bad feeling about this.*

"Enemy units are right on top of us!" Grant cried out.

Colin heard a loud rushing sound coming from above his head. He looked up to see seven humanoid figures descending from the sky. They were clad in shiny, metallic armored suits. Their suits' bulbous helmets had black visors that totally concealed their faces. Mounted on their backs were two broad metallic wings. Each wing had two long cylindrical jets attached to them, spitting out blue jets of flame with loud roars. Each of these men, except for one, was armed with long barreled assault rifles. The one that Colin focused on was holding a larger weapon with a long, thick cylindrical barrel.

The group of armored men landed in the middle of the street, seeming to be oblivious to the approaching vehicles at the left and right, which came to a screeching halt to avoid a collision. The squad of men looked about the street. Then one of them pointed a finger in the group's direction.

"Here we go," Colin muttered to himself. At this point, it would seem a fight would be unavoidable.

Several screaming people in the area began to scatter. The armored men aimed their weapons towards the group. "Get down!" Diane shouted.

Everyone dove to the ground behind parked cars for cover as the armored squad opened fire. A hail of bullets shattered car windows and punctured their sides. Colin, in his crouched position, charged up his power. His hands were crackling with electrical energy. He looked to his left. Diane, down on her knees, had taken her laser gun from its holster. Kelly and Ava were crouched down at Diane's left. Colin took a brief glance over to his right. Grant, Markus, and Gaylie were kneeling close beside him. Colin was waiting for the right opportunity to take the offense against these men, but for the next several seconds their barrage did not abate. Then the gunfire stopped. Colin took the moment to pop his head up from behind the car and see if he had his chance to strike. Gaylie also lifted her head. She let out a gasp, then uttered a name. "Shockwave."

The man holding the large weapon aimed it towards the car that Colin was hiding behind. A bright white flash spat out from its barrel, along with a loud boom. Colin's vision suddenly blacked out as his body was

Barry K. Nelson

struck by a powerful impact that hurled him backward. The next second, his body was searing with pain as he struck a hard surface. While there was a sharp ringing in his ears, Colin opened his eyes and looked over to the car that he was hiding behind. The entire middle section of the car was completely torn apart. Grant and Markus were still crouched down at the car's rear section. Colin found that he was hurled away from it and had slammed into the building several feet away. He found himself covered by metal and plastic shards from the damaged vehicle. Pain seared through Colin's back as he tried to rise to his feet. He recalled the name that Gaylie had mentioned. *Shockwave. Makes sense*, he thought.

Colin rose to his knees. The ringing in his ears was now subsiding. He glanced over to his right to see that Gaylie was lying next to him. She was not moving. Colin looked over at Shockwave, the armored man with the large and powerful weapon. He was slowly advancing in Colin's direction. He aimed his weapon.

"My turn," said Colin. He reacted quickly, raising his hand and firing a bolt of electrical energy that sent Shockwave flying backward several feet, onto the windshield of a car, shattering it on impact.

Diane was able to rise and fire two shots at one armored man. His body jerked back as the weapon's crimson laser bolts struck his chest. He remained standing and raised his weapon at Diane. Diane followed up on her attack by continuing to fire laser shots at the man until he dropped to his back. Kelly, still crouched down behind the car, took this opportunity to attack. Aiming his hands at the car, he released a basketball-sized orb of fire that easily burned through the car and flew on to strike one of the armored assailants. Kelly's fireball exploded on impact. The man's entire armored upper torso was

49

destroyed, leaving the lower portion of his body in flames.

Colin looked over to Grant and Markus, who had now taken pistols out of their pockets and were still crouched down behind the remnants of the car. "Stay down," came Colin's stern warning to them. He stood up and directed a stream of energy to the ground. As he quickly raised his hand, the electrical charge that he planted in the sidewalk began to travel through the ground towards another one of the armored men. Bolts of energy shot up from the man's feet and shredded his armor. A plume of black smoke rose out from the man's body. His skin was scarred with severe electrical burns.

Shockwave was now recovering from Colin's attack, still holding onto his weapon. He stood up on the hood of the car and aimed it at Kelly. He opened fire. There was a loud boom and a white flash from its barrel. The car that Kelly was hiding behind exploded into a cloud of shards while Kelly was hurled backward. Shockwave aimed at two other cars parked in front of that one and began shooting. The energy from his weapon ripped the front section of one car apart while turning it on its side. The second car was ripped into scattered fragments. Shockwave then turned his weapon to the car that Diane was standing behind. Diane, seeing this in time, dove to the right just as Shockwave opened fire. The car was pushed back as its front section was ripped apart.

Colin crouched back down as the remaining members of the armored squad began to spray the area with gunfire. Grant and Markus began shooting at them from the protective cover of a red car. Colin rushed over to Diane, who was kneeling to avoid a hail of bullets.

"We have to end this fast," Colin told Diane. He looked over at Kelly, laying still on the sidewalk. "We have to get to Kelly."

"Only if these idiots let us," Diane replied. "That one guy's weapon is pretty wicked."

Colin looked over at Shockwave. He had jumped off the roof of the car and was now walking in their direction. He raised his weapon. The surviving members of his squad began to join his advance.

"That weapon fires some sort of concussive force," said Colin.

"Concussive force?" Diane replied. "Is that all?"

Diane rose up and began to charge towards Shockwave. During her run, she began to fire her laser gun at one of Shockwave's comrades standing at his left. Diane's aim was accurate as she sent multiple laser shots into his helmet's visor. The man staggered backward, dropped his machine gun, then fell to his face. Shockwave aimed his weapon at Diane and fired. Colin watched as the weapon emitted its boom and bright flash. Diane stopped in her tracks, quickly raising her forearms up to her face. The energy from Shockwave's weapon blew back every scrap of debris on the street around Diane as if they were caught by a gale force wind. But Diane stood firm on her feet. Her long black hair was whipped back by this force.

Colin held his breath in amazement at this sight. He surmised that Shockwave was also equally amazed. He lowered his weapon and remained still as he gazed at Diane. Then, as Diane lowered her hands, he began to step back.

"Are you out of your mind?" Colin shouted at Diane.

Diane looked over at Colin. "Hey. Concussive energy. It's just pure force," she replied in a casual manner. "It's not like he's shooting bullets or something."

Colin could not accept Diane's logic for taking such a dangerous risk. And there was no time to argue with her about it now. There was still Shockwave and his three cohorts to deal with.

Shockwave looked back at the surviving members of his squad. He waved a hand forward. The jets mounted on their wings spat out streams of fire. The men were then lifted off their feet and propelled forward. Kelly returned to his feet, as did Gaylie. Gaylie wasted no time taking quick aim with her machine gun and opening fire at the oncoming armored threats. Colin raised his hands and fired twin electrical bolts at the men, but their spiraling movements in midair prevented him from getting a clear shot. His attack missing completely. Kelly's aim was much more accurate as he released a stream of flame from his hand that caught one of the armored men and set him ablaze. He began to spin out of control and crashed to the pavement. He rolled for several feet before crashing into the side of a building and laid still while engulfed in flames.

With the protection of his armor, Shockwave was flying unhindered through the combined gunfire from Grant, Markus, and Gaylie. Gaylie continued shooting as Shockwave was flying on a direct course towards her. He slammed into Gaylie and knocked her to the ground. He landed on his feet next to her, grabbed her by her arm, then flew up into the air with her. Markus and Grant began shooting at Shockwave and the two remaining members of his squad as they began to fly towards the top of the buildings.

Colin feared that their gunfire might put Gaylie in danger. "Stop shooting!" Colin shouted. Waving his arms in the air. "Stop! You might hit Gaylie!"

Grant and Markus stopped shooting. Colin watched as the flying men soared above the buildings and, within seconds, were out of sight.

Ava rushed over to Colin, while not taking her gaze away from the sky." Gaylie. They've got my daughter."

"Not for long. We'll get her back." Colin assured her.

Markus also approached Colin. "You see this? You see all this chaos? I was afraid that something like this would happen." He pointed a damning finger at Colin's face. "This is all your fault."

"Fine. Sue me," Colin's reply. He turned his attention to Kelly. "Can you track these guys on your sensor pad?"

"I've already got them," Kelly replied. He tapped his finger on the device in his hand. "They're heading east."

"So are we," Colin added. "Markus. We need a car."

"You want one of my cars after you put my operation at risk," Markus shouted. "Is there anything else I can give you?"

"There's no time to argue. And I wasn't asking," Colin told Markus.

Ava approached Markus. "They have my daughter. Please."

Giving in to both Ava's plea and Colin's stern demand, Markus threw his hands up and relented. "Alright. You can take one of my cars. Just one. Go get the girl. I don't want to see you again after this. You've already threatened my operation enough."

Colin ignored Markus as he joined Diane and Kelly following Ava, while hoping that they would not lose the second of Ava's two daughters.

CHAPTER FOUR

Traveling in the blue car that they rode in from the airfield, Colin remained tense as they were heading down the road away from the city and into the country. Ava, sitting next to Colin in the driver's seat, was following directions from Kelly as he was sitting in the back seat with Diane. Kelly's sensor pad still had a solid fix on Shockwave. He was traveling eastward, and the sensor reading also indicated that Gaylie was still with him. Colin felt that this was encouraging, but at this point anything could still happen. Shockwave seemed to be ruthless enough to kill Gaylie for any reason. Colin could only imagine the level of distress that Ava was withholding. On the outside, she was maintaining her hard, strong demeanor, but on the inside, she was no doubt fearful that her last surviving daughter could die at any moment.

Colin looked back at Kelly. "What's their status?"

"They're about twelve miles ahead of us now. They appear to be slowing down."

"If Gaylie is still alive, then where could they be taking her?" Colin wondered. "Ava. Are there any Guydrun bases out here?"

"There could be. I don't know the layout of the land.," Ava replied.

"Well wherever they're taking her, let's hope it's not too heavily fortified. Otherwise that might make things a little more complicated.," Colin warned.

The car continued driving along the road with vast, green fields at its left and right. After driving for another mile, the road began to lead up a small hill with a dense growth of trees at both sides. Then at the top of the hill, the road leveled off and the car continued traveling for another mile before coming to a line of cars that were stopped up ahead.

"What the hell is this?" Colin asked. Peering out through the windshield, he saw the last two vehicles in the line before them. A red car and a black pickup truck. Then several feet beyond these two vehicles he caught the familiar sight of two Guydrun soldiers dressed in their dark blue uniforms and black metal helmets. With their assault rifles in hand they were at the left side of the road, approaching the stopped cars.

"Oh great," Ava moaned. "A checkpoint."

That's all we need now, Colin thought. "Everybody, stay calm."

Colin continued to watch the soldiers as they went from car to car. Stopping for a few moments at one, then going on to the next.

"Maybe they just want to ask some questions," was the theory from Kelly.

The soldiers walked up to the red car. They both stopped moving for a moment. Then one of then raised his weapon at the driver's side door. The occupant, a young, black haired white female in a blue dress, got out of her car and raised her hands above her head. Then the soldier fired a rapid burst from his weapon into the woman's chest. She fell back against her car, then collapsed to the ground.

"I don't think we're going to like the questions they'll be asking," Diane said.

A third soldier rushed onto the scene and dragged the woman by her feet to the side of the road. The other two soldiers now walked up to the pickup truck. They stopped for a moment to speak to its male driver. Colin observed him handing something to one of the soldiers. The soldier examined it, then gave it back. Now the two armed soldiers began to approach the next car. The one currently occupied by Colin and his friends.

"They're coming to ask us for our identification and travel permits," Ava informed the group. "We have neither."

"Just relax. We got this," Colin assured Ava. "If there's any problems we'll just talk it out with them."

There was complete silence in the car as the two Guydrun soldiers slowly walked up to the car, one approaching at its left. The other stopped and stood just a few feet away from the front passenger's side door, and Colin. His partner went over to the driver's side and addressed Ava.

"Identification and travel permit for this area."

Ava hesitated for a moment before she gave an answer. "Just a minute." She looked to Colin.

"Let me handle this," Colin told her. He raised his hands up to his head and turned to speak to the soldier at his left. "Hi. We're not from around here, and we don't have any ID, or this travel permit you're talking about. But if you give us a chance, we can explain."

Colin was startled when the soldier at his right gave the driver's side door a sharp kick. His partner at the left leaned down to address Colin. "That's not what we want to hear. The woman in that car up ahead didn't have her ID or permit either. Step out of the car."

"Are you sure you want me to do that?" Colin asked.

The soldier stepped back away from the car. "All of you, get out. Now."

"Have it your way," Colin calmly told him.

Colin slowly opened the door and stepped out of the car. He pointed a hand at the soldier that was keeping him covered and released a bolt of electricity that lifted him off his feet and hurled him backwards into a tree that was several yards away. This action took the second soldier completely by surprise. His moment of hesitation gave Kelly the opportunity to point his hand to the passenger's window and shoot out a bolt of fire that instantly burned through the glass and exploded upon impact with the man. The explosive force knocked him backward for several feet while setting him ablaze. Colin saw the third soldier further up the road running toward the scene. It was a simple matter for Colin to fire a bolt of energy that engulfed the man in a bright white flash and an explosion of sparks, then sent him flying into the trees.

Colin rushed over to the front of the car and looked down the road to see if there were any more soldiers. Far up ahead there was a military truck parked at the left side of the road. There were two more Guydrun soldiers blocking the road. Colin caught sight of one pointing in his direction. Then both soldiers dashed around to the other side of the truck.

"I think we're going to have company," Colin warned the others. "We'd better go."

"Go?" said Ava. "Where?"

"To wherever they're taking Gaylie," Colin told her. "We'd better leave the car. Kelly, are you still tracking our targets?"

"I've still got them," Kelly returned. "I'm also picking up an installation of some kind. Due east. Apparently, that's where they're headed."

"Then that's where we're headed," Colin returned. "I just hope we're not too late."

The group abandoned the car and ran into the woods. Colin looked back to see if there were any soldiers in pursuit. So far, he saw no one. He assumed that the other two Guydruns were calling for help. If that was the case, then the group had to get out of these woods as soon as possible.

The group continued their fast trek through the woods for several minutes. During this time, they encountered no other enemy presence. Colin knew that their luck would not hold out. Following Kelly's direction, they proceeded to move up a hill with a dense growth of trees. When they reached the hilltop, all they saw were more trees.

As they continued to proceed, Colin was wondering if there were now any Guydruns in pursuit. "Kelly, are you picking up anybody following us?"

"Nothing. We're the only ones in the vicinity," Kelly reported. "But I am picking up a faint radio signal."

"A signal?" asked Colin. "Why am I thinking that means trouble? Ava. Would they have any kind of defenses protecting this installation?"

"It would be likely," Ava returned. "But what kind of defenses, I can't really say."

"That's encouraging," Diane's comment. "I guess we'll have to be ready for anything."

"Story of our lives," Colin mumbled to himself.

The group continued moving through the forest for several more minutes. Colin could not help but notice how quiet it was. There were no sounds of any birds chirping in the trees. Nor the appearance of enemy soldiers in pursuit.

"It's odd how there's no Guydruns combing the woods to find us," said Colin.

"Yeah. I noticed that," said Diane. "Either we're too far ahead of them or they're waiting for us up ahead someplace."

"Kelly are you still picking up that signal?" asked

Colin.

"Yeah," said Kelly, after glancing at his data pad. "The signal is getting stronger."

"Stronger?" asked Colin. "I don't like this."

As they advanced further on, they came upon an area where the trees were starting to become denser. Suddenly, Kelly stopped while staring at his data pad. "This is where the signal is coming from. And it's still getting stronger."

Being more cautious, the group continued to push ahead. They came to a spot where several trees have grown close together. They were covered in long, thick vines that were entwined around their trunks and hanging down from their branches. Colin remained tense as the group continued to proceed into the area. With this thick cover of trees, he was expecting any threat to appear without warning.

They moved closer to a tree that was surrounded by thick, five-foot-tall bushes. A thick sheet of vines hanging down from the tree's branches intermingled with the bushes. Upon moving in closer, Colin noticed that there was also a dark shape among the bushes and vines.

"What the hell is that?" Colin asked.

"According to the data pad, that's the source of the radio signal," Kelly reported. "And now I'm getting several more."

The figure in the bushes began to move. There was the loud, sharp crack of dried branches and the rustling of leaves as the figure began to emerge from the bushes and out into full view. It appeared to be a man wearing a Guydrun soldier's uniform that was marred by muddy stains. The soldier was wearing a round, silvery helmet. Beneath the helmet was a fleshless skull covered by mud and dead leaves. The soldier had a metal harness strapped to his torso, arms, and legs. A system of cables led down from his helmet to each section of the harness. As the soldier continued shuffling forward, he raised his skeletal hand to reveal the machine gun that he was holding. The soldier raised his weapon at the group.

Before the soldier had a chance to open fire, Diane drew her laser gun and fired two shots at his chest. The soldier staggered back. His movements threw off his aim and he fired at the ground. Seeing that the soldier was still on his feet, Diane shot him two more times, striking his head. The soldier stumbled back again, then fell onto his back. Before anyone had the chance to react there was the sound of more rustling from the bushes. Another armed Guydrun soldier came shuffling forward. This one also having a fleshless skull under a metal helmet connected to the harness it was wearing. The soldier raised his machine gun and fired. Everyone ducked behind the trees for cover. Colin acted swiftly, moving from behind his tree and sending a bolt of electricity from his fingertips that shoved the soldier backward. His helmet exploded and he dropped to the ground, remaining still.

Everyone stood back up and moved in to take a closer look at one of the dead, skull-faced soldiers. Black smoke was rising from the hole burned into it by Diane's laser shot. The second soldier, lying six feet away, had his entire skull smoking from the remnants of his shattered helmet.

"What the hell are these things?" Colin asked. "Are the Guydruns using zombies?"

"Not exactly zombies. These are just drones. Corpses manipulated by the computers in their helmets," explained Ava. She pointed to the small round lens on the center of the soldier's helmet. "The computers are programmed to attack any target that's not carrying a friendly ID signal. These harnesses send electro impulses that manipulate the corpses motor functions. Basically, walk and shoot. They're used until the corpses deteriorate to a point where they're no longer useful."

"The perfect renewable security system," said Colin. "Just hook up a dead body to one of these things, give it a gun, and send it out into the woods."

The loud chatter of machine gun fire suddenly filled the air. Bullets penetrated the trunks of the trees at Colin's right. "Get down," Colin shouted.

Once again, the group ducked behind the trees for cover as the gunfire continued. Colin peered from around his tree and saw three drones in the distance emerging from behind the trees, firing their machine guns as they walked. In the far distance behind them, he was able to make out the image of three more drones moving. The sound of cracking branches at his left caught his attention. He turned and counted four more drones slowly advancing in this direction.

Colin looked to Ava, down on her knees behind the tree at his left. "How good a shot are these things?"

"I've heard they're not very accurate shooting at a distance," replied Ava.

"Let's not give them any closer targets," Colin returned. "Our destination is up ahead. Let's keep moving."

The group quickened their pace through the trees. Several drones appeared ahead of them. Their slow movements, walking and aiming their weapons, proved to be a slight advantage to the group. Colin and Kelly were able to use their powers to disable any drones before they could take an accurate shot. Diane, using her laser gun, took careful aim at the drone's helmets. A well-placed shot disabled the computers within and instantly shut the drones down.

The group emerged from the trees and came

upon an area that was surrounded by a ten-foot-tall fence that was composed of long, six-inch-wide metal bars in between ten-foot-tall metal poles.

"A fence?" Diane scoffed. "They think this is going to keep us out?"

"I'd be a little more cautious. No doubt this fence is electrified," warned Ava.

"So am I," Colin simply said. He had no desire to waste any time dealing with this crude barrier. He pointed a finger and sent a continuous arc of energy into the fence. Through this energy, Colin established a link between himself and the fence, enabling him to utilize his ability to manipulate electrically conductive material. Sparks began to shoot out from a large section of the fence as it began to rapidly disintegrate into a pile tiny metal shards.

Colin disengaged his energy, then led the group through the newly created breach in the fence. Ava laughed as she walked over the pile of metal shards. "I can just imagine what this war would be like if we had more fighters like you on our side. We could kick these invaders back out into space within a week."

"Don't praise us just yet," Colin told her. "We haven't gotten Gaylie back yet."

The group proceeded into the airbase. They passed by four large, rectangular buildings at the far left and right. Parked in front of the buildings at the left was a row of large, wedge shaped ships with white hulls. At their rear sections were large vertical fins and two smaller horizontal fins. Guydrun gunships, looking as intimidating inactive as they are when flying in to attack. There was no enemy movement in this part of the base, but further ahead in the distance there were several men moving about near two more of the large buildings. There were also four gunships parked in front of these buildings.

"So, what do we do now?" Diane asked Colin.

Good question, Colin asked himself. *Maybe going in with guns blazing isn't the answer here.* Colin stopped walking. He decided that their next course of action would be to do something daring. "Let's wait here."

"Wait?" Diane cried.

"We'll use a little psychology," Colin explained. "Let them come to us. If Shockwave is here, then I'm willing to bet that he might be curious about us. His ego might compel him to come out and tell us how much of a tough guy he is."

Kelly offered an alternative to Colin's scenario. "Or they could fire their artillery at us and blow us away without getting too close."

"There's always a naysayer in the group," Colin muttered.

The group stood and waited. As the seconds passed, Colin was hoping his theory about the enemy's behavior would prove to be correct. Watching the men in the distance, he could see their numbers increasing. They began to spread out and make a slow advance towards the group. As they were moving in closer, Colin could now make out their uniforms. Then, armed soldiers began to emerge from the buildings at the far left and right. They halted several feet away from the group and aimed their weapons.

Kelly walked over to Colin and tapped his shoulder. "This is getting worse. We've got more company coming. The sensor pad is picking up a bunch of drone signatures heading our way."

Colin turned back and looked towards the breach in the fence. The sight of a mob of drones shuffling forward confirmed this.

"Colin, I hope you know what you're doing," said Ava in a quivering voice.

So do I, Colin thought in agreement. He and the others continued to wait as the Guydrun soldiers at the left and right began to move in closer. Then they all stopped. Several of the soldiers in front of the group turned their heads and looked back. Near the buildings a shiny, humanoid figure emerged. The figure launched itself into the air and flew on a direct course towards the group, then landed in front of the line of soldiers. *Shockwave,* Colin thought. The enemy had answered his call.

With his large concussive weapon in hand, Shockwave took a few steps forward. He stopped. His helmet's visor opened to reveal his scowling face. Then he spoke. "You again. How did you find me? And how the hell did you get through the drones? And through the south fence?"

"Finding you wasn't hard," Colin told Shockwave. "You left the back door open, so we walked in."

"So, you're McKenzie," said Shockwave. "Central command warned me and my team about you. We're equipped to handle hard targets, but we weren't prepared to deal with you freaks back in Devarow. And here you are now on our home turf."

Colin grinned. "I'll take all that as a complement. So now you probably know why we're here."

"My daughter," Ava shouted. "Where is she? Where's Gaylie?"

"You mean the resistance girl?" Shockwave asked. "Yeah, we have her. I'll let you see her." Shockwave raised his left arm up to his face and spoke into a small red disk on top of his hand. "Bring the girl."

A second figure in shiny armor back near the buildings rose up into the air and flew towards the group. Colin watched as he came closer, appearing to have another person in tow. The armored man stopped just a few feet above Shockwave's head. With him was Gaylie, carrying her by her arm. He hovered for a second, then descended to a slow, soft landing at Shockwave's right. He dropped Gaylie's limp body to the ground.

"Gaylie!" Ava cried out in anguish. She started to rush towards her. Shockwave and the soldiers all raised their weapons. Ava halted.

Colin looked down at Gaylie, seeing that she was wearing the same computerized helmet and harness as the numerous drones that were now staggering into the base and massing behind him. The sight of Gaylie laying still on the ground angered Colin. He raised a finger at Shockwave. "You're all going to die for this."

Shockwave glanced down at Gaylie, then back to Colin. "Take it easy. She's still alive."

The armored man who had brought Gaylie out was holding a small, black pad. He tapped a finger on the pad. With slow, awkward movements Gaylie rose to her feet. She stood with her torso leaning to the right. Her arm hanging limp with a machine gun in her hand. Her eyes were closed while her mouth was gaping open. She let out a faint wheeze.

"The helmets and harnesses can weaponize an unconscious person just as good as a corpse," Shockwave explained to the group.

Shockwave's armored accomplice tapped his pad three times. Gaylie's body spun around and she raised her weapon towards Ava.

"I bet you didn't plan on coming all this way to get killed by the girl you were rescuing," Shockwave's taunt. "Or even the possibility of killing her. Maybe we should just step back and let the drones do the job."

Colin turned his head and saw the mob of drones behind the group. They were all moving in closer. Raising their weapons, ready to fire. While Colin was relieved to see Gaylie still alive, he and the others now had to find a way out of this trap that was closing in on them.

"We seriously need a plan here," Diane said.

"Hold on. I'm working on it," Kelly replied.

Kelly began to tap his fingers on his sensor pad. The drones all stopped moving, but kept their guns trained on the group. Kelly tapped his data pad two more times, and then the drones all froze.

"What the hell's going on?" Shockwave demanded to know. "Why aren't they firing?"

The drones all began to slowly turn and face the Guydrun soldiers that were flanking Colin and the others. Even Gaylie, still unconscious, spun around and aimed her gun at Shockwave.

"What are they doing?" Shockwave asked.

His armored comrade was repeatedly pressing his fingers on his pad. "They're not responding."

The drones began to open fire at the soldiers. Complete chaos broke out as several of the soldiers to the left and right were being cut down. The surviving soldiers began to

scatter while returning fire on the drones. Gaylie fired her machine gun at Shockwave. He raised his arm to his face as his helmet's visor closed. Ava dashed forward and tackled Gaylie to the ground. Colin, Diane, and Kelly all dove down to avoid getting caught in the crossfire between the drones and the soldiers.

Laying on his stomach, Colin looked over at Kelly. "What the hell's going on?"

Kelly shouted over the sounds of the gunfire to explain, "I used my sensor pad to jam the Guydruns' ID signals and broadcast it from our location. The drones think that the Guydruns are enemy targets."

Colin could not prevent himself from cracking a smile at Kelly's ingenuity. "I'll be damned. What a smart assed trick."

"Thanks, but we're still not out of the fire yet," Kelly returned.

Colin looked up at Shockwave and his partner.

Shockwave was stepping backwards as the soldiers around him were fighting to remove the threat of the rogue drones. His partner was still tapping on his pad in an attempt to reestablish control over them, but to no avail. Colin relieved him of the effort by aiming his hand and blasting the soldier with an electrical bolt that sent him flying back towards the buildings in the distance. The man's armor exploded during his flight, transforming him into a human fireball. He continued burning as he landed on the ground among the parked gunships. Shockwave leaped into the air. The jets on his wings spitting out fire as they lifted him into the sky at a rapid speed, then propelling him back towards the buildings in the distance.

"He's getting away," Diane said. She raised her laser gun up to the sky but did not fire at the fleeing Guydrun.

Colin was more concerned about Gaylie's condition then catching Shockwave. He crawled over to Ava, who was kneeling over the girl. "How is she?"

"I think she's ok," Ava told him. She removed the drone helmet from Gaylie's head. "I think they just had her drugged. She should be fine."

"Well we won't be if we don't get out of here," Colin told her. "Everyone, follow me."

Colin spun to his left. He swiped his hand out in front of him while discharging a bolt of energy that lifted three soldiers off their feet and sent them flying backwards. He turned to his right and swept the area of three more soldiers. Colin looked back to analyze Gaylie's condition. She was in a groggy state as Ava lifted her to her feet. Colin rose and dashed forward. Diane and Kelly ran to catch up to Colin as he was heading towards the buildings. Kelly was able to rapidly launch large balls of fire at both soldiers and drones to their right. All of his targets burst into flames upon impact. As the three were drawing closer to the buildings, Colin looked to the sky above them and saw Shockwave circling overhead. He stopped, then hovered. Then one of the gunships began to rise into the air. Hanging just five feet from the ground it propelled itself forward on a direct course to attack.

"I got this one," Diane shouted. She sprinted forward ahead of Colin and Kelly. Colin was amazed to watch Diane running forward with such a burst of speed. He was even more amazed to watch her running towards the gunship as the two large machine guns at the craft's nose began to open fire in her direction. Diane leaped high into the air to avoid the gunship's fire. It's rapid hail of bullets strafing the ground but missing her completely. The gunship stopped firing as Diane landed on the ground several feet away and did not break her stride as she continued running. When Diane and the gunship both met, she gave it a shove with her hand that was powerful enough to send it flying backward. The gunship flew back towards the buildings. It skidded against the pavement, then crashed into a second gunship that was parked in its path. The impact caused the second gunship to explode into large burning fragments, while the other gunship smashed through the wall of the building, then exploded.

Diane stopped running when Shockwave descended to a landing in front of the now burning building. He took aim at her with his concussive energy weapon and fired. With a bright flash and a loud boom, Diane was pushed backwards for just a few feet. She then managed to bend her knees and lower herself down in order to brace herself against the power of his weapon. With her hair being blown back and gnashing her teeth, Diane was now rooted firmly into place as Shockwave continued his assault.

"This is getting old!" Diane shouted.

Colin watched as Diane suddenly bolted forward against the onslaught of Shockwave's weapon. His weapon continued to discharge its power, but it was inadequate against Diane's strength. When Diane reached Shockwave, she quickly raised her fist and sent a solid punch into his armored chest. The power of Diane's blow was more than enough to send Shockwave flying back several yards, into the nose of a parked gunship. Still holding onto his weapon, Shockwave bounced off the gunship and dropped to the ground. Colin watched as Shockwave was laying still. Colin was expecting him to be out of the fight after he had taken this punishment from Diane. But to his amazement, Shockwave began rising to his feet.

We have to end this, Colin thought. Shockwave, now standing, aimed his weapon at Diane again. Colin whipped out his hand and fired an electrical bolt at the weapon. The weapon exploded in Shockwave's hands. The blast was powerful enough to shatter the visor on Shockwave's helmet. Shockwave cried out in pain, clasping his hands against the front of his helmet. He staggered backward, slamming against the gunship. He bellowed out again, then removed his hands to reveal the streams of blood pouring down his face. His left eye was closed. He gritted his teeth and opened a small compartment in the upper thigh of his right armored leg to bring out a small, black egg-shaped device. A grenade. "You freaks! I'll make you all burn for this," he snarled at Colin and the others. He pulled a small pin out from the top of the grenade, but before he could make another move, Diane raised her gun and shot six laser bolts into Shockwave's legs. He howled in pain as the laser fire burned through his armor with ease. He dropped to his hands and knees, also dropping the grenade, which landed on the ground right under him.

"Dammit! Dammit!" Shockwave yelled. His hands groped across the ground to try to reach the grenade. Then it exploded. Shockwave was engulfed in a blast that scattered flaming fragments of his armor through the air. Through a curtain of fire, the remains of Shockwave's burning body was barely visible. He was now permanently out of the fight.

"How many more of these idiots are going to have to die before the day is out?" asked Kelly.

"That might include us if we don't get out of here fast," Colin told him. From the distance, the gunfire between the Guydrun soldiers and the drones was beginning to subside. Colin looked back to see that the remaining drones stopped shooting and were now walking this way. They were also being joined by the soldiers, who were now regaining order. "Looks like your trick with the drones has worn off."

Ava was helping Gaylie, who was still in a groggy state, with her arm draped around Ava's shoulder. Ava pointed at two olive grey military trucks that were parked at the side of a building on the far left. The backs of both trucks were covered by tarps. "This way. We can take one of these trucks."

Ava, assisting Gaylie to move faster, led the way to the trucks. Colin went to the back of one truck and pulled away the tarp so he could take a quick look inside. The truck was empty. Colin helped Ava lift Gaylie inside. While Diane was climbing in the back with Ava and Gaylie, Colin and Kelly ran to the front. Colin climbed into the truck and sat in the driver's seat. Kelly quickly opened the passenger's side door and sat next to him. Colin looked at the right side of the steering column and was relieved to see the key card was still plugged into the ignition. He pressed a large green button above the card. There was the loud whine of the truck's engine coming to life. Colin glanced down at the stick shift lever protruding from the floor at his right. As his hands grasped the steering wheel a nervous, tight knot began to tighten in the pit of his stomach.

"Can you drive this thing?" Kelly asked Colin.

Keeping his gaze locked on the steering wheel Colin smiled. "Sure. No problem."

There was the sudden loud chatter of machine gun fire. The glass on the driver's side window shattered. Several small bullet holes appeared in the windshield. Colin did not bother to see where the gunfire was coming from. He grasped the stick shift lever and pulled it all the way back. He and Kelly were suddenly pushed back in their seats by the trucks forward momentum as the truck lurched forward. Colin drove the truck past the building and on a direct course towards the base's front gate in the distance. And the two soldiers standing guard in front of it. Colin could still hear gunfire coming from behind. With the truck coming under enemy fire, he was concerned about Diane, Ava, and Gaylie. "Are you guys okay back there?"

Diane's voice called out in response. "We're alright."

"Great," Colin said to himself. He pressed his foot down on the accelerator pedal. The truck began to move faster.

"Those guards up ahead are going to give us a problem," Kelly informed Colin.

"Not as much as that gate," Colin's response. Despite both obstacles, he did not reduce the truck's speed.

"I'm on it," Kelly quickly said. He pointed his hand and produced a bolt of fire that instantly burned through the windshield with a burst of sparks and glass shards. The fire bolt flew out of the truck and towards the gate. Colin was caught off guard by this unexpected action and jumped in his seat.

"Hey. What the hell?" Colin shouted at Kelly.

"Sorry," Kelly briefly apologized.

Traveling faster than the truck, Kelly's fire bolt continued flying directly towards the gate. It exploded on contact, ripping the gate apart. The two soldiers standing near the gate both dove to the ground when the explosion went off. Before they had a chance to get back to their feet, the truck came racing out of the newly created entrance and out of the base. Colin heard the more gunfire going off behind the truck. He imagined that the Guydruns would muster a force to give chase. He was intending to gain as much distance from them as possible.

"Where to now?" Kelly asked.

Back to the airfield. And our ship," Colin's answer. "We've still got our original mission to find the missing task force. Our best solid lead so far are these transmissions out in space."

"If we make it out to space. I don't think that these assholes are going to just let us stroll off this planet without giving us a problem."

Colin gave Kelly's words some thought. But his determination remained adamant. "I think they know us by now. We'll give them a bigger problem."

CHAPTER FIVE

Colin remained on edge as he was driving the truck back to the airfield despite there being no enemy forces chasing them. Once he got a good enough distance away from the Guydrun base, Ava instructed him to go off the main road and travel through a forest to avoid detection. When they finally reached the airfield, Colin was still feeling uneasy. Before them was the open gate to the airfield's parking area, empty and without a single Guydrun soldier or vehicle present.

"Look at this. Nothing," Colin quietly said. "I was expecting to see an army of tanks and soldiers waiting for us. But there's nothing. Not so much as a single soldier. Reaching the Black Raven can't be that easy."

"Don't complain," Kelly told him. "If we're getting away without any trouble, then enjoy it while you can."

"If only I could," Colin mumbled. He was still fearful that anything could happen when they reached the Black Raven.

Colin drove the truck into the parking area,

parked it and got out to scan the area. As the others were getting out of the truck, Colin carefully looked over the other vehicles in the parking lot. So far, he had seen no evidence that an enemy was hiding in wait, ready to strike at any second. Everyone followed Colin out of the parking area and over to the runway where they left the Black Raven. As they approached the ship, Colin saw his fears were not in vain. There were four Guydrun soldiers standing in front of the ship. Among them was the young red headed man that they had seen in the café back in Devarow. He and the soldiers were gazing directly at the group as they were approaching. Still walking purposefully towards the ship, Colin looked about to see if there were any other Guydruns in the area, but these five were the only ones.

Colin stopped just six feet away from these men. The others stopped with him. With a grin on his face, Colin addressed the enemy standing before him. "Lieutenant Drake. Thanks for watching over our ship while we were gone."

Drake glanced up at the Black Raven, then smiled as he looked back at Colin. "This is an impressive vessel. I've never seen anything like it before."

"Is that a fact? I've got a feeling that if you saw more of these ships coming your way, you Guydruns would drop your weapons and run," Colin taunted.

Drake held his smile. "I don't doubt that. So, I take it that you and your friends are leaving."

"That's right. You don't think you can stop us with just these four guys, do you?"

Drake laughed as he shook his head. "No. I wouldn't dream of trying to stand in your way. I know all about you, Colin McKenzie. The man that wields lightning as a weapon. You and your friends are quite unique, same with your ship. I was warned about people like yourselves. And where you come from. From outside the known quadrant."

Drake's statement surprised Colin. "So you know that?"

"We're not stupid," replied Drake. "We've been trying to trace human origins in space for decades. We know that there's other life far out there. But that's not important. The real question is why are you here?"

Colin thought that he'd withhold the true information from Drake about human origins, that the entire human race has been manipulated by an alien scientist who is now in exile in the dimension beyond mirrors. "Let's just say that our mission here involves more of these ships that you're so impressed with. If I were you, I'd start running now. Unless you're willing to make the same mistake that your pal Shockwave did."

Drake's smile faded under Colin's second taunt. Colin suspected he had struck a nerve. Drake gave a nod. "Yes. I've heard about the incident at our forward outpost. Alright, you're getting off scot-free then. Providing that you can get past our orbital patrols. I know just how powerful you people really are. We could assemble a big enough force to properly deal with you, but we agreed to follow the Gatherers' directives and limit our forces and activities in certain areas. But take this as a warning. Eventually that will reach its limit. We will find a way to destroy you."

Drake said nothing else as he and his men turned and walked away from the Black Raven. Colin and the others watched them as they left the parking area.

"Well, that was charming," came Diane comment.

Ava frowned. "Too bad you didn't kill that man. I've heard he's done some very terrible things. He's no better than Major Vormeister."

"I've got a feeling that we'll meet up with him again," Colin told Ava. "When that happens, he's not walking away. But in the meantime, we've got to get out into space before we run into any more trouble."

It took only a few minutes for the group to board the Black Raven and then take off into space. Colin, sitting into the seat next to Diane, watched as she once again performed her piloting with flawless precision. Ava and Gaylie both stood behind Colin and Diane, watching the scene through the forward window. Kelly once again took his place at the computer station. Through the forward window, the details of the scenery below quickly grew smaller as the Black Raven climbed higher into the sky. Within minutes, the darkness of space appeared as the Black Raven was climbing away from the planet Sidra.

Colin kept Drake's warning in mind, expecting to run across some form of enemy opposition. "Kelly, are you getting anything on the scanners?"

"I'm picking up eight spacecraft heading on an intercept course," Kelly reported. "Four of them are Guydrun. The other four are Tritian. Distance is fifty-three kilometers and closing."

"Looks like Drake kept his word," said Colin. "We've got a head start on them. Let's make it a little bigger. Diane, send us into a short warp jump."

Diane pressed several keys on the control panel in front of her. "Get ready," she said. She pressed one final key. The view from the forward window was filled by a bright white flash. Seconds later the darkness of space returned.

"Where are we?" Gaylie asked.

"Too far out for those patrols to reach us," Colin answered. "Kelly, any other ships in this area?"

"I'm not picking up anything."

"That's a relief," said Colin. "Give Diane the coordinates of this transmission. Let's see if this pans out or if we're just wasting our time."

Kelly's fingers rapidly typed on his computer

touchpad to transfer the coordinates to Diane's pilot controls. Diane typed on her control pad, then glanced over the small monitor above it.

"I have the coordinates. Our estimated time of arrival is one hour, ten minutes," Diane reported to Colin.

"They're not far," Colin uttered. "Let's hope that there's no surprises waiting for us."

The time passed quickly as the Black Raven traveled to the location in space where the mysterious Protectorate signal was originating. Colin and Diane both gazed out through the forward window. In the darkness of space, there was a shiny object in the distance.

"What the hell is that?" Diane asked Colin.

Colin turned his head back to look to Kelly. "Kelly, are you getting any readings on this? "

Kelly looked at his monitor. "I'm picking up a large metallic object. Most likely a starbase. Origin unknown. It doesn't have the same organic wood material as the Tritian base we came across earlier. It could be Guydrun."

"And this could be a trap," Colin added. "Are you certain that these are the coordinates that you got from Markus' people?"

"According to their data, this is the spot," Kelly replied.

Colin turned back to the forward window. "There's nothing out here except that thing. This makes no sense. Are you picking up anything else on the scanners?"

"Nothing. I'll try sending a message." Kelly tapped his keypad to access the controls to the ship's communications. Then he spoke out in a loud clear voice. "This is the United Protectorate ship Black Raven. Sending out a message to any Protectorate ships. Please respond."

Everyone listened to several seconds of silence. Kelly repeated his message.

"This is the United Protectorate ship Black Raven. Sending out a message to any Protectorate ships. Please respond."

There was still no reply.

"This is the United Protectorate ship Black Raven. Sending out a message to any Protectorate ships. If you're out there, please respond."

There was still no reply.

"This is the United Protectorate ship Black Raven. Sending out a message to any Protectorate ships. Any ship, please respond."

Then Kelly received a response in the form of a male voice.

"Black Raven. This is the United Protectorate destroyer, Hemlock. Come in, please."

Excited to hear this reply, Colin and Diane both smiled.

"Hemlock. It's good to hear from you," Kelly returned. "This is Kelly Lytton. Who am I speaking with?"

"This is Captain Paul Everton. It's good to hear from another Protectorate ship. What are you doing way out here? I don't recognize you as a member of our task force."

"We were sent out to this quadrant to find you. You guys were reported missing. Where exactly are you? How far are you from our location?"

Everton hesitated. "It's hard to say. We're trapped in some sort of strange dimensional space. We can't get out. We're separated from the rest of the task force. I don't even know if they're alive."

Colin rose up from his seat and approached the computer station. "Everton. This is Colin McKenzie of the Black Raven. What exactly happened?"

"We were with the other ships in the task force when

we entered this quadrant. We came upon this alien starbase. We tried to hail them, explaining that we were on a peaceful mission. Then they sent out these ships to attack us. Naturally we defended ourselves. We destroyed the alien ships, but then the starbase fired some kind of energy weapon at us, and we were somehow transported here. Wherever the hell *here* is. Several of the ships split up to try to find some way out of here. That's when we were attacked by these creatures. They swarmed over us. Almost ripped the Hemlock apart. Several of our major systems are out. Our engines and weapons are down. We have just enough emergency power to maintain life support and to try to send out a distress call. We have heavy casualties. Most of my crew are either dead or missing. All we can do is try to hide from them until help comes or they do."

Colin shuddered at the thought of what Everton and his crew had gone through, and the possibility of experiencing the same ordeal if they could find the Hemlock. After listening to Everton's story, Colin was hoping that Kelly could have some answers to this mystery. "They're trapped in some kind of dimensional space after confronting that starbase? How is that possible? And how is it possible that we can communicate with them?"

Kelly looked over his computer monitor. He typed on his keypad. "Give me a minute. I'm running a scan." Kelly's eyes were glued to his monitor. His finger tapped a key. He tapped three more times. He froze as he watched the monitor. Then he revealed his findings. "My scan is picking up a small wormhole in space. It's only a few inches in diameter. My guess is that's how we're able to pick up the Hemlock's signals. But the wormhole's stability seems to be fluctuating. Getting smaller. I don't know if it will stay open or close all together. As for the cause, it's obvious that this starbase is responsible. They have hyperspace technology the same as ours. But in this case, they can use it as a weapon."

"That's a comforting thought," Colin muttered. "Now the next question is who's behind this? From what we've seen so far, I don't think that the Guydruns or the Tritians are capable of this."

"But the Gatherers are," revealed Ava. "They have this technology that you described. This is part of their efforts to try to free Kimdrack."

Colin pondered the information before him. "Then that has to be a Gatherer starbase."

"So now what? We go and assault that thing?" Diane asked Colin.

"We don't have a choice," Colin told her. "This is our biggest lead to finding the missing task force. If the Gatherers have the power to send them to this weird dimension, then they should have the means to free them."

"True," Ava's comment. "But knowing the Gatherers, I don't think they're just going to give us what we ask."

"That's ok," Colin replied. "We're not going to ask." Colin returned to his seat next to Diane. "Take us to that starbase."

Diane pressed a button on her control panel, then pulled back her two control sticks. As the Black Raven was racing forward, the view of the starbase's shining form was getting larger and becoming clearer, but they were still too far away to make out any of its exact details. As they continued to draw closer, Kelly announced the emergence of a threat that Colin was expecting.

"Guys, we've got company. They've sent out four ships on a direct course for us."

"They didn't waste any time," Colin said.

Diane pressed several buttons on her control panel.

"Weapons hot. We're ready for them."

Through the forward window, the onrushing forms of four, dark, disk-shaped spacecraft appeared. They were flying in close formation as they approached the Black Raven. Then they began to spread out and stage their attack by firing crimson beams of energy at the ship. The impact of their weapons fire rocked the ship but caused no damage.

"That was a rough hit. But our shields are still holding," Kelly reported.

"They look like the same drone ships that we ran into back at the valley of mirrors," said Colin.

"I'm tracking them on our scanners. It looks like they're trying to surround us," Kelly warned.

For a second time, the Black Raven was shaken by the drone ships' weapons fire.

"This is your moment, Diane," Colin told her.

Diane said nothing as she pulled back on the flight control sticks, then shifted them to the right. Colin held on tightly to the edges of his seat while riding the momentum of the ship's sharp turn. Ava and Gaylie both had to kneel while hanging on to the back of Diane's seat to keep themselves from falling. Colin watched as Diane steered the ship into sharp zig-zagging maneuvers, then flying directly behind one of the drone ships. Her thumbs pressed red buttons on the sides of her control sticks to fire the Black Raven's four plasma cannons. A blue glow flashed around the drone ship as it was hit by the four red beams of plasma energy. A reaction of its defensive shields absorbing the attack. The drone ship veered off to the right. Diane put the Black Raven in a sharp turn to stay on its tail. At the same time, the Black Raven took more hits by the firepower of the other drone ships.

"Our shield strength is down to seventy four percent," Kelly cried.

"Diane. You've got to take these things out," Colin told her.

"I'm on it," Diane replied. "He's not going to just stop and wait for me."

Diane continued piloting the Black Raven in wild zig-zags to keep on the drone ship's tail. She fired several more bursts from the plasma cannons but missed. She executed a sharp loop with the drone, then fired the plasma cannons. Diane hit her target. The defensive energy shields at the drone ships rear section again flashed. Then its rear section exploded as the plasma fire penetrated it's shields and burned into it's hull. The drone ship began to spiral out of control. The Black Raven, matching it's speed and movements, stayed on its tail. Then a final burst of plasma fire caused it to explode.

Diane jerked the control sticks to the right. The ship veered off and a second drone ship came into view. Diane wasted no time firing the plasma cannons, striking the underside of the enemy ship. With it's shields standing up to the attack, the drone ship flew upward until it was out of view.

"Damn. These suckers can move," said Diane.

Kelly gave a report on the drone ships actions. "It looks like they're all scattering. Breaking off the attack. And I'm picking up some kind of energy surge building up from inside that starbase."

"An energy surge?" inquired Colin. "What the hell are they up to?"

Kelly continued. "The surge is getting stronger."

With the drone ships clearing away from the Black Raven and this strange energy surge from the starbase, Colin suspected they were being set up for a trap.

"The surge is getting stronger," Kelly warned.

"Get us out of here," Colin told Diane.

Diane jerked the control sticks sharply to the right. The Black Raven steered away just as a wide beam of light flashed by the forward window.

"Damn. That was close," Diane exclaimed.

"What kind of weapon was that?" asked Ava.

"I'm thinking maybe this hyperspace weapon of theirs," Colin's theory. "That's probably what happened to the Hemlock and the rest of the task force."

"If this weapon of theirs transports ships to an alternate dimensional space, then there's no defense against it," Kelly explained.

"Wrong. Our only defense is to not get hit," Colin argued. "Diane, see if you can catch up to one of those drones. Get as close to one as you can."

Diane began to pilot the ship into wild loops and spirals in order to close in on one drone ship. Through the forward window, the drone ship came into view. Its form growing larger as the Black Raven came closer. It executed one sharp turn and loop after the other, but Diane was able to keep close to it.

"The energy surge is decreasing," Kelly reported. "It appears to be staying at a lower level."

Colin considered this to be good news. "I hope they're holding off their weapon in case they don't want to take out one of their own ships."

"Yeah, but how long are they going to keep this up?" Diane asked Colin. "They might just say to hell with it and sacrifice their ship to get us."

Colin knew that Diane was right. They could not keep this up for very long. He had to come up with a new tactic. "Ok, then. Break off and head straight for the starbase. Top speed."

"What?" Diane squawked. "Are you high?"

"I'm testing a wild theory. Just trust me," Colin told her. "Do it."

Diane shifted the control sticks to the right. Then pulled them back. The Black Raven veered away from the drone ship and headed on a rapid course towards the shiny form of the starbase. As the Black Raven was drawing closer to the starbase, the details of its form were coming into clear view. Its huge, silvery, cylindrical body had four long, rectangular arms protruding from its sides. At the end of each arm, was a large scythe-like blade that reached up past the top of the base's main body. On the sides of the base's cylindrical form were columns of small red lights. In the middle of the cylinder was a single larger red light. At the bottom of the cylinder, there appeared to be a large rectangular opening.

As the Black Raven continued its rapid approach to the starbase, Kelly informed Colin about its activity. "The energy surge is building up again. They could fire their weapon at any second."

"Dive," Colin ordered Diane. "Go under the base."

"Are you sure about this?" Diane cried.

"This is no time to argue," Colin scolded.

Diane put the Black Raven into a sharp dive and headed on a course for the bottom of the starbase. Through the top of the forward window, Colin saw the white beam of the starbase's weapon flashing. *Another miss,* he thought. The Black Raven continued its fast dive to reach the underside of the starbase. Once it was underneath, Diane put the Black Raven into a wide turn to the left, while at the same time reducing speed. The Black Raven flew in a wide circle underneath the starbase, out of its weapon's range of fire.

They escaped the threat of the weapon up above. But even underneath, there was a second threat that they had to face. Several metallic globes emerged from the starbase's hull. Twin gun barrels extended from each of these globes, which then began to swivel around to aim their guns at the Black Raven. In seconds, the guns all began to open fire with blazing red energy bolts. Inside the Black Raven, everyone was being shaken as the ship endured the force of the combined firepower.

"These guns are hitting us pretty hard," Kelly shouted. "They're wearing our shields down. Shield strength is down to fifty three percent. We can't take much more of this. And now we've got company."

The form of two drone ships appeared in the distance, flying underneath the starbase with their weapons blazing as they headed directly towards the Black Raven. Diane pushed her control sticks forward while her fingers pressed their firing buttons. The Black Raven's four plasma cannons blazed away at the enemy ships as it was racing towards them. One of the drone ships veered off to the right to avoid the attack, while the other one was caught by the full force of the barrage. The concentrated plasma fire caused the ship to quickly explode. Diane turned the Black Raven around to pursue the second drone ship. They both began to fly in a wide circle underneath the starbase. The Black Raven was firing its weapons while holding a close pursuit on the drone ship, and at the same time being actively bombarded by turret fire.

"Shields down to forty two percent," Kelly cried out. "We seriously need to get out of here or we're going to be toast in space."

Colin already had another risky plan in mind. "Diane, get us out of here. Take us up into the base."

"What" Diane shrieked.

"That's our only refuge. And we might take them by surprise."

The Black Raven broke off the pursuit and headed for the edge of the starbase. Once it flew out from underneath, the Black Raven headed up along the side of the starbase to reach the large rectangular opening. The Black Raven flew through the opening and reduced its speed as it entered. Through the forward window, the group was able to get a clear view of the starbase's interior. They appeared to be in a large hangar for the drone ships. Along the ceiling, were two rows of large cylindrical mechanisms ending with three short metallic clamps. Attached to the clamps were more of the same drone ships that the Black Raven was battling outside. Colin caught the sight of one drone ship being released from its clamps and preparing to fly off.

"Diane. take out those ships," Colin ordered. Pointing at the forward window.

Diane opened fire with the Black Raven's plasma cannons, quickly destroying the drone ship. Diane did not stop with that single drone. She took the Black Raven lower and closer to the other drones that were still secured to their clamps, then she opened fire with the plasma guns, destroying them one by one.

Colin was now hoping that they could get a moment's respite now that the threat of the inactive drone ships was removed. But there were still two more of them to deal with. The Black Raven was shaken by the impact of enemy fire. Diane spun the ship around and opened fire on the two remaining drone ships that now entered the starbase. The battle was brief as the Black Raven destroyed them both.

Colin, gaping out through the forward window, saw no signs of any more drone ships. "I hope that's it. Kelly, are you picking anything up on the scanners?"

"I'm not getting any readings that resemble those drones. I think we've got them all. But my scans are picking up two life signs. Both human."

"Human?" said Colin. "That has to be two of the Gatherers. The ones operating this place."

"I can't imagine that they're going to be very happy about us breaking into their place and trashing their hardware," Diane pointed out.

"They can be pissed at us after they help free the Hemlock and the other ships from that dimension they're stuck in," Colin returned. "Kelly, is the air outside breathable?"

"I'm doing a quick scan. The air outside is breathable."

"Then let's go out and met our hosts," said Colin. We've got a lot to talk about."

Diane found a clear spot for the Black Raven to land. The group disembarked and began to explore the large hangar area with its silvery metallic walls and floor. With his Sensor pad in hand, Kelly led the way past the wreckage of the destroyed drones. Far above their heads were the mechanisms where the drone ships were secured. Black smoke was rising out from their now damaged forms after the Black Raven's assault.

"These life form readings are getting closer," Kelly informed the group. He turned to his right. "They're coming from this direction."

Colin was surprised to hear this. "They're coming to us? Then maybe we should wait for them."

"Do you think that's wise?" asked Ava.

"At this point we don't have much of a choice," Colin told her. "They're the only chance we have to find out how to get the Hemlock and the other ships back."

The group stood and waited for several tense seconds for the arrival of the base's occupants. Colin dismissed the possibility that their meeting would be pleasant but was fully prepared to deal with it. At the distant wall, a metal door before them slid open and three individuals dressed in white hooded robes appeared. Two of them walking in front of a taller person. Their hoods were draped over their heads, concealing their faces.

Colin looked to Kelly. "I thought you said that you picked up two humans. There's three."

Kelly's gaze switched from his sensor pad to the three robed figures. "I'm still getting the same reading."

The three robed figures stopped several feet away from the group. The two up front pulled back their hoods to reveal their faces. They were both middle aged men with short black hair. Colin was fully prepared to take offensive action against these two. But for the moment, he was curious to see what their intentions were.

The robed man on the right spoke to address the group. "So, you are the interlopers who have caused so much destruction against us. And now you dare to come here to one of our most sacred and holy places?"

"If it makes you feel any better, we'll put a donation into the collection plate before we leave," Colin jested. "But right now, we need you to help us release our friends from the dimensional space they're trapped in."

The man on the left gave out a laugh. "Are you referring to those other interlopers? They posed a threat to us. Same as you do. We dealt with them in a humane fashion. You won't get that luxury when we deal with you."

Colin scoffed at that threat. "Just the two of you? You must be pretty confident."

"Not us, you fool," the man rebuked.

Both robed men stepped aside as the taller person behind them stepped forward. Colin and the others watched as this person's transparent glass-like right hand reached up to pull back his hood to reveal his features. His entire head was as transparent as glass, save for the network of glowing green lines inside that resembled printed circuitry. His large, unblinking eyes were glowing bright green. He extended his left arm out to the group, revealing it to be a glassy gun barrel.

This explains why Kelly only picked up two life forms, Colin thought. *That thing's not human.*

Kelly dropped his sensor pad and held out both hands to create a large wall of his red reflecting energy just as the creature's gun arm spat out a burst of blue fire. The attack instantly bounced off Kelly's shield and was sent back to the creature. The creature staggered backward as its robe was engulfed by the strange fire. It grabbed the burning garment and ripped it away from its body. Tossing the burning robe aside, the creature now revealed its full glass-like body laced with the glowing network of printed circuitry inside. Attached to its back was a large glass cylinder.

"Devastator! Kill them!" one of the robed men commanded.

Devastator began to walk forward. The cylinder on its back began to shrink as it quickly morphed into a pair of broad wings. Devastator then leaped into the air and took flight. Colin was surprised to see that the creature's instant wings were able to keep it aloft without the benefit of any type of visible propulsion. *Another flier. Great,* was his thought.

Devastator circled in the air high above the group. Then, from its gun arm, it launched a blue fireball down at Kelly. Kelly extended his hands above his head and again erected a large panel of his red energy. The fireball created a huge explosion when it collided with Kelly's shield. Its force was enough to knock everyone off their feet. Laying on his stomach, Colin rose to his knees and looked up to see Devastator circling around. "Everybody, scatter," he shouted to the others.

The group all jumped to their feet and ran off in different directions just as Devastator launched another explosive fireball. It hit the floor just several feet in front of Kelly just as he was running off. The force of its blast hurled Kelly into the air and threw him against the side of a wall that was several feet away. Colin, taking refuge behind a mass of wreckage from a destroyed drone, watched Devastator circle around and fly off into the distance. Then, as it came flying back, it shot three fireballs down into the area. A quick succession of three powerful explosions went off, hurling metal debris in all directions. Colin looked about to see if he could locate the other members of his party. To his far right, Kelly had recovered from his collision with the wall and taken refuge behind a large mass of metal debris. At Colin's far left, he saw Gaylie, who was also hiding behind a mass of torn metal. Diane and Ava were nowhere to be found.

Colin decided to go on the offensive. He sprang up from his cover and aimed his hands up at Devastator, who just turned around and was beginning to circle away. Firing his first twin lightning bolts from his hands, he missed Devastator. His second shots also missed as Devastator ducked under them. Devastator made a sharp turn and then came soaring in to make another strafing run. That was when Colin's third set of shots hit their mark. There was a bright white flash and a huge burst of sparks when Devastator was hit. Colin was expecting to see the wreckage of the creature dropping to the floor. Instead, Devastator was simply hovering in the air, apparently unharmed by Colin's electrical attack. Then, it dashed forward and launched a fireball straight at Colin's position. Colin made a mad dash to his right and dove to the floor to escape the deadly explosion in time.

One of the Gatherers bellowed out a loud taunt. "You mindless fools! You cannot hope to escape!"

Colin was determined to prove him wrong on that boast. To his right, a large, red ball of fire flew up towards Devastator. It executed a wide loop to avoid being hit. Colin turned to see Kelly shooting up a second fire ball at Devastator. He fired a third and then a fourth, but Devastator was able to avoid each one with its agile maneuvering. At his left Colin caught the sight of rapid laser fire streaking up into the air towards

Devastator. He was relieved to see that Diane was unharmed and was joining the fight with her laser gun. She managed to hit Devastator twice, but then it began to fly in a series of wide loops and spirals to avoid both her and Kelly's assault. It turned and began to fly from the area. Colin thought that this would be a perfect moment to make a move that would catch the robotic menace by surprise. He charged up his right hand, feeling it tingling with power. He aimed his hand to the metallic floor and sent a surge of power into its surface. He quickly directed the energy down across the floor towards a huge mass of metal debris. Exercising his control over electrically conductive materials, Colin engulfed the metal wreckage in streams of a powerful electromagnetic force. Raising his hand, he sent the debris flying up into the air at Devastator. It was caught by this unexpected barrage from below, battered several times by the heavy metal fragments. It then dropped to the floor.

Devastator was lying face down, but already starting to rise. Colin was not going to let this advantage go to waste. He quickly walked towards Devastator and used his power to take control of another huge chunk of metal. With a wave of his hand, he levitated the metal fragment and sent it crashing into Devastator just as it rose back to its feet. The fragment smashed Devastator into a wall with the sound of a loud thud. The fragment made an equally loud thud when it dropped to the floor, leaving Devastator standing against the wall. As Colin, Diane, and Kelly began to cautiously advance towards Devastator, it began to stagger away from the wall. With its head sloping down, it shuffled forward. Colin pointed a hand and hit Devastator with a bolt of electrical energy while Kelly hit the creature directly in its chest with an intense stream of fire. A powerful explosion against its body caused Devastator to stagger back against the wall. Then it stood unmoving.

Colin was still cautious as he, Diane, and Kelly moved in closer to see if Devastator was now disabled. The robot remained still, its head leaning down and its arms hanging limp. There was a gaping chunk of glassy material blasted away from its chest, the fragments laying across the floor at its feet.

Colin froze, taking the time to examine the disabled creature. He was sure that it was no longer a threat. "That takes care of that thing."

"Don't get overconfident," shouted the Gatherer. "This battle is far from over."

Colin had reason to doubt the man's boast, until he looked on at Devastator's immobile form and the fragments from its body laying at its feet. Suddenly, the fragments began to break into smaller sections. Each section continuing to break down into smaller pieces until they became even smaller fragments. These fragments amazingly sprouted tiny legs and began to crawl up along Devastator's legs and up along its torso in order to reach the gaping hole in its chest. Once they reached this spot, the individual crawling fragments began to link together until they filled the hole, effectively repairing Devastator's damage.

"Well that's something new," Diane quipped.

The Gatherer laughed out loud. "You see? You idiots. You have no chance against our technology. Your only option now is to decide who dies first."

Devastator raised its head and took a step forward. It swung its gun arm around and aimed it at the trio. Kelly moved fast, raising his hands to create a wide wall of his reflective red energy just as Devastator's gun arm shot out a stream of blue fire. The fire scattered into five separate streams as it bounced off Kelly's energy wall. One of these streams flew back, striking the two

Gatherers. Both men screaming out in agony as their bodies burst into flames. Devastator halted its attack and turned to watch as its masters thrashed on the floor. Colin took advantage of the robot's hesitation, raising his right hand to send a powerful bolt of energy into its head. Kelly's energy wall instantly faded as he launched a fireball at Devastator's chest. Colin's bolt seared through the top of Devastator's head while Kelly's exploding fireball blasted another large hole in its chest, severing its right arm. Devastator staggered back against the wall. Once again, the severed fragments of its body broke down into smaller components and crawled back up to repair Devastator's damaged body. Even it's severed arm broke itself down and its pieces moved back to reform with the robot's body.

How the hell do we beat this thing? was Colin's thought. *As fast as we break the thing it fixes itself.* Colin had to think of some means of effectively dealing with Devastator. The robot was now fully repaired and stepping forward to get back into the fight. *What happens if all those pieces can't get back together again?*

"Kelly. Hit him again," Colin ordered. He and Kelly both concentrated their attack. A powerful, fiery explosion engulfed Devastator's body. When the flames dissipated, there was a large hole blown clear through Devastator's torso. This time both of its arms were blown off. Already, the glassy broken fragments were starting to break themselves down and reform. But this time, Colin used his power to electromagnetically levitate a six-foot-long, twisted beam of metal. The beam sprang into the air and flew spinning towards Devastator. It struck the robot in the hole through its body, driving itself clean through. Colin watched as Devastator's fragments crawled up over its body and swarmed over the metal beam. Colin did not stop there. He caused the beam's metal to disperse into dozens of tiny streams. Moving under Colin's direction, these streams began to spread throughout Devastator's torso. Then they penetrated his legs and head. With jerky, clumsy steps it moved away from the wall. Colin could see the robot's form growing darker as the foreign metal was filling its body. Devastator's head thrashed to the left and right, then the rest of its body reacted in the same manner. The individual fragments of Devastator were still swarming around the metal beam in a futile effort to rejoin with the robot's body. Devastator dropped to its knees, it's head still thrashing about. Then it fell to its face on the floor. For several seconds, its legs were twitching, then stopped. At the same time, the swarm of Devastator's fragments also stopped moving. Abandoning their mission to repair the damaged robot, they collapsed into an inert heap of powder.

Colin, with his hands still aimed at the seemingly deactivated monster, slowly walked towards it. Diane and Kelly also moved in closer. Diane keeping aim with her laser gun, while Kelly's hands glowed red with an aura of fire. Colin studied the robot for several seconds. Within that time, there was no reaction. Satisfied, he lowered his hands and exhaled a deep breath.

"Alright. I guess he's down," said Colin.

Ava and Gaylie both approached the robot. "How the hell did you do that?" asked Gaylie. "How did you kill it?"

"It was a long shot. When I watched this thing repair itself, I was wondering what would happen if it was infected by some foreign matter from the inside," Colin explained. "My long shot paid off. This metal wreckage somehow disrupted its functions. Sort of like having a few pounds of molten metal poured down your throat."

Gaylie shuddered. "This is another reason why I'm thankful that you guys are on our side. So, what is this thing? It looked like a robot. But not like any that I've ever seen."

Kelly offered his explanation. "Judging by the way it kept putting itself back together, I'd say that this is some form of advanced Nano tech."

"Nano tech?" Gaylie inquired.

"Nano tech comes from the use of nanites. Nanites are tiny machines that can be engineered to merge and create larger components, even complex things like this robot. But seeing it operate on this scale is amazing."

Colin agreed. "This is no doubt technology that the Gatherers have taken from Kimdrack. Just like that hyperspace weapon of theirs."

"And what about that weapon?" asked Diane. "I doubt we're going to get any technical advice from those two Gatherers. They're both crispy fried."

Colin turned to his left and saw the blackened, smoldering bodies of the Gatherers, both burned beyond recognition. "I think we're going to have to improvise. Let's explore this place and see if we can find some sort of control room."

Kelly ran back to retrieve his sensor pad that he dropped among the rubble. Then he joined the others as they headed for the doorway the Gatherers emerged from. The group entered a square corridor with the same silvery walls and floor as were in the hangar. Kelly tried to take some readings with his sensor pad but could not find anything helpful. They passed by one open doorway on the left side of the corridor that revealed a sleeping quarters with two small, white beds. At the foot of both beds were large white footlockers.

"These guys won't be sleeping here again," Colin said in a quiet voice. He and the others moved on.

Walking further down the corridor, they came upon another open doorway on the left. When they entered the room, its contents appeared to be more encouraging. It was a large square room. Positioned against the surrounding four walls were six-foot-tall, three-foot-wide, silvery columns. At the top of each column was a square, blue holographic monitor displaying rows of strange symbols. In the center of the room were four columns grouped together. Their holographic screens displayed scenes of the empty space outside the starbase.

Diane looked about the room and then turned to Colin. "This looks like some kind of control room."

Colin agreed. "That was my guess too. But just what does this place control?"

Kelly held his sensor pad up against one of the columns in the middle of the room. "I have no idea what these things do." He pressed a finger against the side of one column. He quickly jerked his hand back as a blue holographic keyboard appeared below the monitor. Kelly examined the keyboard, his finger hovering close to its surface from left to right. He then looked to Colin. "This technology is over my head. I have no idea what these things do."

Colin walked over and glanced at the keyboard and monitor. "There has to be some way to find out what these things do."

Kelly frowned. "Not unless you want to risk trial and error. Error might prove to be fatal. If we touch the wrong controls, we could end up activating a self-destruct sequence, and we'd never even know it until the base blows up. And look at these symbols on the keyboards and monitors. I have no idea what these things mean. This has to be some form of Gatherer language."

"Or Kimdrack's," Colin added. He looked around at the other columns in the room. "That hyperspace weapon of theirs has to be controlled from here. If not somewhere else in this base. We need some way to decipher these controls."

"Not without a Gatherer to English dictionary," Kelly returned. "And the only Gatherers that could have helped us are practically cremated."

True, Colin thought. The accidental deaths of the two Gatherers was a loss to their cause. But in Colin's mind, there was still hope. "Then we'll go get some new ones."

"What?" Diane exclaimed.

"We're going to go grab two or more Gatherers and make them work this technology and help us free the task force. Have you forgotten that we just came from a planet that's loaded with them?"

"You make it sound as easy as picking apples," Diane rebuked. "And we don't exactly know where to find them back on the planet."

Colin grinned. "We don't. But we know someone who does. Let's go back and pay another visit to Markus."

CHAPTER SIX

"You want what?" Markus bellowed out to Colin's face. A red spot suddenly appearing on his forehead.

This was the reaction that Colin predicted from Markus when they returned to his building lobby in Devarow to ask him this favor. "You heard me. We need your help in kidnapping some of the Gatherers. We don't need a mob. Maybe just two or three of them."

"Oh, is that all? And would you also want me to provide a four-course dinner for them too? And maybe treat them to an evening at the theatre?"

"If you think that will make them more cooperative, then I can go with that," came Colin's humorous reply.

Markus scowled at Colin. "You're a real funny man, McKenzie. You know that? You're a combination of comedian and mental patient. What the hell could you possibly want with the Gatherers?"

"We made contact with the Hemlock. They're trapped in this alternate dimensional space. We need the Gatherers to operate a hyperspace weapon and free them."

"Even if you were able to get one or more Gatherers, there's no guarantee that you can make them cooperate," Markus pointed out.

Colin was fully aware of that fact. "We'll cross that bridge when we come to it."

"My advice is to burn that bridge," Markus countered. "You have no idea how dangerous these people are. And you want me to help you piss them off? It's all that we can do to keep ourselves under the radar while we're operating in one of their installations."

"We're not asking you to invite them here for coffee," Colin angrily returned. "We just need to know where we can find them, and we'll do the rest."

Ava walked over to Markus and placed a hand on his shoulder. "Markus, you must help. This is very important to our friends who have done so much to help us."

"You mean help you," Markus corrected. "These aliens haven't done anything for me except put my operation at risk."

Ava simply repeated her plea. "Markus, please. As a favor to me. This means a lot."

Markus spent the next several seconds staring into Ava's eyes. Then he lowered his head and heaved a loud sigh. Then he looked up at Colin. "Fine, but you aliens keep in mind that I'm doing this as a personal favor to Ava. I know where you can get access to the Gatherers. They have a base just a few miles outside the city of Tennison. It's about thirty miles away from here. Now we know very little about what goes on inside this base, but the outside is heavily fortified. The whole place is surrounded by a mine field that's nearly a quarter of a mile wide. It has more defensive gun emplacements than you can count, as well as patrols by flying drones. The base itself is surrounded by a twenty-foot-high wall that's also fortified by some sort of defensive energy shield. And let's not forget even more guns."

Colin considered this information to be foreboding. "Sounds like this place is tighter than the Tritian detention camp."

"Going against this place will be a nightmare," Markus commented. "You'd need ten times the army that you'd need to take on the Tritians. It would be insanity. But there is still a way to get to the Gatherers. They keep themselves quarantined in their base all the time, but occasionally come out and travel to the city. That is where they are at their weakest."

"So, we strike at them when they leave," said Colin. "Just like our plan with the Tritians when they move their prisoners. We can make that work. What about their security?"

"We have no way of knowing. They usually travel in a small caravan of two or three cars. I'm certain that they have armed security, but overall, nobody has ever dared try to threaten them. Not when you consider the fact of reprisals from their chief enforcer."

Colin knew full well who that enforcer was. He winced at the thought of her name. "Deevor. Have any idea where she is right now?"

"She's disturbingly close," Markus said. "She's up north. We're keeping her movements closely monitored. Just like we're keeping the Tritians monitored when they're prepared to transport their prisoners."

"We'll deal with Deevor when the time comes," Colin told Markus. "But now we need you to give us the location of this Gatherer base. From there, we can set up an ambush."

Markus once again guided the group down to his underground command center. Once inside, he took them over to the male technician who was working at the station near the tall column with the three holographic screens projected in front of it. Markus ordered him to bring up a detailed map of the area surrounding Devarow. A map appeared on the center holographic screen. It had six red circles. Markus pointed to one of the circles.

"This is the base in question. It has no known name or classification. All we know is that this is the home of the Gatherers in this region. Like I said before; Trying to break into this place won't be a picnic. So, if you want to try to get some Gatherers as hostages, then your best bet is to try to get them on the road. But you never heard that from me."

Colin studied the map, paying attention to the roads near the Gatherer base. "Too bad we don't know what they do inside this place. Have you ever tried to find out what goes on in there?"

Markus laughed and threw his hands up into the air. "Oh sure. They give guided tours of the place at least once a week. I should have taken down notes the last time I was there."

Suddenly the holographic screen turned black, as did the other two at its left and right. Followed by all the other screens in the room.

"What happened?" asked Markus. Pointing a finger at the black screen. "Get that back."

The technician pressed several keys on his computer touchpad but yielded no progress. "I'm trying to get the image back, but so far nothing is working. It's like we're locked out."

"Locked out?" Markus cried. He turned to the other technicians sitting in front of their black screens. "How about the rest of you? Are you getting anything?"

Several technicians throughout the room responded with a resounding no. Colin, looking about at the black screens, could not help but to take this as a bad omen. Standing at his right, Diane voiced what he was fearing. "I've got a really bad feeling about this."

On the holographic screens across the room, the

image of a middle-aged man with a graying beard and moustache, wearing a white hooded robe appeared. He spoke out in a loud, baritone voice.

"You filthy trespassers. You mindless animals. You dare to defile this sacred place with your diseased presence? And you actually think that you have the mental capacity to understand how to manipulate that which our lord Kimdrack has left behind? Let alone tamper with this technology for long without us being able to trace you to this location? It pains me to think that you fools managed to discover this facility before us. Just as it pains me to now consider this entire location to be expendable. Our lord Kimdrack demands your destruction. So, we must make the sacrifice."

After the Gatherer was finished making his address, the screens in the room all turned black again. Colin's sense of foreboding grew worse.

Ava frowned. "What does that mean?"

"Trouble," Markus spat out. He walked over to the other columns to inspect their screens. "They're all still down. We're now effectively blind."

"Blind?" said Diane. "Then we have no way of knowing what they're going to do next."

"I think we already know what their next move will be," Colin told her.

Markus frowned. "I was afraid something like this would happen," He turned away from the group and faced the technicians, then blared out an announcement. "Everyone. We're evacuating. Take what you can and clear out now. We're regrouping at location Zeta."

"Location Zeta?" Colin inquired.

"It's another Gatherer facility that we've unearthed. This place isn't the only one," Markus explained. "Zeta is a facility with artifacts similar to this one. But smaller. It's hidden far away from the Gatherers and you."

Colin was surprised. "Us?"

"Yes," Markus snapped. "You aliens aren't coming

within a mile of the place. You've already caused enough damage. I blame you for all this."

Colin was insulted by Markus' accusation, but he was also developing a lingering feeling that Markus was right.

"Markus. You can contact the mayor and civil defense. If we're going to be under attack, then you must warn them to evacuate the city," Ava told him.

"I'll get in touch with them at once," Markus answered. He rushed out of the room with the rest of his staff.

"We'd better get out of here too," said Colin. "Ava, can you get a car from Markus and drive Diane back out to the airfield so that she can get the Black Raven? We're going to need it for a fast get away."

"What are you and Kelly going to do while I'm gone?" asked Diane.

"We're going to stay behind and try to give the people a chance to evacuate," Colin explained. "I don't know what's coming, but maybe we can try to hold it back."

Everyone left the command center and exited the building. Colin had a strong feeling of dread as he ventured outside. The people were still going about their normal routines. Traffic on the streets was still moving normally. The people were all unaware that there was an impending threat to the city.

Diane ran off with Ava to get a car. Gaylie remained behind. "I'm staying," she told Colin.

"No," Colin disagreed, "We need you to go. If there's a fight coming, then you know the kind of people we deal with."

"Yeah," said Gaylie, pointing a finger at Colin. "And I've been fighting them long before you guys showed up. I'm not sitting out this fight. You can't make me leave."

Colin   admired   Gaylie's   courage   and

determination. He was also in no mood to argue. "Ok, fine. You stay. Just be careful. We're not losing you too."

"I'm a big girl, Colin. And I'm also a soldier," Gaylie scolded. "I may not have powers like you guys, but I can still fight for my world. It's my job."

I just hope that your job doesn't end up getting you killed, was Colin's dire thought.

Suddenly, the air was filled with the sound of a siren, blaring so loudly that it was nearly drowning out Colin's thoughts. *Now it begins.*

The people on the street all froze and looked up to the sky. Then they began to scatter and run. The vehicles on the road began to speed up and move faster to drive away from the area. Stepping forward and standing at Colin's left, Gaylie raised her machine gun up to chest level. Kelly, at Colin's right, charged up his power. His hands taking on a red glow of fire. As the trio stood and waited in the middle of the sidewalk, a small crowd of people ran past them. They waited for the next few minutes while watching the people running through the streets in a blind panic. So far, the threat to the city had yet to emerge. Then up ahead, there was the sound of an explosion.

"Get ready," Colin told Kelly and Gaylie.

The sounds of more explosions could be heard. This time, they were closer. More people were running through the streets in a screaming panic, as well as rushing out of the buildings. Then the source of the explosions revealed themselves. Three of the Gatherers' dark, disk shaped drone ships came flying above the rooftops. They began to fire their red energy weapons, setting off explosions on the buildings and the street below. People trying to flee the area were hurled into the air as they were caught in the blasts. The drones continued their onslaught as they progressed deeper into the city, getting closer to Colin, Kelly, and Gaylie, who were standing in wait.

"Hold your position," Colin told Kelly and Gaylie. He saw that Kelly's hands began to glow brighter. Colin took this time to build up his own power, feeling his hands tingling with his rising energy.

The very moment that the drones came within range, Colin and Kelly both released their powers. Colin sent up twin electrical bolts up at one while Kelly assaulted a second drone with rapid fire balls. Both drones instantly halted in mid-flight as they were struck by the attacks. Their energy shields flashed as they absorbed the firepower. Colin and Kelly both launched a second attack. This time with more devastating results as they penetrated the drone's shields and ripped into their metal hulls. Both drones exploded into a hail of burning fragments that scattered about the area below. The third one appeared no sooner than the first two. It fired its energy weapon down at Colin and Kelly. Kelly quickly created a large, square panel of his red deflecting energy shield which sent the drone's firepower streaming back at it upon contact. When the drone was hit by its own attack, it wobbled in the air while its shield flashed. Colin fired two of his electrical bolts up at the drone, piercing its shields and causing the front section of its hull to explode. The drone began to make a rapid descent to the ground. A hail of fragments flew out from the drone as it hit the pavement. It came to rest as a smoking wreck.

Gaylie pointed up to the sky. "There's two more," she cried.

Two more drones came flying above the rooftops. When they came within range, they both began firing their energy weapons at the trio below. Kelly again erected his red energy shield the deflect the drones' attack back at them. Both drones stopped in midair as their shields were battered, then veered off to the right and flew away from the area. Colin fired two more blasts at the fleeing drones, but they began flying in wild spirals in order to evade being hit. The drones flew back over the city, then separated and dove down among the buildings.

With the drones now out of view, Colin remained on the alert. "Keep an eye on the buildings. I think they're circling around for another attack."

Colin remained tense as he was watching the street, waiting for the drones' next attack. So far, there was nothing in the distance, save for a few abandoned cars. Then he spied the sight of one drone ship flying down the street on fast approach. *There's one. Where's number two?* he asked himself. He spun around and looked to the rear to see the second drone also flying low on fast approach from far away.

"They're coming at us from both sides," Colin warned Kelly and Gaylie.

Colin was not about to wait until the drone up ahead was in range. He aimed his right hand to the ground and sent a powerful surge of electricity into the pavement. Utilizing his ability to direct his power to any specific target, Colin sent his stream of electricity coursing underground until it came within range of the fast approaching drone. Colin then directed his underground lightning bolt to split apart into several smaller bolts. All of them streaming up from the ground and striking the underside of the drone. The drone began to spin out of control. The bombardment of electrical power weakened the drone's shields and ripped it apart with a fiery explosion.

Colin turned away from the destroyed drone's burning fragments and watched as Kelly was dealing with the second attacking drone ship. The drone was still half a block away but approaching fast. Kelly held out his right hand and a tall, thick wall of his blue energy suddenly appeared on the street, directly in the path of the oncoming drone. Flying too fast and unable to stop or evade in time, the drone crashed headlong into the wall, exploding instantly. The impact and explosion put several small holes through Kelly's shield wall. But standing among the flaming wreckage it had endured.

Colin, with his hands still coursing with electrical power, looked up to the building's rooftops to see if any more drone ships were coming to attack. For the next few seconds, he continued looking up at his left and right, but the skies were clear. Colin powered down but remained on alert.

"So that's it?" asked Kelly. "For all the trash talking, I expected more."

"Maybe it's not over," said Gaylie.

The sound of movement caught Colin's ears. He turned to the right and saw a young black woman in a blue dress running out from her cover behind a white pickup truck. She had shoulder length red hair. Her black high heel shoes made rapid clacks on the pavement as she was rushing towards Colin, Kelly, and Gaylie. She was accompanied by a young white male with long black hair. He was wearing a black T-shirt, blue pants, and black sneakers. He was holding up a small, dark video camera, pointing it directly at the trio.

"That was amazing," The woman exclaimed. A smile beaming on her face. "That was incredible. Who are you people? What are you?"

Colin was surprised by the woman's presence. As well as confused by her questions. "Who are we? Who the hell are you?"

"I'm Linda Jones. A reporter with Central Media," She revealed, still smiling. "This is Al Sharpie. He's my video tech. We need to do a story on you. Who are you?"

"I'm Kelly Lytton," Kelly stated, returning a smile.

"Are you serious?" Colin shouted out. "Lady, we're in the middle of a war and you want to do an interview?"

The sound of a loud boom now attracted Colin's attention. Everyone turned their heads to see that the noise was coming from the drone ship that crashed landed on the street several feet away. Another boom came from the drone. Colin was expecting the drone to succumb to the extensive damage that it had suffered and finally explode. Instead, there was the sound of a third boom. Then a large section of the drone's hull flew off and landed across the street. The source of the disturbance climbed out of the drone ship and onto the street. Deevor the Destroyer. Brushing her long black hair away from her face after breaking out of the drone ship, she turned her head to meet the eyes of Colin, Kelly, and Gaylie. An evil grin appeared on her face.

Now Colin understood the true force behind the Gatherers threat. Deevor. The last person he was expecting to see here now.

"McKenzie," Deevor called out. "I knew that eventually I'd run into you again."

Despite his fear at the notion of facing Deevor again, Colin displayed a calm demeanor. "We were hoping to see you one more time before we left this planet."

"It will be the last," Deevor told him. "I see that you're not all here. Where's your girlfriend? That bitch, Christy?"

"She's on her way," replied Colin. "I imagine that you're not too thrilled for a reunion with Diane. Considering she pretty much kicked your ass in our last fight."

Deevor scowled at Colin's taunt. "You bastards were lucky. But now your luck just ran out."

Deevor raised her hands. Her palms took on a bright red glow, then then a huge burst of fire erupted from them. Kelly quickly countered by raising his hands and creating a large wall of red reflecting energy to repel her attack. Deevor's blast created a loud and powerful explosion when it hit Kelly's shield wall. The blast was powerful enough to hurl everyone back to the ground. Colin, laying on his back, could still hear the boom of the explosion thundering through his head. He turned to see that everyone was down. He looked over at Deevor. She was holding a sinister grin on her face while her body was taking on a bright white glow as she absorbed the energy that was fed back to her. Colin had to think of something to at least hold off this monster who could absorb all forms of energy-based attacks. And with electricity being his prime weapon, the job would not be easy.

Deevor laughed as she began to walk towards Colin. "Too easy. I wish that Christy was here to watch me kill you all before she gets her turn."

Gaylie sprang to her feet and began to fire her machine gun at Deevor. She continued her rapid, full auto assault until her weapon's clip was empty, but Deevor was unharmed. Gaylie quickly removed her empty clip and replaced it with a full one, then resumed firing at Deevor. Deevor's only reaction was to laugh.

Colin felt grateful to Gaylie buying him a few vital seconds to take action. He sprang to his knees and pressed his hands onto the pavement. He activated his ability to manipulate the electrically conductive ground in order to create a wide, growing fissure that rapidly spread from his hands to where Deevor was standing. Deevor stepped back away from the fissure, but it was opening too fast for her to avoid being swallowed. Colin jumped back to his feet, as did Kelly and the two reporters. He knew that the fissure would not hold Deevor for long. While she was already starting to climb out, he sought to take a creative approach to using his power. He looked to his left at an abandoned blue car. He thrust out his right hand and fired a bolt of energy at the vehicle, causing it to instantly explode. Still exercising his power, he seized control over the car's metal parts and drew them towards himself. The mass of metal debris stopped just six feet in the air from Colin. He then thrust his hand out towards Deevor, causing the mass of debris to fly towards her. Deevor was pummeled by the debris, causing her to step back towards the fissure.

Kelly thrust his hands out towards Deevor and created a thick, blue wall of energy directly in front of her. His effort to block her proved to be futile when she punched her fist through the wall. She then tore the wall apart with a single swipe of her arm. Its blue fragments scattered about and faded away.

Deevor pointed a finger at Kelly. "Is that the best you can do?"

Colin was thinking the same thing. Against Deevor, their options were limited. Stand and continue to fight a futile battle or run. Assuming that they were able to run very far from her. Then Colin heard the whooshing of air behind him. He turned and was surprised to see the Black Raven flying in on a fast approach. To Colin, it was a welcoming sight. The Black Raven, piloted by Diane, rapidly reduced its speed, coming to a quick stop. As it hovered several feet above Colin's head, its four plasma cannons began to open fire upon Deevor. The rapid fire of plasma energy exploded over Deevor and the area surrounding her.

While she was being hammered by the attack, Colin saw this as the perfect opportunity to make an escape. "Let's get out of here. Move it," he shouted to the others.

Everyone ran back away from the area as the Black Raven continued to pound Deevor with its plasma cannons. Colin ran down the street several yards away from the scene. Then he stopped and turned to see that the Black Raven was still raining plasma fire down on Deevor until she fell back into the fissure. Then it stopped and spun to the left, facing a tall building. Two missiles were fired from its front. They struck the side of the building and exploded. The twin blasts were powerful enough to completely wreck the building's base. The structure began to collapse upon itself, sending tons of concrete and metal crashing to the ground and burying Deevor while she was still inside the fissure.

Colin's view of the area was obscured by the thick clouds of dust that was churned up by the collapsing building. He was certain that Deevor was buried under the massive rubble but knew that she would survive. He was not sure how long she would remain buried, but this gave himself and the others enough time to board the Black Raven and leave before she dug her way out. Despite all this, Colin knew that the next encounter with Deevor would be inevitable. There would be no running next time.

CHAPTER SEVEN

Colin was growing impatient as he was standing with Kelly, Gaylie, and reporters Linda Jones and Al Sharpie beside a country road flanked by large grassy fields and groves of trees. They were waiting here for almost two hours as they were expecting the Gatherers to travel from their base that was several miles up the road. Colin was not expecting an encounter with these people to be easy or pleasant. But considering the urgency of their mission, he was also in no mood to be pleasant.

Colin could tell that Kelly was also getting impatient with waiting. An indication given by the loud sigh that he was heaving. "You think that they're going to show up?" he asked Colin.

"Markus said that they use this road to travel into town," Colin told him. "He didn't say when. So, our best bet is to just wait."

"It's the waiting part that bothers me," Kelly replied. "What if Deevor finds us out here? You heard what she did in Devarow."

Colin frowned. "I know." During their flight, they listened to the radio transmissions that Linda received. Deevor had completely destroyed the Fenwig building where Markus and his people were working, and the hidden Gatherer installation with it. During the process, she also caused extensive damage to half the city. Colin could not help feeling guilty over what happened. "Markus was right. All that destruction is our fault."

Gaylie approached Colin, looking up to him so that her gaze could meet his. "Nothing is your fault. Deevor is a monster. You're not responsible for what she does. Markus and his people knew the risks they were taking when they took over that Gatherer installation. It was only a matter of time before they would be found. These are the risks that we have to take in this war."

Colin took little comfort in Gaylie's words. "I still feel bad about all that death and destruction. All because she's looking for us. Me, Diane, and Kelly. How many more innocent people have to die before we stop her?"

"*If* we can stop her," Kelly corrected. "She seemed pretty badass back there."

Gaylie responded with a laugh. "No. *You guys* are badass. Together you can beat her."

Linda and Al approached Colin. Linda was beaming a wide smile on her face while Al was holding up his video camera, actively filming. "We got footage of the whole fight between you and her. It was incredible. You wouldn't believe the ratings we got when we were transmitting the whole thing live. The whole planet loved seeing you kick her ass."

"We didn't kick her ass. We cut and ran," Colin angrily corrected her. "Maybe next time the whole planet will watch us get ourselves killed. And remind me why I let you guys come along."

Before Linda had a chance to answer, Kelly pointed to the road up ahead. "Check it out. Cars are coming."

"Here we go," Colin responded.

A caravan of three long, black cars came racing down the road at a high rate of speed. Colin walked out onto the middle of the road and stood with his arms folded against his chest. Kelly and Gaylie followed close behind him and stood at his right. Gaylie raised her machine gun, aiming it at the approaching cars. As the caravan was drawing closer, it began to reduce its speed. Colin was not concerned about the caravan stopping on its own accord. He had already set in motion the perfect means of getting these cars to halt.

From the field at the far right, the Black Raven flew up from behind a grove of trees and soared towards the road. It stopped and hovered in the air high above the trio's heads. Its plasma cannons opened fire at the lead car. It only took a short burst of rapidly fired energy to blow the car apart. As the lead car's burning fragments scattered about the road, the other two cars behind it both swerved to an abrupt halt.

"I think that got their attention," was Colin's smug comment. He watched as three individuals wearing white hooded robes jump out of the lead car. A young white male with long black hair. A white female with short blond hair. And a tall black male. Colin wasted no time addressing them, speaking in a loud, clear voice. "Sorry that we had to be a little extreme in order to get your attention. But my friends and I are pressed for time and we're in no mood to screw around."

The robed black male took a step towards Colin while pointing a damning finger. "You. Do you know what you've done? Our friends were in that car."

"We won't be available for the funeral," replied Colin. "Like I've said. We're pressed for time. But if it makes you feel any better, you won't be going to their funerals either."

The man's eye's widened, he gnashed his teeth. "Is that a threat? You dare to think that you can threaten us?

Do you know who we are?"

Gaylie took a step forward, raising her machine gun. "Yeah. You're our hostages."

Colin grinned. "I'd listen to the young lady if I were you."

"You don't threaten us," the man's angry reply. "We're not some helpless vagabonds on the street. We dictate terms to entire armies. You think you can be a threat to us?"

The man turned and looked back at the second car. The driver's side door opened and a tall figure wearing a white hooded robe stepped out. The hood was covering his head, but he pulled it back to reveal that he was a robotic creature composed of transparent material with a network of green printed circuitry inside. Exactly like the robot that Colin, Diane, and Kelly fought back at the Gatherer starbase. The robot's glowing green eyes stared at Colin. He raised his left arm, revealing it to be the transparent barrel of a gun.

"One of these things again," Colin calmly muttered. Back at the Gatherer starbase, Colin, Diane, and Kelly had difficulty in dealing with that robot, until Colin discovered a way to effectively deal with it. He was now intending to use the same method to deal with this one.

The black Gatherer pointed at Colin and the others. "Kill them," he shouted. "Kill them. All of them."

Colin extended his right hand out and fired a bolt of electricity directly to the robot's face. The robot staggered backward for a few steps as a small explosion from Colin's attack ripped a gaping hole into its face. As with the other robot, Colin was expecting its separated fragments to rejoin with the robot's body, repairing the damage. But Colin countered this function by aiming his hand at a mass of twisted metal debris from the destroyed car and causing it to break down into a swarm of tiny metal fragments. The metal swarm flew over to the robot and penetrated its damaged face. From there, Colin directed the metal fragments to break into smaller components and permeate the robot's entire head. Under this infection, the robot staggered backward. It thrashed its body to the left and right as if it were in pain. Colin continued directing the minute metal particles throughout the robot's body until it fell onto its back. Its legs thrashed for several seconds. Then the robot was still.

All three Gatherers looked on in wide eyed amazement at the sight of their robotic guardian being defeated so quickly and easily. Satisfied that the robot was completely disabled and no longer a threat, Colin grinned as he looked back at the Gatherers. "Looks like your road trip is going to be a bit longer than expected."

CHAPTER EIGHT

During the trip to the Gatherer starbase, Colin kept their three captives in the dark as to where they would be taken or what would happen to them. After landing inside the starbase and everyone disembarking from the Black Raven, Colin felt that now was the time to reveal his plans for the young Gatherer captives. Colin, Diane, and Kelly were walking ahead of the three Gatherers as they were heading down the Black Raven's ramp. Gaylie and Ava were walking behind them while keeping their machine guns trained on their backs. Reporters Linda and Al were walking close behind Gaylie and Ava. Al keeping his camera up to his eye while actively filming.

"You guys are probably wondering why we brought you here," Colin addressed the Gatherers. "You're going to help us with something very important."

The young black Gatherer sneered at Colin. "Help you? With what? And what have you done to this place? Where are the custodians?"

"By custodians I assume that you're talking about

those two guys in the robes that were here. They had an accident and ended up dead. You're here to take their place. What are your names?"

"I'm Martin," the man answered.

The female Gatherer answered, "Audra."

"Kerwin," the white male Gatherer answered. "Tell us why you brought us here."

Colin stopped, turning to face them. "Well Kerwin, you're here because we're hoping that you know how to work this hyperspace weapon that's aboard this starbase, and free our missing task force of ships that are trapped in this alternate dimensional space."

Martin laughed. "And just why should we help you? You're all nothing more than defilers. Trespassers."

"You're going to help us because if you don't, then we'll kill you," Colin's stern revelation to the Gatherers. "We'll kill you all then start over with a fresh group. And kill them if they refuse to cooperate. But I'm hoping that you'll be reasonable and spare us the inconvenience of having to travel back and forth."

Colin led the way to the control room with its silvery columns projecting their holographic monitors. Colin pointed a hand to one of the columns. "We assumed that this controls the hyperspace weapon. We have no idea how to operate this technology, let alone how to read the language on these monitors. But considering this starbase is your turf, I'm willing to bet that you can."

Kerwin looked about at the columns. "You display your ignorance when you state that we have a hyperspace weapon, as you call it. This is a research installation devoted to finding some way to breach the barrier between our universe and the dimension beyond mirrors where our great lord Kimdrack is imprisoned. This weapon that you speak of is called a warp converter, designed for that purpose."

"Only thing is that it didn't work," Kelly added. "Kimdrack is still locked tight in that dimension. But you have used this warp converter as a weapon. That's how our task force ended up trapped in that dimension. And it was nearly used on us."

"If you can send ships into this dimension, then you can bring them back," Colin told Kerwin. "Can you operate these instruments?"

Audra answered, "We are familiar with this technology. As well as what happened here. Your task force strayed too close to this starbase and was considered a threat. So, the personnel here used the warp converter to banish your ships to the alternate dimension."

"Then I'm certain you'll want to cooperate with us so that you can go back to your lives of working towards the futile goal of freeing Kimdrack," said Colin. "Bottom line: You help us get our task force ships back and then we leave you here in peace. You say no and then I give you to Ava and her daughter. After the loss that they've suffered, I'm sure that they have every reason to want to kill you all."

For a moment Kerwin, Audra, and Martin all looked at each other. Then Audra turned back to Colin. "Alright. But you have to give your word that you'll let us go."

"After we get what we want, then you all get to live," Colin replied. "But also keep in mind that if any one of you tries anything, then we'll kill all of you without hesitation."

Audra walked over to one of the columns and pressed her fingers onto it. A glowing blue holographic touchpad appeared below the monitor. As she began to tap her fingers onto the touchpad, Martin went to the column at her right and activated its touchpad. Colin and the others stood by and watched as the two Gatherers began their work.

"Charging up primary unit," said Audra. "Unit power level at twenty percent. Thirty five percent.

Fifty percent."

"Activating gravimetric stabilizers," said Martin. "Synchronizing with electromagnetic capacitors."

"Unit charge now at seventy percent. Now at one hundred percent," Audra reported.

"Synchronizing with dimensional and gravitational displacement modulators," said Martin as he continued tapping his touchpad. "I'm now filtering out electromagnetic distortions."

Audra's fingers rapidly tapped her touch pad. Then she stopped. "I'm ascending the unit to target coordinates minus four, three, seven, zero. These are the coordinates where your task force was banished into the subspace dimension."

"Are these the same coordinates where we found a tiny wormhole out in space?" Asked Kelly. "Our ship, the Hemlock, was able to get a signal out through this. That's how were able to communicate with them."

"That minute wormhole was no doubt a residual effect," explained Audra. "This technology is still experimental, so we haven't been able to correct that yet." Audra waited and watched the symbols flashing across her monitor. "Target coordinates are now set. How are the distortion readings?"

"Electromagnetic distortions are at zero percent," Martin answered. "Gravitational distortions at zero. You can fire when ready."

Audra tapped her finger on her touch pad. A large, black holographic monitor materialized above the first monitor. Audra tapped the touchpad again. Watching the black monitor, Colin realized that it was showing space outside. A familiar white beam of light began to streak across the monitor.

"Unit has displaced target coordinates," said Audra.

"Rift stability is at one hundred percent," Martin's report. "Electromagnetic and gravitational distortions are still zero."

Audra turned to Colin. "There's your rift to the subspace dimension. You can now travel freely between this space and ours."

"It wasn't our intention to commute there," Colin told her. "But now we can get our task force out of there. Kelly, go to the Black Raven and see if you can contact the Hemlock."

Colin watched the monitor as Kelly rushed off. The white streak of energy from the hyperspace generator was maintaining a steady presence. "So how long can you keep this rift open?"

"As long as the primary unit maintains its full power level and we continue to filter out any electromagnetic and gravitational distortions, then we can keep it open as long as we need to," Martin explained.

Diane held up her hand as she stepped forward. "Wait. Everton from the Hemlock told us that they were under attack by monsters. What do you know about that?"

Audra and Martin both glanced at each other. Then Audra explained, "We have picked up the presence of life forms that inhabit this subspace dimension. We managed to capture a few of them for study, but their origin is a total mystery to us. All we know is that they are extremely dangerous. If they've found your task force and its people, then you may have done all this for nothing. They may all be dead."

"We're not going to take your word on that," Colin's defiant reply.

Linda looked on, smiling as Al continued filming every activity. "This is all just incredible. Al, are you sure you're getting all this? Colin. What are your thoughts now?"

"Are you kidding me?" Colin shouted. "This isn't the news at eleven."

Kelly ran back into the room. "Guys, I got in

touch with the Hemlock. All I got was a few words from a girl who said that they were under attack. I heard shooting. Then we were cut off."

To Colin, this was dire news that he did not want to hear. But given the details that he knew so far, he thought that this was to be expected. "They were under attack? Did you try to get in touch with any of the other ships?"

"I tried," said Kelly, nodding. "I didn't get anyone else."

Colin heaved a sigh and rubbed his brow. "God. This is turning into a bigger mess."

"So, what do we do now?" Diane asked Colin. "We can't just stand here."

"Yeah," Colin muttered. He looked up at the monitor displaying the continuous white streak of energy. Then he turned. "Ava, Gaylie. Keep a close eye on our friends here. Don't let them touch anything unless there's a threat to the rift. If any one of them tries anything, then you know what to do."

"Why? Where are you going?" Ava inquired.

Colin looked back at the monitor. "Inside the rift."

CHAPTER NINE

Deevor was once again inside the circular chamber with its reflective floor and walls, located within the Temple of Mirrors. She was humbly kneeling in front of the platform where Gatherer Crayden was standing. He was holding a crystalline helmet in his hands. Behind him was a large, square mirror. Deevor knew full well why she was summoned here, and why Crayden was holding that helmet. Kimdrack was displeased with her progress in finding and dealing with McKenzie and his friends. Now she was about to see what punishment Kimdrack had in store for her.

Crayden raised the helmet to his head. For a moment he gazed at it in silence. Then he spoke out. "Lord Kimdrack, I accept this gift with my profound thanks."

Crayden put on the helmet. He then gnashed his teeth and let out a grunt in pain as he staggered back against the mirror. Then both the helmet and mirror turned black. seconds later the huge face of a lizard-like creature appeared in the mirror. Crayden stepped away from the mirror and looked down at Deevor.

His eyes began to glow bright red while small, red veins began to spread across his face. Then he spoke. "Rise."

Deevor stood and faced Crayden, who was now being used as an instrument by Kimdrack to communicate with her from the dimension beyond mirrors.

"You have failed me again," said Crayden. "You still have not destroyed McKenzie, Christy, and Lytton. These germ samples who have caused me so much trouble."

"I am sorry, my lord," Deevor stuttered out. "I came close to killing them in Devarow, but they managed to escape."

"I know that!" Crayden shouted. "You have wasted valuable time searching from city to city trying to find these alien germs. While you were on tour across this germ-infested planet, they were colluding with these maggots in this so-called resistance movement to tamper with the technology in one of my lost facilities. A facility that had to be destroyed in retaliation for their trespass. The facility was deemed expendable. But still, the trespass was an insult. This will not stand. What do you have to say?"

"I am truly sorry, my lord."

Small streams of smoke began to rise from the veins across Crayden's face. "Sorry? Sorry does not help me!" he bellowed out in anger. "You're wasting time chasing these fools across this planet. You must make them come to you. You must go to their home. The United Protectorate. Coordinates nine, nine, eight, nine, epsilon. This is where you will find their home sector. You will go to this place and destroy it. City by city. Planet by planet until they have no choice but to come to you."

Crayden's body burst into flames. He dropped to his knees, then fell onto his back. Upon witnessing Crayden's death, she gave no further thought to his loss. This was a sight that she has seen here in this room on more than one occasion. She was now only focused on Kimdrack's commands. She rose up and strode out of the room. She paid little attention to the sight of her own reflection moving along the walls and floor of the corridor as she walked. At the end of the corridor, she reached the opening to the outside. Resting on the reflective ground just a few feet away was the black, disk shaped drone ship that transported her and Crayden here.

Deevor entered the round open hatch at the side of the ship and walked through a short, round corridor that led to a small, circular room that was illuminated by rows of dim white lights along the walls. There was a dark, cushioned seat in the center of the room. There were no controls or instruments aboard this ship, as its fully automated systems were at Deevor's full command.

Deevor sat down and crossed her arms against her chest. "Take me to warp gate three."

The baritone male voice of the ship's computer system gave a quick reply. "Acknowledging command. Setting course for warp gate three."

Deevor heard the faint, low hum of the ship's engines being activated. The light from outside the ship began to fade as the hatch began to close. A moment later, she felt the slight jerk of the ship rising into the air. She closed her eyes and waited for the ship to travel to the Gatherers warp gate station that was located at the far edge of this star system. It was there that her journey to the United Protectorate would begin. The trip would take less than an hour. During that time, Deevor would contemplate all that she would do to the home of McKenzie, Christy, and Lytton in order to force them out of hiding. She was hoping that it would take less time to destroy them than it will take to destroy their world.

As time passed, Deevor opened her eyes to the

sound of the ship's computer reporting their status.

"Now arriving at warp gate three."

A holographic screen materialized in front of Deevor. It displayed the image of a huge, white, cylinder shaped structure floating out in space. This was warp gate three. One of seven special installations that the Gatherers have across the quadrant. Their purpose was to provide the Gatherers with a greater means of traveling through the vast distances of space beyond their drone ships. The ship that Deevor was traveling in was warp capable. But it did not have the power to take her to the great distance that she needed to travel in such a short space of time.

Deevor spoke out to hail the warp gate. "This is Deevor. Identity code prime, five, five, three, zero, six."

The sound of a male voice responded through the ship's communication system. "Identity confirmed."

"Set warp for coordinates nine, nine, eight, nine, epsilon," Deevor ordered.

"Stand by."

Deevor watched the screen. A large glowing blue ring began to appear on the front of the warp gate. A moment later, a huge white disk appeared in front of the ring. It began to grow until it matched the warp gate's size. Then the voice called back.

"Powering up all systems. Now entering target coordinates nine, nine, eight, nine, epsilon. Coordinates are now set."

"Shall we proceed?" the ship's computer asked Deevor.

"Take us in," was her command.

Deevor continued watching the screen as the ship began to fly closer to the glowing disk. The ship increased its speed, reaching the disk within seconds. The moment that the ship made contact with the disk a white flash filled the screen. Then it was replaced by the darkness of space. The warp gate was nowhere in sight.

An expected occurrence considering that the Gatherers, using the warp gate's advanced technology engineered by the Dark Masters, transported the ship far off into a new quadrant in space.

"We are now at coordinates nine, nine, eight, nine, epsilon," the computer reported.

Deevor nodded in approval. "So, we're here. In the heart of this United Protectorate."

Deevor continued watching the screen. It was displaying the image of a large, blue orb. The computer reported its findings. "Planet detected. Distance, ninety-seven thousand, five hundred kilometers. Also detecting a large presence of unidentified ships in the vicinity."

"They're of no concern," said Deevor. "Take us down."

Deevor continued watching the screen as the orb was steadily growing larger as the ship was flying closer. Within minutes, its features as a planet were becoming more defined. Large, grey land masses sitting among huge, blue oceans. She watched as the ship passed by a squadron of six jet-styled spacecraft flying in a tight triangular- formation. The ship continued its descent to the planet. As it entered the planet's atmosphere, it stayed on course towards a large continent with massive, rocky mountains reaching up to the sky. As the ship continued descending, the landscape below was becoming clear. The forms of tall buildings could be seen. The ship was heading down towards an expansive city. Deevor grinned with anticipation as she watched the buildings coming closer into view. She would have great enjoyment in obliterating a city this large.

On the screen, a busy street below came into view. It was filled with a long line of vehicles. It was here that Deevor planned to begin her work. "Open the hatch, then go into orbit around the planet and wait for further orders."

Deevor rose from her seat and strode through the corridor to reach the hatch, which was now fully open. Without slowing her stride, she leaped out of the hatch and dropped down to the street below. The ship was hovering low. Her fall was short. She landed on her feet onto the pavement, coming to a crouched position. She then stood upright in time to see a red car coming to a screeching halt directly in front of her.

As Deevor looked at her surroundings, she was amused at the similarities between the buildings of this alien city and the ones on the planet Sidra. She was keeping in mind that both human civilizations developed this way because of Kimdrack's manipulation with their development. Although, the humans of the United Protectorate were far more technologically advanced.

The horn from the red car that stopped in front of Deevor began to blare out. Several of the other cars behind this one also began honking their horns. Deevor turned her head and grinned, looking directly at the car's driver, a middle-aged black male wearing a black suit. *This will be a good place to start,* was her thought. The driver continued honking his horn as Deevor walked up to the side of his car. She kneeled down and placed her right hand under the car while her left hand had a firm grip on its hood. With little physical effort, she picked the car off the ground, then hurled it towards the upper level of a tall, grey building across the street. The driver let out a prolonged scream as his vehicle went soaring through the air and crashed through the wall of the building. Deevor finished the job by raising her hand in the air and releasing a huge blast of fiery energy at the hole that the car made in the side of the building. Her energy blast caused a massive explosion that tore completely through the entire building.

Upon seeing the destruction of the red car, the other

drivers began to panic and abandon their vehicles on the street. Deevor turned her attention to them. She aimed her right hand to the street and let out an energy blast that burned through the long line of cars. Dozens of the vehicles exploded into fragments while their occupants and humans on the street were instantly obliterated. Now a full-blown panic was spreading throughout the area. Screaming humans were scrambling to escape the super powered threat that was among them. Deevor found their efforts of escape to be amusing, just as their attempts to fight against her would be. She began to walk down the street. She casually aimed her hand to the right and fired an energy blast at a line of storefronts there. Each location was destroyed by a powerful explosion and left flaming. Deevor spied a mob of humans to her left that were running down the street to escape. She spun around and aimed her right hand, firing an energy blast that incinerated every human on contact.

So far Deevor was facing no opposition here in this alien city. She began to wonder if there were any more super powered beings here like McKenzie, Christy, and Lytton. If so, then they would easily die, along with the rest of this planet's other defenders. She continued walking down the middle of the street. As she approached any abandoned vehicle that was in her way, she simply swatted it to the side with a swipe of her fist or picked it up and threw it into the side of a building. As she continued walking, three men in black uniforms ran out into the street and stopped several feet in front of her. They had guns drawn and aimed directly at her. One of the men spoke out.

"Hold it right where you are! Get down on the ground now."

Deevor laughed at the man's bravado, without knowing the power that he was addressing. She kept walking.

"I said stop!" the man yelled out. "Stop where you are and get on the ground!"

"There is only one force in this universe that I would kneel to," was Deevor's first reply to the man. Her second reply was a fiery blast from her hand that burned all three men. They screamed briefly as their lives were snuffed out, leaving charred bodies.

Deevor saw another man in a black uniform approaching her from her far right. He aimed the weapon in his hand and fired four laser shots at her. As with any weapon, this laser fire proved to be ineffective against her. Deevor began to walk towards the man as he continued shooting at her. She began to quicken her pace. The man continued shooting, but so far, his efforts were useless. Deevor approached the man and swatted the weapon out of his hands with a quick backhand swipe. She then grasped him by his neck and squeezed. Under her tight grip she felt the vertebra of his neck separate as they were being crushed. Jagged bone fragments penetrated out from his skin. His blood started to run down along her fingers. Deevor heard a wailing siren. She turned to the left and saw an approaching white car with red flashing light bars on its roof. She raised her left hand and fired a blast of energy that burned away the car's entire front section. Its now flaming rear half sped out of control and crashed into the side of another car.

Deevor heard more sirens in the distance. She dropped the body of the man she had just slain and anticipated more of these humans coming to oppose her. This was a large alien world and its people had yet to learn the full scope of the power that was among them. Deevor had little patience in taking a prolonged time in order to teach them. She was here to send a message to McKenzie and his friends; A message that would reach out beyond the stars in order to gain their attention. Deevor held both hands out at her sides. At her left hand appeared a bright red orb of glowing energy. At her right hand appeared a yellow orb. Both orbs were basketball sized, and then continued to grow in diameter. They were two powerful opposing charges of energy that would create a devastating explosion when brought together. Deevor was determined to make this entire planet burn until McKenzie answered her call.

As the two powerful charges of energy continued to grow, Deevor brought her hands, and both charges together. A devastating explosion followed.

CHAPTER TEN

Once again strapped to the seat next to Diane inside the Black Raven's cockpit, Colin was still feeling the lingering nervousness that began when they departed the Gatherer starbase. Looking out through the forward window, he could see the ship following the white stream of energy fired from the warp converter. It was his understanding that all they had to do was follow the energy stream until they came upon the rift itself. Then once they entered the rift, they would be facing a true unknown. Colin was still trying to grasp how he, Diane, and Kelly came to this point. They were light years away from their home quadrant, about to fly headlong into an artificially created rift to a mysterious subspace dimension inhabited by unknown hostile life forms. Colin's only comfort at this point was to think back on Captain Melony Carter's words to them just before they left the United Protectorate. *Don't screw up.*

"It's not much further," Kelly announced as he was carefully monitoring the situation at the ship's computer station. "I can't believe we're doing this."

"Neither can I," Diane said in agreement. "What do you think we'll find in there?"

Colin was tempted to laugh at her question. "With our track record, trouble. Lots. High emphasis on the lots part."

The Black Raven continued following the energy stream as it ended at a huge circle of white light. Diane pulled back on the control sticks, bringing the ship to a stop in front of this anomaly.

Kelly reported his findings. "That rift is right at the exact same coordinates where we were getting the signals from the Hemlock. This thing is pretty big. Big enough for a destroyer to pass through."

"See if you can raise the Hemlock," Colin ordered.

Kelly tapped the controls in front of him. "This is the Black Raven calling the Hemlock. Come in, please. This is the Black Raven calling the Hemlock."

There was no reply.

"Again, this is the Black Raven calling the Hemlock. Please respond."

There was still no reply.

"No answer. We can take this as a bad sign," said Diane.

"What if they're dead?" Kelly asked. "What if they're all dead? The whole task force?"

"We'll never know until we see for ourselves," Colin told Kelly. He pointed a finger to the rift. "Take us in."

Diane slowly pushed the flight control sticks forward. The Black Raven began to move towards the rift. There was silence inside the cockpit as they watched the ship moving closer to the rift. Then the forward window was filled with a bright white flash. After that, the space outside the forward window was silvery and shimmering instead of black with the small twinkling of stars in the distance.

"Well this is different," Diane said.

"Kelly, what are the sensors picking up?" asked

Colin.

"I'm getting a lot of weird interference. It's preventing me from getting any accurate readings. But I am picking up a large object about thirty-five thousand kilometers away."

"A large mass? Any other details about this thing?"

"Nothing," Kelly's answer. "This space is screwing with our sensors. All I can pick up is a large mass."

Great. Then we're flying blind, Colin mused. "If it's something big then it just might be the Hemlock or one of the other missing ships. Give Diane the coordinates so that we can go check it out."

Diane tapped the controls in front of her. Then she pushed the control sticks forward.

After several minutes of traveling through this strange alien space, the form of a dark object appeared in the forward window. The Black Raven continued to move closer.

"There she is," said Kelly. "That has to be the Hemlock."

The Black Raven moved in closer. The object was now coming into clearer view. It was the form of an enormous, dark hulled spacecraft. It had a huge triangular front section with a long cylinder shape at its rear. At the rear end of the cylinder were two broad swept forward wings. Attached to the tips of both wings were smaller cylinders. The ship was still. There were no lights shining from alongside its hull. But the most striking feature of this ship was the huge mass of bright blue coils that were embracing the ship's rear section and both wings. They resembled the coils of a snake, but with a smooth surface instead of scales.

"What the hell is that?" Colin asked.

Kelly studied his computer readouts. "I'm not sure. Sensors are still not functioning. I'm not picking up any readings."

"I hate going into this completely blind," said Colin.

134

"And something that big can't be good. Look at it. It's got half the ship covered."

"I'm taking us around to get a better look at this thing," Diane told Colin.

The Black Raven moved in closer and then flew along the side of the huge ship. Getting a closer view of the ship, they saw markings along the side of its hull. *622UP Hemlock*. Colin pointed a finger at the ship. "There's the ID marking. This is it. The Hemlock. A ship that big here has to have somebody still alive inside."

"There's a landing bay underneath the ship," said Kelly. "Assuming that they didn't seal the bay doors, or that the bay's force field is working to keep the air inside, then we've got a way in. But do we really want to?"

"We don't have a choice," Colin told him. "We're not getting any replies from whoever's inside. And this might be our biggest clue regarding the whereabouts of the other missing ships."

The Black Raven moved in closer to the Hemlock. It dove down along the massive ship's hull to reach its underside. There, it came upon a huge, rectangular landing bay. The Black Raven moved in closer. Rows of white lights along the landing bay's square entrance were shining, but, from the inside, the lighting was dim.

"Take us in slowly," Colin told Diane.

The Black Raven made a slow and steady approach to the landing bay, then safely passed through the entrance. Inside the landing bay, the ship hovered above a large, clear area that was flanked by two rows of small triangular-shaped fighter crafts. Inside the cockpit, Colin looked out through the forward window at the dimly lit area outside. There were no signs of any of the crew. Not even so much as one body lying on the floor.

"We've got a small bit of luck. I am able to take an atmospheric reading," Kelly said. "Outside atmosphere is normal. The life support in the landing bay is working. But still no long ranged scanning because of the interference."

"Great," moaned Diane. "So, we have no way of knowing if anybody is even aboard this thing."

"Somebody is aboard," Colin told her. "We spoke to them. And the only way that we're going to find them is to go out and look for them. Kelly, activate the auto transponder signal. Maybe we can raise the other ships."

Colin was sensing that Diane and Kelly were sharing his apprehension as they were departing the Black Raven, walking down its ramp and stepping foot upon the Hemlock's landing bay. Looking around this huge area with its dim lights and no other living presence was unsettling. Kelly had his sensor pad in hand and was trying to get any readings. The frown on his face was an indication that he was having no success. Diane had her laser gun in hand. Holding it out in front of her.

Colin stood and looked at the rows of inactive fighter crafts at his left and right. Then he shouted out in a loud voice, "Hello!"

There was no reply other than the faint echo of his own voice reverberating through the landing bay. He called out again.

"Hello!"

He waited in silence for a minute to listen for any reply. There was still nothing.

"Kelly, are you able to pick up anything?" Colin asked.

"Nothing," said Kelly. "Even the sensor pad is getting the same interference."

"Great," Colin grumbled. "Then that means if there's anyone or anything alive on this ship, they'll have to find us before we find them."

Diane pointed her gun to the far side of the landing

bay. "I see a corridor over there."

The trio strode through the landing bay and headed for the corridor. Once there, they found the corridor to be just as void as the landing bay. And the atmosphere was just as dark.

"Nobody here," said Diane, still holding her weapon up and ready to open fire at a second's notice.

"Maybe they evacuated," Kelly theorized.

"Possibly," Colin replied. "Maybe we'd have a better chance of finding out what happened here if we get to the bridge."

The corridor was suddenly shaken by a strong force that nearly knocked Colin, Diane, and Kelly off their feet. It was accompanied by the sound of a loud, prolonged boom and the creaking of metal. The disturbance stopped just as suddenly as it started.

"What the hell was that," Diane asked.

"It felt like the ship was breaking apart," Kelly said.

"That doesn't make sense," Colin told him. "Unless it has something to do with that thing wrapped around the outside of the ship."

"Well, do you think we should still go on," Kelly returned. The rising pitch in his voice displaying his nervousness.

Colin also began to question the safety of their mission here. "It might be ok. But just in case maybe we won't go too far."

As they continued heading forward in the corridor, they came upon several metal doors at the left and right. Colin approached one of the doors, expecting it to open automatically. But it did not move.

"Door's not opening," said Colin. "Either it's been locked, or the power is out. That could also explain why the lighting is so low. The ship must be running on emergency power. Just enough to maintain life support and minimal lighting."

"Maybe one of us should open it," Diane suggested.

Colin considered that. Between their super-powers, getting through this door would be a simple task. But Colin decided not to tarry here in this corridor. "Let's just keep moving."

They continued to press deeper into the corridor, still finding no signs of human life. Colin stopped to shout out again. "Hello!"

There was still no reply. He, Diane, and Kelly resumed moving forward.

The corridor came to a four-way intersection. Colin decided that they should keep moving forward. As they continued going deeper into the corridor, Colin spotted a dark object laying on the floor several feet up ahead. As they were drawing closer, the shape of the object in the dim light became clearer. It was a human shape. A body lying on the floor. They stopped six feet away from this gruesome find. It was a body wearing the shredded remnants of a grey camouflage uniform with black boots. The body was horribly mangled with its head and an arm both missing. Its right leg was bent backward and resting on its chest. Several ribs could be seen protruding from its side. The body was lying in a wide pool of blood that was spread across the floor from one wall to the other. Both walls were also splattered with blood.

Colin felt nauseated as he was looking down at this body.

Diane lowered her weapon. "My God. What could have done this?"

"Obviously one of those hostile life forms that the Gatherer told us about. It would be just our luck that all the humans did leave the ship and left us alone with whatever did this."

There was a sudden banging noise coming from behind. Colin, Diane, and Kelly all spun around, expecting to find an enemy but seeing nothing.

"What the hell was that?" Kelly asked, speaking rapidly.

"Wasn't one of us," Colin told him. "It was back down the corridor."

Colin led the way, moving to return to the intersection. He looked down the left and right corridors but saw nothing. He decided to call out again. "Hello!"

From the left corridor, there was a second banging noise. Colin turned and pointed. "It came from down there."

"So, what do we do?" asked a wide-eyed Kelly.

"You want to stand here and send whoever it is an E-mail?" was Colin's sarcastic reply. "We go and investigate. That's what we're here for."

Colin, Diane, and Kelly entered the next corridor. They traveled for several feet before discovering two more corpses laying on the floor. Both of them were missing their heads and were as horribly mutilated as the first body.

"More bodies," said Kelly. "I'm not sure that I want to run into whatever did this."

"We might not have a choice if it means that we can get some answers," Colin told him.

There was another banging sound. Then a few feet ahead, the door to the right slid open and a woman dressed in a grey camouflage uniform and black knee-high boots stepped out into the corridor. Her face was obscured by the shadows. She stepped forward and raised her hand, aiming a gun at Colin, Diane, and Kelly.

"Hello," Colin greeted.

"Who are you?" the woman yelled out, taking a step closer with her gun still raised.

Colin raised his hands. "Take it easy. We're friends. My name is Colin McKenzie. My friends here are Diane Christy and Kelly Lytton. We're with the CID."

"The CID?" the woman asked. "Are there any more of you here?"

"No. There's just us."

"Just the three of you?" the woman replied. Keeping her weapon raised she moved closer, stepping out of the shadows.

"There's just us," Colin told her. "And you can lower your weapon. We're here to help. What's your name?"

The woman moved closer. Coming into a clearer view she revealed herself as a young black woman with short hair. She lowered her weapon down to Colin's feet. "My name isn't important. But what matters is that you're here to help. I can certainly use it."

"What happened here?" Colin asked her. "These bodies all torn apart. Where's the rest of the crew?"

"The crew are all back in the engineering section," the woman explained. "They're all being held prisoner by those things. The creatures that invaded the ship. They came at us so fast. There was no way we could have stopped them. We can't waste any time here. You have to help me save them."

Colin was glad to meet with at least one member of the Hemlock's crew. But for some reason, her presence was making him feel more uneasy. "We spoke to a Captain Everton. Is he still alive?"

"Captain Everton is dead," the woman quickly said. "And the others will be dead too if we don't do something to help. Now we're wasting time. Follow me."

The woman quickly strode past Colin, Diane, and Kelly, leading the way down the corridor. Colin still had several questions to ask this woman, but for now decided that it would be wise to accompany her.

The woman led them back down the corridor and to

the intersection. They made a right turn and headed back down the corridor where they encountered the first dead body. They passed by the body and continued down the corridor. Colin thought that he would take the opportunity to ask this unnamed woman more questions.

"We still need to know what happened here," Colin told the woman. "How did you manage to survive? And what about the other task force ships?"

"You ask too many questions," the woman snapped. "We have no time for this. We have to get to the engineering section up on the next level. The longer we delay will hurt our chances of saving the crew."

"Can you at least tell us your name?" Colin implored.

The woman ignored Colin and continued walking.

As they were hurrying down the corridor, there was a banging sound coming from behind. Colin, Diane, and Kelly all stopped.

"What was that?" asked Kelly.

The woman stopped and turned around. "That might have been one of those things. The ship is crawling with them. We can't stay in this corridor. We have to keep moving and reach the engineering section."

The woman stopped at a metal door on the left side of the corridor. She pressed a button on a panel at the door's right side, causing it to slide open. "This elevator will take us up to the next level."

The woman stepped into the elevator. Colin, Diane, and Kelly were about to follow her when there was another banging noise coming from behind. Then the sound of running footsteps. They all turned around and were greeted to a shocking and unexpected sight. A black woman dressed in a grey camouflage uniform and black knee-high boots came running down the corridor. She had the exact same face as the woman who had just stepped into the elevator. There was a laser pistol in her hand, aimed at Colin, Diane, and Kelly.

"Don't move," the mysterious woman demanded. She continued walking forward.

Colin was confused. He held out his hands. "Hold on. Take it easy. Just who the hell are you?"

The woman ignored Colin. She stopped in her tracks just as her twin stepped out of the elevator. The woman aimed her gun at her twin and immediately fired three laser shots into her face. The duplicate stumbled back into the elevator as she was hit. The woman stepped closer and shot three more times, hitting the duplicate in her chest. She dropped her gun and slammed into the wall, then slid down to the floor while a clear liquid seeped out from her wounds. The woman then stepped away from Colin, Diane, and Kelly, aiming her weapon at them.

"Who are you people?" the woman forcefully inquired.

After witnessing the violent incident, Colin sought to pacify the woman. He could easily use his power to subdue her. But he was hoping that she could provide any answers as to what was going on. "Take it easy. Just calm down. We're friends. But do you mind telling us what the hell is going on?"

"I asked who you are?" the woman again demanded. "You're in civilian clothes. And I saw a ship from a lower port side window where we were hiding out. Was that you?"

Colin nodded. "Yes, that was our ship. I'm Colin McKenzie. My friends here are Diane Christy and Kelly Lytton. The CID sent us out here to try and find your task force."

The woman studied Colin for a moment. Then lowered her weapon. "The CID sent you out here? Ok.

That makes sense. I'm lieutenant Clara Skyhook. Tactical officer for the Hemlock. And that thing I just killed wasn't me. It was one of them trying to pass itself off as me."

Colin took a quick glimpse into the elevator at the body lying in a pool of thick, clear liquid.

Clara continued with her story. "They're monsters that can make themselves look like us. My guess is that they live here in this dimensional space. Just like that thing outside. Six weeks ago, our task force came out of a hyperspace jump to explore this sector when we came upon this alien starbase. We tried to communicate with whoever was aboard the thing when they launched a small group of fighters to attack us. They weren't much of a threat and we fought them off pretty easily. After that, the starbase fired this weapon at us. Then we ended up here, trapped in this weird space. Shortly after that we were attacked. These creatures kill their victims and then take their place."

"That sounds familiar," Colin quipped, recalling his own origins as a Reploid. "And what about that thing wrapped around the outside of the ship?"

"That thing attacked us first. I don't know what it is, but it was too powerful. It attached itself to the ship and began draining off our power. I think it's feeding on it. Then the smaller ones came with it. It didn't take them long to infiltrate the entire ship. I was lucky to escape. But that's not going to hold out for long. We've got to get off this ship."

"Wait. That thing told us that there were survivors being held prisoner in the engineering section," Colin informed Clara.

Clara shook her head. "No. That was a trick. It was trying to lead you into a trap. The others are all dead. Now we can't waste any more time. We have to get to your ship and get out of here before it's too late."

Considering the information that Clara had given him, Colin decided that it would be wiser to cut their mission here short instead of pressing forward. "Maybe it is best that we leave."

Clara said nothing else and lead the way down the corridor to reach the landing bay. The group traveled down the corridor until the entrance to the landing bay was just a few yards in the distance. Then the entire corridor began to shake. The group stopped just as a blue mass burst through the wall and blocked half of the corridor. As this mass penetrated the ship, it also ripped a large hole in the corridor's right wall, creating a sudden explosive decompression of air. The powerful force of the sucking air was strong enough to nearly pull everyone off their feet. Colin and Kelly pressed themselves against the right wall of the corridor to try to stay on their feet while Diane and Clara moved close to the left.

"We have to go back," Clara shouted over the sound of the rushing air. "Back to the elevator."

The group made their way back down the corridor, groping along the walls. Another strong force shook the corridor. As they gained distance from the breach in the hull, the power of the decompression pulling against them began to weaken. When they reached the intersection, they were able to break away from the walls and return to the elevator.

"That thing," Kelly gasped. "It was that thing on the outside of the ship."

"Yeah. And now we're cut off from the landing bay," Diane said.

"Not so," said Clara. "We can go to one of the upper levels and make our way to an aft section elevator that will take us directly to the landing bay. But we have to hurry. That thing might be ready to tear this entire ship apart."

Clara dragged the corpse of her twin out of the elevator, leaving a short trail of the clear liquid. Colin, Diane, and Kelly joined her in the elevator. She pressed a button on the panel at the right side of the door. The metal door slid shut, leaving the group standing in the dark space as the elevator began its ascent.

The door slid open when the elevator stopped. Clara stepped out. "This way."

As they were following Clara, Colin was feeling that all too familiar impending doom pit in his stomach tightening. "I hope the landing bay is still intact. If we lose the Black Raven, then we're pretty much screwed."

They continued following Clara. Along the way, they passed three mutilated bodies lying in the corridor. All of them dismembered and missing their heads. Clara instructed Colin, Diane, and Kelly to ignore them and keep moving on. As they came to a four-way intersection, Clara was still going forward. Then the faint sound of a scream caught Colin's ears.

Colin stopped. "Hold on. What was that?"

Clara stopped and turned. "What are you doing? We have to keep moving."

"I heard something," Colin told her. "It sounded like someone crying out."

"It was nothing," Clara insisted.

"Wait," Colin's firm reply. He took a step into the left corridor and listened. He heard another scream. A female voice. "It's a woman. There's somebody down there."

"There's nobody there," Clara snapped. "We don't have time for this."

Colin was certain that what he heard was accurate. "There's somebody down there in trouble. We have to go see."

Colin bolted down the corridor. Diane and Kelly

ran to follow. There was another scream. This time it was louder. Colin paid little attention to the mangled body lying on the floor as he was rushing by. His focus was on whoever was crying out. Colin stopped running when he heard the woman's screams again. This time sounding as if they were just a few feet away from him. He approached a set of large, twin metal doors.

"That came from behind here," Colin said. He approached the doors, but they did not open automatically. He went to the door's control panel at the right. Its buttons were dark. He pressed one button after another but there was no response. "Controls aren't working. The door's sealed shut."

"Not to us," Diane reminded him.

Diane stepped up to the doors and pressed the fingers of her hands in between them. With a swift effort she pulled the doors apart from each other. There was the sound of grating metal as the doors were being forced open. Now that they had an entrance, the trio stepped through.

Past the doors, they found themselves inside of a large room. It appeared to be a storage area, with rows of tall shelves holding dozens of large dark, plastic crates. But the first feature of the room that caught their attention was that it was completely enshrouded by thick sheets of a strange white material resembling a spider's webbing. The webbing covered everything from the floor to the ceiling. Sheathed within the webbing were dozens of men and women in grey camouflage military uniforms. All of them wrapped up like trapped flies. Colin, Diane, and Kelly were all startled by a sudden scream at their right. They turned and were horrified at the sight of three men and a woman hanging upside down, wrapped up to their necks by the webbing. Among them were three strange creatures.

They were tall. Six feet according to Colin's estimate. They had large heads that closely resembled the bleached white skulls of cattle, with white strands of tendons attached to the sides of their faces and their lower jaws. Their small, yellow eyes were sunk back inside their sockets. Clusters of long spines were protruding from the back of their heads. Their long necks were a combination of white vertebra and connecting tendons. Their gaunt bodies were covered by large, white, overlapping scales. In place of arms, they had four long, thin, insect-like legs ending in long serrated spines. They were standing on spindly, reverse-jointed legs with long three-toed feet ending in sharp talons. Clusters of long spines were protruding from their backs and running down to their long, thrashing vertebra tails.

The creatures were biting at the captive humans. Tearing away chunks of flesh from their torsos. Their victims were wide eyed with pain and terror during this ordeal. One of them, the female, extended her one free arm out to Colin, Diane, and Kelly. When Colin looked at her face, he could not believe what he was seeing. She had a familiar face. The face of Lieutenant Clara Skyhook. She let out a moan just as one of the creatures clamped its jaws down onto her head. Before anyone could make a single move, the webbing next to Clara spread open and one of the creatures burst through and leaped towards Diane. Diane cried out in surprise and fell to the floor with the thing on top of her. It brought two of its arms down on Diane, their serrated tips aiming for her face. Diane, reacting quickly, managed to grab the tips of the creature's arms and avoided having her head impaled. She then drove her foot into the creature's chest, knocking it back towards Clara and the others. It landed on the floor but quickly recovered and stood back to its feet. It let out a long, low toned hiss at Diane. Its brethren stopped tearing at their human prey and began to hiss.

The creature let out a high-pitched screech as it lunged for Diane a second time. Moving as fast as the creature, Kelly shot out a bolt of fire from his hand that burned completely through the creature's chest while knocking it backward again. For the next few seconds, the creature continued its piercing screech as its arms were wildly flailing in the air.

As Diane was returning to her feet, she, Colin, and Kelly were given no respite as four more of the creatures began to emerge from the same mass of webbing where the first one appeared. That creature had now stopped its flailing and became still and quiet. Several more of the creatures began to crawl down from the sheets of webbing reaching up to the ceiling to join the number. All of them letting out the unnerving, low pitched hiss. All throughout the room, swarms of the hissing creatures were now emerging from their hiding places within the webbing and crawling towards their fresh prey.

CHAPTER ELEVEN

Kelly thrust out his hand and blasted another powerful bolt of fire, this one burning off the head of one approaching creature. Diane took aim with her laser gun and began shooting into the growing crowd of monsters, hitting three of them. Colin was about to raise his hands and use his electrical power to assault these creatures when they all began to let out a collective high-pitched shriek and charged forward.

"Let's get out of here. There's too many," shouted Colin.

Colin, Diane, and Kelly all retreated back through the open doors. Once they were out of the storage room, they sprinted down the corridor with the mob of screaming monsters chasing after them. Their ultimate hope of escape was to reach the landing bay and board the Black Raven. They stopped when they reached the intersection.

"Which way?" Diane asked in a hurried voice.

Colin's head swiveled to the right and left. He pointed a finger. "Left," he exclaimed, hoping that his choice was the right one.

As they bolted down the next corridor, another of the strong tremors rocked the ship. They were nearly thrown off their feet as the corridor shook but managed to keep moving. They ran for several more feet before coming to the familiar sight of an elevator door on the left. Colin stopped in front of the elevator and began pressing buttons on the control panel on its right wall. He was gasping for air while desperately urging the elevator to move quickly.

"Come on, come on, come on!" Colin rapidly muttered.

To his joy, the elevator door slid open. He, Diane, and Kelly dashed inside the elevator just as two of the monsters were upon them. Diane quickly turned and delivered a kick to the face of one creature, sending it crashing back into the second. Colin pressed a button on the control panel, and the elevator door began to close just as three of the crazed monsters were charging forward.

Diverting his focus from his heavy breathing, Colin could feel the slight momentum of the elevator going down. He let out a quick gasp of air and then looked at Diane and Kelly. "God. We were lucky to get away."

"We're still not free yet," added Kelly. "They're bound to come after us. We have to get off this ship."

"Where is this thing taking us?" Diane inquired.

"For now, someplace safe," Colin told her. "Maybe this is the elevator that Clara was talking about. The one that will take us directly to the landing bay."

"And what about Clara?" Diane asked. "Where the hell did she run off to?"

"That thing we were talking to wasn't Clara," Colin cheerlessly told her. "The real Clara is still up above with the rest of those people being held by those monsters."

The elevator stopped and the door slid open to reveal a dark corridor. And to Colin's relief, no attacking monsters. He pressed two of the lower buttons on the elevator's control panel. "One of these has to take us down to the landing bay."

"Let's just get there fast. Those things aren't going to give up the chase," Kelly reminded him.

The elevator went down to the next level. Colin peered outside when the door opened to see a huge area in the background. He caught the sight of two fighter craft in the distance. "We're here. The landing bay," he exclaimed.

Diane and Kelly followed Colin out into the landing bay. They headed directly for the Black Raven just a short distance away, but then they stopped when a figure stepped out from behind a fighter craft that was parked to the right. The mysterious figure remained standing in the shadows. *Clara,* Colin surmised. He was wondering about her whereabouts. She was waiting for them here in the landing bay.

"You're here? You're still alive?" said Clara, projecting a clear tone of surprise in her voice. "I told you not to go near that storage area. I thought I'd seen the last of you."

Colin was immediately angered by Clara's masquerade. "Cut the shit. We already know that you're not the real Clara."

Clara stepped out of the shadows. "You're wrong. I am the only Clara Skyhook on this ship. The one I killed back in the elevator was using that form to lure you into the upper level so they could take you. Or perhaps she was planning to keep you for herself. I don't blame her if she was. This place... This limbo that we live in is like hell. It's cold and empty. We have to feed off each other in order to survive. Or scavenge the scraps left over by the Hydra when it sleeps."

"Hydra?" Kelly inquired. "Is that what that thing is outside?"

"Yes," Clara hissed. "Hydra rules everything here. We're all children of the Hydra. We bring the Hydra food when we can find it, or offer up ourselves. Life here is a never-ending cycle of hunger and death. I can't stand it here. I need you to take me out of here. I can't fly any of these ships. But you can. You can take me out of this hell."

Colin had no intention of fulfilling Clara's demand. "Sorry. We're not taking any passengers."

Diane raised her gun up to Clara's face. "The hell with this. Let's just kill this bitch and get out of here."

An evil scowl appeared on Clara's face. She hissed at Diane and then leaped high into the air. During her flight, her arms quickly split into four long, spindly appendages. Her face began to turn pale, while at the same time growing into the elongated form of a bovine skull. Her grey camouflage uniform changed into white, overlapping scales, and she sprouted a long, vertebra tail. Within seconds, Clara transformed into one of the creatures that were in the upper level storage room. Clara leaped so high that she was able to reach one of the huge metal beams that spanned across the ceiling, grabbing hold and hanging on with her long insectoid arms. Hanging upside down from the beam, she quickly scurried off into the shadows while avoiding the rapid laser fire from Diane's gun.

Kelly raised his hands and sent twin bolts of flame reaching up to the ceiling. The light from the fire bolts cut through the darkness as they washed over the beam but missed touching Clara. Kelly's attack was cut short when the entire landing bay began to shake. Colin, Diane, and Kelly were nearly thrown off their feet. Things got worse when the landing bay began to tilt forward. Long cracks began to form across the middle of the floor and a wide, gaping hole began to form. There was the sudden sound of a strong wind as the air in the landing bay was being sucked out through this opening. As the landing bay continued tilting, the fighter craft in the vicinity were sliding down towards the hole, including the Black Raven.

Diane charged forward, sprinting to the Black Raven and grabbing onto one of its huge metal landing legs with her left hand. She held up her right hand with her laser gun, keeping it ready in the anticipation of an attack by Clara. Being held under Diane's grip, the Black Raven stopped sliding. Colin stood in total awe of this sight, watching Diane not only holding back the ship with one hand, preventing it from sliding down into the hole, but she started to swiftly pull it back, showing little effort in the process. The low tone of the Black Raven's legs scraping across the floor filled the room. Colin began to wonder just how powerful Diane really was, but there was little time to admire her feat of strength. He could hear a loud banging of metal and multiple high-pitched screeching from behind him in the distance. It could only mean that Clara's inhuman brethren were reaching the landing bay.

Diane continued pulling the Black Raven back away from the hole. She turned her head to Colin and Kelly. "Quick. Get in. This will buy us some time."

Colin needed no further prodding. He bolted for the Black Raven's open ramp with Kelly running close behind him. As soon as they were inside the ship, Colin turned to see Diane running up behind them. Colin pressed a button on the ramp control touchpad on the wall and the ramp began to rise shut. The trio rushed into the cockpit. Diane quickly took her place in the pilot's seat, Colin sitting down next to her in the copilot's seat, not bothering to strap himself in, and Kelly taking his seat at the computer station. Colin watched as Diane's hands pressed the touchpad controls before her. There was the low hum of the ship's engines coming to life. Diane jerked the flight control sticks back. Colin was also jerked back into his seat as the ship suddenly lurched upward. Diane pulled back the left control stick. Colin watched through the forward window as the ship spun around to face the opening to space. He could also see that the landing bay was still tilting. An obvious sign that the entire ship was listing.

"Hang on," Diane cried. She pushed the control sticks forward, sending the Black Raven speeding towards the opening.

The Black Raven safely passed through the opening and exited the ship. They all screamed out in unison when they saw the form of a gigantic creature appearing through the forward window. It had a head like a bovine skull, similar to the creatures aboard the Hemlock, but only blue in color. With thick bands of blue, connecting tendons at the sides of its face. On the back of its head were clusters of long, pointed spines. The monster's head was attached to a long, blue, serpentine neck. The bright yellow glow of its eyes was burning from deep within its large eye sockets. The monster opened its gaping mouth and lunged for the Black Raven. Diane jerked the control sticks to the right, causing the ship to veer away and avoid the monster's jaws snapping down on it. While the Black Raven avoided this monster, it was flying headlong into the face of another one. Exactly like the first.

"Look out!" Colin shouted.

Diane steered the ship to the left to avoid contact with this second monster, only to fly towards another one. Diane steered the ship downward to avoid this third monster. Colin was wondering what kind of situation they had gotten themselves into. Then as the ship was hurtling down, he received his answer. He was horrified at the sight of six of these huge, skull headed creatures with their long, squirming necks, all connected to a blue serpentine body. The six thrashing necks of this hideous creature began to spread apart from each other as a huge maw began to open in between them. It was ringed by a collection of pointed teeth that appeared to be ten times larger than the Black Raven. The maw itself appeared to be large enough to swallow the entire ship whole. And the Black Raven was flying straight towards it.

"Look out!" Colin shouted to Diane.

Diane jerked both control sticks to the left. The Black Raven made a sharp turn away from this huge thing and then headed upward. Colin was unnerved seeing two of the monster's huge heads snapping at the ship. The Black Raven continued to head out into open space and away from the danger.

"That was a close one," said Colin. He was shivering in his seat. "Kelly, anything following us?"

"Give me a second," Kelly returned in a high pitched, nervous voice.

Colin waited to hear Kelly's report after checking the ships scanners.

"There's nothing," said Kelly. "Whatever the hell that thing is, it's not following us. It's staying with the Hemlock."

Despite his fears, Colin was now morbidly curious about the thing. He issued an order to Diane. "Take us back. Nice and easy. I want to see what the hell we're facing."

Diane steered the ship in a circle in order to head back towards the Hemlock. Then she brought the ship to a full stop. From a safe distance, they were able to get a full view of the monster. It had entwined its enormous serpentine body around the full length of the Hemlock and was now constricting it to a point where its hull was being crushed. Colin recalled Clara's name for this monster. Hydra. Its six heads were all staring in the Black Raven's direction.

Their long necks slowly waving about. Then the Hydra opened its huge maw and turned its body towards the Hemlock. It bit down onto the aft section of the ship. Its teeth penetrating the Hemlock's armored hull with ease. Its snake-like necks entwining themselves around the Hemlock to help crush its hull.

Colin was just as silent as Diane and Kelly as they were watching the Hemlock being destroyed before their eyes. Colin was wondering if they were feeling just as helpless as he was.

"Look at it. It's tearing the Hemlock apart," Kelly said in a low voice. "And the crew. All those people we saw. There has to be something we can do to try to save them."

"Maybe we can try an attack," Diane suggested. "We might be able to drive it off or something."

Colin shook his head in disagreement. "That would be futile. The Hemlock is a much bigger ship than the Black Raven. Obviously, it was no match for that thing. We'll be even less effective against it."

"So what? We're not going to do anything?" Diane demanded to know.

Colin shook his head again. "Even if we did try to fight it, we might run the risk of doing harm to the people onboard the Hemlock."

"I just don't like the idea of running away," Diane's testy reply. "We can't try to do something?"

"Like what?" Colin snapped. "There is nothing we can do now." Colin considered this retreat to be a bitter pill to swallow. But he saw no point in languishing on the issue any further. "Just take us back to the rift," he told Diane.

There was a grim silence in the cockpit for several minutes during the flight back to the rift. Colin was still disappointed over not being able to save the Hemlock and its crew. Then Kelly made an unexpected announcement.

"Guys check it out. There's a message coming in. I think it's from one of the other task force ships."

Colin sprang up from his seat. "A message? Are you sure?"

Kelly smiled. "Yeah. It's from the Medusa. I'll patch it through."

Kelly tapped his fingers on the controls before him. The clear sound of a female voice came through.

"Attention Black Raven. This is the United Protectorate destroyer Medusa. Please respond. Black Raven. Come in, please."

Kelly spoke out. "Hello Medusa. This is Kelly Lytton of the Black Raven. Who am I speaking to?"

"I'm Captain Lara Kozak. I'm surprised to see another Protectorate ship way out here. And especially in this subspace."

Colin stepped closer to the communications station. "Hello Kozak. I'm Colin McKenzie. My friends, Kelly and Diane Christy were sent here by the CID to find your task force after you were reported missing. Are you alright?"

"We're all fine here," replied Kozak. "We were wondering what the hell was going on when we picked up your transponder signal."

"Where are the other task force ships?" Colin asked.

"Battle cruiser Perseus and battle carrier Tsunami are right behind us. The status of the Hemlock is unknown."

"The Hemlock is lost," Colin sadly told Kozak. "There were these creatures. Swarms of them. And this huge one that's ripping the ship apart."

"We know about them. We were attacked by the big one with the six heads first. Then the smaller ones came in full swarm. We found out early on that they were shape shifters. Sneaky, vicious bastards.

We were barely able to eliminate them completely. But apparently the Hemlock wasn't so lucky. We tried to deal with the big one, but it was too powerful. It shrugged off everything we threw at it. We were forced to pull back, and then we were lost. I don't know if there are any more of them like it in here."

That's understandable, thought Colin. "Hopefully the Hemlock will keep it busy long enough for us to get out of here. Contact the other ships and tell them to follow us. We have a way out of here."

Colin was elated that his mission was not all for nothing. While the loss of the Hemlock was unfortunate, contacting the remaining ships in the task force partially made up for it.

The mood in the cockpit was now more upbeat, knowing that they would soon leave this limbo while being followed by the ships from home. After several minutes, the sight of a huge, white disk appeared through the forward window. The rift back to normal space. It was rapidly growing larger in view as the Black Raven was speeding towards it. Colin was hoping that they would not have to wait long for the Medusa and the other ships to catch up to them and exit the rift. He dreaded the thought of that giant multi-headed monster and its smaller brethren escaping into this universe.

The Black Raven flew into the rift and emerged back into the darkness of normal space. Diane flew the ship several miles away from the rift and then turned the ship around so that they can see it through the forward window. A few minutes later, the form of an enormous spacecraft similar to the Hemlock emerged through the rift.

"There is it. The Medusa," said Colin. He took notice of the large rips and tears along the front section of the ship's hull. "Looks like they've taken on damage from that thing."

"Let's hope we can get all the other ships through

and then close this rift so those things can't get through," Diane told Colin.

Colin listened to Kozak's voice as she transmitted a message.

"Medusa to Black Raven. It's good to be back into normal space again. I thought we'd never get out of there."

"What about the other ships?" Colin's reply to Kozak. "How far are they? We'd like to get all of you out and close this rift as soon as possible."

"We've contacted the Perseus and Tsunami. They're just a few minutes away. I'll tell them to pick up speed."

"Sounds good, Medusa. We're heading back to the starbase that created this rift. It's under our control. We're going to wait until all ships are through and then close this rift for good. Black Raven out."

Diane piloted the Black Raven back to the Gatherer starbase. Once the ship returned to the landing bay, Colin, Diane, and Kelly were greeted by Linda and her camera man, Al, who was filming them the very second that they were walking down the Black Raven's ramp.

Linda rushed up to Colin. A smile beaming on her face. She began speaking rapidly. "So how did it go? You actually went into an alternate dimension. Can you tell our audience back home what you saw?"

Colin was in no mood to give an interview. "Guys. Give us a break. We'll answer all your questions later."

Everyone followed Colin to the control room. There they saw the Gatherers Audra and Martin were standing at their columns while Ava and Gaylie were keeping a close watch with their weapons in hand. They both smiled when they saw Colin and the others.

"You're back," said Ava. "How did it go? We kept a close eye on these three so that they wouldn't try anything."

"We were partially successful." Colin told her. "It was a horror story. We couldn't save the Hemlock. But we did manage to contact one of the other ships. The Medusa. It's coming through the rift and bringing the rest of the task force with it."

"Thank God for that," replied Ava. "I was hoping that you all would come back safely."

Audra approached Colin. "So, your grand mission was largely successful. And so now that we've held up our end of the bargain, I assume you'll let us go unharmed."

Colin grinned. "Not just yet. We still need you to keep that rift open until all of our ships are through. Then you're going to close it before the monsters that live in that subspace come through to our universe. Then we're going to blow this entire place to hell."

Audra's mouth gaped open. She let out a gasp. "No. You can't. This Starbase, this equipment. This is all of our years of research. If you destroy this base, then the loss will be catastrophic."

"Not to us," Colin's reply. "Stopping you Gatherers from bringing Kimdrack back is a secondary mission. And as far as I'm concerned, that mission is still ongoing."

"We won't help you with this," Audra told Colin. Standing firm on her position.

Colin stood firmly on his own. "Yes, you will. Helping us will greatly decrease the chances of your burned corpses floating through space with the rest of the wreckage. I promise that none of you are going to leave here alive."

Diane aimed her laser gun at Audra's head. "The way I see it, maybe we won't need these three to keep the rift open until the other ships get through. And we sure as hell won't need them to help us blow this place up. So maybe we can see how eager they are to die for their God."

The standoff was suddenly interrupted by a sharp chiming sound coming from Kelly. He reached into his pocket and brought out his sensor pad. He examined it, then looked to Colin. "There's an incoming message to the Black Raven. It's from Markus. I'll patch it through."

Kelly tapped his thumb onto the controls of his sensor pad. The next moment it transmitted the sound of Markus' voice for everyone to hear.

"Hello. Ava. McKenzie. Hello. Come in."

Ava was the first to speak out in response. "Markus. This is Ava. I hear you."

"Ava? Where are you?"

"I'm aboard the Gatherer starbase with Colin and the others," Ava answered. "What's happening?"

"An urgent matter has come up. It took us a while to get things up and running at our new facility with this Gatherer tech. But when we did, we found out that the Tritians have already made their prisoner transport. This happened two hours ago."

"What?" Colin shouted in disbelief. He moved closer to Kelly and his sensor pad. "What the hell do you mean they left?"

"They left," Markus repeated. "Our instruments here recorded them leaving the planet with a larger than usual group of escort ships. Tritian and Guydrun. We've never seen that before. They must realize that this shipment of prisoners must be special. Sorry that we couldn't have gotten the news to you sooner. Now It's too late."

Colin was immediately angered by this news. "Dammit. We missed them," he yelled out.

"Maybe we can still catch up to them," Diane told him. "The Black Raven is faster than anything they've got."

Colin agreed. "Yeah. Ok. Markus, I need you to send us the coordinates to Osidra. We're going after them right now."

"Sure, I can send you the coordinates. But are you insane? By our count, the escort is composed of thirty ships. And they're probably already to Osidra by now."

Colin ignored Markus. "Ava, Gaylie. I need you to stay here and continue keeping an eye on our friends here. And to make sure that the task force ships get through the rift. Then try to contact Captain Kozak of the Medusa. Tell her to get you all off of this starbase, then destroy it completely so that the monsters living there can't escape through. We're going after those kids."

"But are you sure that you can do this?" Ava questioned. "You heard Markus. You will be terribly outnumbered."

"I don't care," Colin snapped. "We're getting those kids back. No matter what it takes."

Colin, Diane, and Kelly turned and quickly headed out of the control room. Linda again badgered Colin for an interview, but he ignored her. As well as ignoring Al, who continued filming the group's every move. Returning to the landing bay, they approached the Black Raven. Before they could reach the ship's ramp, they were taken by surprise by one of the spindly armed creatures that they encountered back at the Hemlock, jumping down from the top of the ship and landing directly in front of them. Within seconds, the creature transformed itself into the human form of Clara Skyhook. Facing Colin, Diane, and Kelly she laughed. "I did it. I'm free. I'm the only one that made it out. I'm free."

Colin could not believe that Skyhook was here with them. But in his mind, the only thing that mattered was killing this monster. He raised his hand and fired an electrical bolt at Skyhook, but the creature was fast enough to leap over his attack while quickly taking on the form of a huge, black stingray. Its broad fins stretching out like wings and flapping rapidly to keep it aloft. The creature began to fly in a wild spiral to avoid the continuous electrical fire from Colin. Then to Colin's amazement, the creature headed towards the entrance to the landing bay and then flew out into space.

"Skyhook," Kelly exclaimed. "How the hell did that thing get here?"

"No doubt it hitched a ride on the ship's hull when we were back in its dimension," Colin explained. "But I'm surprised that it can survive out in space."

"What the hell are we going to do now?" Diane asked Colin.

Despite this unforeseen occurrence, Colin remained focused on their original mission. "We can't worry about that thing now. We've got to get to Osidra and rescue those kids. We're not letting that go."

"Heads up. There's another message coming in," Kelly informed Colin. "It's from the Medusa."

"The Medusa," said Colin. He saw this as encouraging news. "Patch it through."

Kelly tapped his sensor pad. The voice of Captain Kozak came through for everyone to hear.

"Kozak to Black Raven. We've cleared that rift. What is your current location?"

"This is Colin McKenzie. We're aboard the starbase."

"That's good to hear," Kozak replied. "We're heading your way. The other ships are coming up behind us. The Tsunami and the Perseus."

Colin looked up at the holographic monitor above the column. It was displaying the full image of the Medusa. "Kozak. It's good to hear your voice. Glad to hear that the task force is back with us. But now we've got an urgent situation to deal with and we need your help."

"Just name it," Kozak responded.

"First off, I need you to send a detachment of men to take custody of three prisoners. Then after we evacuate this starbase, we need to destroy it. Then we have to go and carry out a rescue mission. Kelly will transmit the coordinates to you. This might be a bit rough, but having you for backup could help."

"I'll send some men over now," Kozak told Colin. "Then I'll get ahold of the Tsunami and Perseus and let them know what's going on."

"Thanks, Kozak. McKenzie out."

There was a determined grin on Colin's face as he looked at Diane and Kelly. "Alright then. Next stop, the planet Osidra. We're going to step on some bugs."

CHAPTER TWELVE

Colin felt more determined than ever to rescue the Willoby children now that he had the support of a large United Protectorate task force. After the Medusa and the other ships emerged through the rift, Captain Kozak sent a small group of soldiers aboard the starbase to take the three Gatherers prisoner. After Colin and the others all boarded the Black Raven and put some distance between them and the starbase, the Medusa opened fire and destroyed it. Now the Gatherers were unable to use the base's warp converter to banish anyone else to the subspace dimension or continue experimenting with ways to return Kimdrack to this universe. After completing that task, the Black Raven and its occupants made an immediate departure to reach the planet Osidra.

Following the coordinates provided by Markus, Diane sent the Black Raven into a hyperspace jump to shorten the trip. Now that they were in Tritian territory, Colin was prepared for anything, except failure. This was a fight that he was determined to win.

Ava, Gaylie, and the two reporters Linda and Al

were all loaded in the ship's cockpit with Colin, Diane, and Kelly. Al was continuously recording everything that happens, while Linda kept badgering Colin for an interview that was continuously declined. Sitting next to Diane, he was too focused on what he would soon see outside the forward window.

"Scanners are picking up a huge alien object about forty-eight thousand kilometers away," Kelly informed the group. "Its composition is that of the Tritian starbase that we ran into a while ago. Part metal, part organic material. I'm also picking up a large number of ships. Beyond that is a planet."

Colin sat up in his seat. "This is it. Brace yourselves. This is going to get ugly fast."

Linda rushed over to Colin. Al keeping his camera trained on them both. "Colin. One more time before we go into deadly battle. Do you have anything to tell our viewers back home?"

Colin's irritation at Linda was increasing. "Are you serious? You want me to give you commentary now? We're about to go to war."

As the Black Raven continued its flight, the Tritian starbase came into view, an enormous, dark pinecone shape covered with large overlapping scales. Lined up in front of the starbase were several silvery wedge-shaped fighter craft with broad swept forward wings and long spines at their rear sections. There were also two huge cigar shaped vessels with broad, triangular lateral fins. Their hulls were covered by long, spiny projections. Also, among these ships was a line composed of several large and small jet styled vessels that Colin recognized as Guydrun. In the far distance beyond the starbase and ships was the green orb of the planet Osidra.

"They're making a show of force," said Colin. "I'm not surprised."

"There's an incoming message," Kelly revealed. "I'm putting it through."

Colin was expecting the enemy ships to make a stand. But he was surprised to hear the familiar voice of Guydrun Lieutenant Drake.

"McKenzie. I assume that you and your friends are aboard that ship. Welcome to the planet Osidra."

Colin rose up from his seat and walked over to the computer station. "Drake. I'm surprised to see that you're here. Maybe this is the day that we get to kill you."

"No doubt," replied Drake. "Just like you killed my colleague, Major Vormiester. You won't be that lucky with me."

"I'm not surprised you know about that," Colin returned.

Drake laughed. "It's not too hard to follow the exploits of three super powered aliens. You three have got a habit of leaving dead bodies wherever you go."

Colin cheerfully agreed with Drake. "You're right. And we plan on adding a lot more to that number before the day is over. I assume that you know why we're here."

"Yes. The prisoners from the town of Willoby. A special shipment. Viceroy Sclero informed me that you have a special interest in this bunch."

"Sclero? Is he here too?" inquired Colin. "Now that doesn't surprise me either. He's been a part of this since day one."

After mentioning Sclero's name, Colin heard the transmission of his gravely toned voice speaking English through his translator. "McKenzie. I assume that this will be our last meeting. I will finish the job that Vormiester and the Gatherers failed to do. Unless you suddenly become wise and decide to retreat back to your home out in deep space."

Colin stood firm. "Not a chance. We're not leaving without those kids and anyone else you're holding down there."

"A laughable boast," Sclero returned. "You talk very tough for someone that's woefully outnumbered. No matter how advanced your little ship is."

Kelly interrupted Colin and Sclero's standoff to deliver some encouraging news. "Heads up, guys. The cavalry is here."

Looking through the forward window Colin saw that the Black Raven was now flanked by the immense, silvery wedge form of the battle cruiser Perseus at the left, and the much larger battle carrier Tsunami at the right. Colin and the others received a better view of the two huge ships as they slowly pulled away from the Black Raven. Flying out from below the Tsunami were dozens of triangular shaped fighters, all forming a long line in front of the two large ships. Appearing from below the Black Raven came the huge triangular shape of the destroyer Medusa's front section. Being this close to these three large ships was an impressive sight. Colin was hoping that the enemy forces would be even more impressed.

"Message coming in from the Medusa," Kelly said.

"Kozak to Black Raven. I hope we're not too late for the party. Where are these kids we need to save?"

"Glad to see that you guys could make it," Colin returned. "The kids have been taken down to the planet. We might have to fight our way through to get to them."

"That all depends on these assholes up ahead and their intentions," Kozak added.

Great point, thought Colin. "We'll give them one chance to step aside. After that, we touch off a war. Stand by."

Colin ordered Kelly to reopen the channel to Viceroy Sclero so that he could relay an ultimatum. "As you can see, we didn't exactly come alone. Now unless you want to see which one of us has the superior force, I strongly advise you to bring us those children or we'll go through you and take them back."

A quick response came from Lieutenant Drake. There was a nervous tone to his voice. "These ships. Where did they come from? They're with you?"

"That's right. United Protectorate task force five," Colin told Drake. "You may have the numbers. But we have the advanced tech and firepower. So, which one of us starts this war first?"

For a minute there was no reply. Then Drake relayed his response.

"There's no need for us to get too involved in this conflict. We're here officially on an observer status."

Colin watched as the Guydrun ships began to peel off from the Tritian forces and move a safe distance away. *So, you Guydruns want no part of this fight,* he thought. The transmission of Sclero's angered voice gave Colin a clear indication of the Tritian's position in this standoff.

"Drake! We don't need you human cowards to defend our territory. Damn you! And damn you too, McKenzie! All of you humans die!"

The Tritian forces began to fly forward while opening fire with their weapons. The battle had now begun.

"Here we go," Colin muttered. He looked back at Ava and the others. "Hang on, everybody. This is going to be a rough ride."

Diane pushed the flight control sticks forward to send the Black Raven on a direct course towards the swarm of Tritian ships. Her fingers pressed the buttons on the sides of the sticks to fire the ship's plasma cannons. At the same time, the other Protectorate ships also began to charge into battle while opening fire. Soaring head long to meet the enemy, the Black Raven destroyed two Tritian fighters, then began to pursue two more as the rest of the enemy forces began to scatter. During the chase, Colin caught more of Linda's commentary. Along with Al, Ava, and Gaylie, she was crouched down while holding on to the back of Colin and Diane's seats.

"We are now engaging the enemy forces in serious, deadly combat. It appears that the Guydrun forces have backed out of the fight, leaving the Tritians to fend for themselves. This is where we see if these aliens from the United Protectorate have the superior power to deal with the Tritians. This battle could be historic, as it could affect the war that our planet is waging against these invaders. Colin, can you please share your thoughts concerning the battle?"

"Why do you always have to pick on me for this?" Colin shouted back to Linda. "I'm not the only one here you know."

"Diane, your thoughts?" Linda asked.

"Sorry, I'm a bit tied up at the moment," Diane cried back in response. She piloted the Black Raven in pursuit of a fleeing Tritian fighter, then destroyed it in an instant with the ship's plasma cannons.

Kelly took the time to respond to Linda's question. "This is probably the hairiest situation that I've been in. And here I thought that we had our hands full when we were up against the Enforcers. You remember that, Colin?"

"Whenever somebody tries to kill me, I don't write down notes to compare who pissed me off the most," Colin shouted. "Let's just focus on who's trying to kill us here and now."

Diane piloted the Black Raven to pursue and destroy one Tritian fighter after another. During the intense dogfight, the impact of enemy fire rocked the ship. Colin was thankful for the ship's defensive shields to absorb the Tritians weaker firepower. And hoped that they would continue to last.

"Kelly, how are the shields holding up?" Colin asked.

"Shields holding at ninety six percent," Kelly reports. "As long as we don't get hit by a concentration of their heavy firepower, we should be ok."

Diane, remaining quiet as she focused her concentration on her flying, followed two Tritian fighters as they were executing wild loops and turns in an attempt to elude her. After a minute of this chase, she was able to get one of her targets in her sights and destroy it with just a few plasma shots. She continued the chase against the second fighter when Kelly patched through an incoming message from the male pilot of another Protectorate ship."

"Black Raven, this is Lieutenant Wenzer of Lance Squadron. We're going after one of those big ships. You're welcome to join our fighter wing."

A smile formed on Diane's face. "I never pass up a formal invitation to kick somebody's ass," she loudly said.

"If I didn't know any better, I'd swear that you're enjoying this," Colin told Diane.

The Black Raven dove down and merged with a large group of fighters as they were flying towards one of the large Tritian ships. Space was thick with rapidly fired laser and plasma fire coming from the Protectorate forces assaulting their huge target. Without the benefit of any protective energy shielding, the ship's hull was ripped to shreds by the Protectorate assault. While this was going on, the Medusa, Perseus, and Tsunami were attacking the ship with their heavy weapons, their plasma cannons spitting out powerful beams of crimson energy that burned completely through the Tritian ship's hull. The Black Raven and Lance Squadron fighters began to fly along one side of the Tritian ship while raining down their relentless attack. Large sections of its hull was torn away as the assault progressed. Then reaching the rear section of the ship and circling back to attack the other side. From beneath the attacking squadron, two more massive plasma beams burned clean through the Tritian ship.

"Wenzer to squadron. Clear the area and proceed to second target ship. This turkey is cooked and done. Wenzer out."

The Black Raven joined the other ships as they veered off to the right and flew out into space for a short distance, then circled back. Through the forward window, the Black Raven's occupants watched as the heavily damaged Tritian ship exploded into a bright red ball of fire, scattering its briefly flaming fragments throughout the area.

Colin was not surprised when he heard the overjoyed cheers coming from Ava, Gaylie, and Linda. This was probably the first major enemy defeat that they have witnessed during this war. However, the frantic message that was relayed from Viceroy Sclero revealed he was less than pleased.

"McKenzie! What have you done? This is an outrage! You humans will pay for this outrage! No one attacks the Tritian Hierarchy!"

Colin was more amused than intimidated by Sclero's threat. "Are you aboard that second ship, Sclero?" he cried back. "Don't worry. You're next."

"Not just yet," Sclero replied.

Colin watched as the Black Raven joined the squadron of Protectorate fighters to engage the second large Tritian ship. Other squadrons were flying about to attack and destroy the Tritian fighters that were now caught on the losing end of a one-sided battle. Sclero's ship turned away and headed towards the starbase. The Black Raven and the other ships began to spread out and open fire at the rear section of the ship. Their combined firepower tore away large sections of the ship's hull. Sclero's ship increased its speed and moved around to the right side of the starbase. The starbase began to open fire with its defensive gun batteries and missiles. The Black Raven was shaken by several hits from the smaller weapons fire. But the incoming missiles would prove to be the greater threat if not for the Black Raven's auto defense guns. They rapidly shot out red energy beams that scored direct hits and exploded four missiles in the distance.

The Black Raven and the other Protectorate ships continued their assault on Sclero's ship as it made its way around the starbase. It was this moment that Colin, Diane, and Kelly were taken totally by surprise at what was waiting at the other side. Docked at the side of the starbase were two huge, dark, manta ray shaped spacecraft that the three instantly recognized on sight.

"Brelac!" Diane exclaimed.

Colin pointed. "Brelac destroyers."

"Brelac?" Linda inquired. "Who are they?"

'They're our enemies," Colin quickly answered. "What the hell are they doing here?"

The Black Raven intercepted the radio chatter coming from the other Protectorate ships. Multiple voices all expressing the same surprise.

"Brelac. Attention all ships. We have contact with Brelac destroyers."

"We have Brelac in the vicinity. All fighter wings pull back."

The Brelac destroyers moved off from the starbase and headed out into space. They then simultaneously turned about and faced the Perseus, Medusa, and Tsunami so that they could fire a swarm of missiles. The three Protectorate ships quickly opened fire with their smaller defensive laser batteries to destroy the incoming missile attacks. But the Brelac missiles, being faster and protected by defensive energy shields, proved to be more difficult targets than their Tritian counterparts. The missiles took on bright blue glows as their shields were bombarded by the Protectorate fire. The shields of several missiles weakened enough for the firepower to penetrate and destroy them. But several more managed to survive and reach their targets.

Everyone in the Black Raven's cockpit watched as the missiles struck and exploded against the hulls of the Medusa, Perseus, and Tsunami. The defensive energy shields of the three ships flashed blue under the force of the powerful explosions. After staging their missile attack, the two Brelac destroyers both turned away and headed off into space. They traveled for a short distance, then they were both enveloped in a bright flash of light and completely vanished.

"What just happened?" Linda asked. "Where did they go?"

"They made a hyperspace jump," Diane answered. "They cut and ran."

"Well, where are they now?" Gaylie asked.

"They could be anywhere," Colin told her. "They could emerge in the next star system or halfway to the next quadrant. But that's not important. What we need to know is why were they here with the Tritians?"

"The Tritians. Sclero's ship," Diane exclaimed. "Where the hell did he go?"

To Colin the answer was obvious. "Where else? Down to the planet. Sclero won't get far. But first, let's help finish the job here and take out that starbase."

Diane turned the Black Raven around and merged with a swarm of fighters that were heading on a direct course to attack the starbase. All ships began to pour their smaller firepower to the huge starbase, as well as the few remaining Tritian fighters. Countless laser and plasma shots ripped away large sections of the starbase's hull, leaving behind briefly flaming craters. As the Black Raven passed over the top of the Tsunami, Colin saw that it had launched several missiles at the starbase. As if on cue, the other Protectorate ships, both large and small, also fired their missiles.

"Firing torpedoes," Diane said.

Diane pressed a button on the side of her right control stick. Four of the Black Raven's fusion torpedoes went streaking out to join the multiple missiles that were flying on their way towards their huge target. The group of missiles struck and detonated on contact with the Tritian starbase. Several powerful explosions went off against its hull. The starbase erupted into a massive fireball; its glowing red fragments scattering in all directions.

There were more cheers in the Black Raven's cockpit after witnessing the Tritians suffer another defeat. But Colin knew that the fight was far from over.

Linda continued giving her commentary. "Oh my God. I hope everyone back home had the chance to see that. The forces of the United Protectorate have just destroyed a gigantic Tritian starbase. Our combined resistance forces wouldn't dare come light years near that thing. But these people, our fellow Humans and new allies were able to blow the Tritians out of space. But the question now is what happens next? Colin. Can you please tell us?"

Linda finally asked a question that Colin could answer. "What's next? We go down to the planet and do the same to whatever is down there. We're here for those kids and we're not leaving without them."

"Message coming in from the Medusa," Kelly said.

Kozak's clear, loud voice came in. "Medusa to Black Raven. Looks like we're done here. Where's our primary targets?"

"The children? They're being transported down to the planet," Colin called back. We're going after them. And Viceroy Sclero. He was on that big ship that got away."

"We'll follow your lead, Black Raven. I just hope that whatever is down there won't be too much for us to handle. Medusa out."

The Black Raven dove down on a course towards the planet, leading the way as swarms of fighters and the three huge ships followed. It only took a few minutes for the ship to enter the planet's atmosphere and pierce a thick cloud bank. A few minutes later, the Black Raven emerged from the clouds and continued soaring downward until the surface of the planet came into view through the forward window. The heavy cover of clouds created a dark scene below. The Black Raven was descending upon a huge land mass with countless tall structures reaching up to the sky. They were round, dark towers covered with large, overlapping scales and topped by long points. On the ground below were long networks of canals filled with green water. At the bottom of some of these towers were beams of bright light shining up to the sky. Also, from the bottom of these towers were swarms of Tritian fighters that began to fly up and engage the invading Protectorate force in battle.

"Here we are now at the Tritian's home planet, Osidra," Linda reported. "It's dark and foreboding. Down below we see a vast Tritian city. There are countless towers all over the place. They're sending up squadrons of ships to attack us. There's no signs of the abducted children."

Diane opened fired with the Black Raven's plasma cannons as three Tritian fighter craft were streaking up towards it on an attack course. All three enemy ships were destroyed one after the other. Diane then steered the ship upward away from the exploding ships to give chase to another fighter. Watching the scene through the forward window, Colin saw several Protectorate fighters scattering and engaging the Tritians in aerial combat. The energy of their weapons fire flashing through the air and exploding their targets on contact. Colin had no desire to spend precious time fighting the Tritians here while there were no signs of Sclero and the children.

"We can't let them bog us down here," said Colin. "Kelly, run a sensor scan for any concentration of humans in the area. They couldn't have gotten far."

"I'm on it," replied Kelly.

Colin waited. During the moments that passed, he sat and watched as Diane was flying the Black Raven in tight loops and sharp turns in order to evade Tritian pursuers while chasing down and destroying other ships. Colin could not help but to be impressed by the level of flying skill that she was displaying. As it was turning out, Diane was not the reckless danger in the cockpit that he feared.

"I have to hand it to you. You really are earning that title, Ace," Colin complemented.

Diane smiled, but kept her focus locked on the scene outside. "Let's plan on celebrating when we get out of here.

Kelly gave a report. "Heads up. I'm picking up a large concentration of human contacts about twenty miles away. Due north."

"Take us there," Colin ordered Diane. "Kelly, contact Kozak and the others and have them follow us. Maybe we can end this quickly and then get out of here before we end up fighting the entire planet."

After shooting down two more Tritian fighters, Diane steered the Black Raven sharply to the right and then flew above the city until they came upon a huge pyramid structure in the distance. Its surface was covered with dark, overlapping scales and long protruding spines. At the top of the pyramid was a thick cluster of the spines. In the middle of these was a huge round shape. It was black, bearing white tiger stripe patterns. Colin was encouraged when he saw the large, cigar shaped vessel bearing the extensive hull damage flying close to the top of the pyramid structure: Sclero's ship. Flying slowly next to it were three huge, dark spacecraft resembling blimps. They had dozens of long spines protruding from their hulls and curving back to their rear sections with twin, glowing red engine ports. Docked at the side of the pyramid was another large ship similar to Sclero's.

Diane reduced the Black Raven's speed, making a slow approach to the pyramid.

"Those three big ships. That has to be them," Colin said as he pointed. "Prisoner transport ships."

"So how are we going to do this?" asked Diane. "If we go in with guns blazing, there's the chance that those transports might get caught in the crossfire."

Colin was well aware of that danger. "Maybe we can try to lure Sclero away from the transports. But first, I'm going to send him an ultimatum."

Colin waited for a moment while Kelly established an open channel. Then he spoke out in a clear, stern voice. "Alright, Sclero. I know you can hear me. This is the end of the line. If you have any prisoners on board those three ships, then we're giving you just one last chance to surrender them to us or its total war. You've already seen what we can do against your forces. You have no chance. So, either we do this the easy way or the hard way. But personally, I'd jump at the chance to ram a fusion torpedo down your throat and up your ass at the same time."

A few seconds later, Colin received a response from Sclero's gravelly voice. Sooner than he expected.

"McKenzie. You dare to hound me here at the heart of our home? This is the Tritian Hierarchy. You do not make demands here. These humans will not leave here alive. And neither will you."

Colin nodded and grinned in the face of Sclero's threat. "Ok then. That's an open invitation to do this the easy way."

Diane also nodded. "I can do it the easy way. The easy way is more fun."

"Do you mind telling me what the easy way involves?" Linda asked in a nervous voice.

"Do I have to spell it out to you?" Colin moaned.

Sclero issued a second threat. "You humans will step no further to this hallowed place. You will stop here, and you will all die! Die by the full power of the Tritian Hierarchy!"

The second large ship began to pull away from the side of the pyramid and slowly moved next to Sclero's ship. Two more large ships moved from around the other side of the pyramid and joined them to form a defensive line. As the Tritian ships were displaying this show of force the huge, round, tiger striped object at the top of the pyramid began to move. Two enormous, black bat wings covered by white tiger stripes rose up from the cluster of spines and spread themselves out. The wings were a part of a massive insectoid monster that resembled a Tritian, but greatly larger. By Colin's rough estimate it was nearly fifty feet tall. The creature extended its eight long legs, with its two forelegs bearing long scythe blades that looked as though they could slice the Black Raven in half with a single slash. Its body was covered by shaggy black fur with patterns of white stripes. Its large round head had four vertical rows of small red eyes. Above the eyes were two long antennae. Its mouth, below its eyes, was composed of two large, serrated mandibles.

The creature bent its head down and faced the Black Raven. It opened its mandibles and let out a loud roar.

"That's one big pissed off bug," Colin exclaimed.

The monster flapped its wings and leaped high into the air. Its entire body was exposed now that it was away from the pyramid, revealing its short tail. It had thick black fur with white tiger stripes that was nearly obscured by thick clusters of long pointed barbs. Each one appearing to be half the size of the Black Raven. The monster raised its tail, aiming it at the Black Raven. Several of its barbs shot out, spraying the area.

"Get us out of here! Move it!" Colin hastily told Diane.

Diane steered the Black Raven into a sharp right turn. The ship was suddenly struck by a powerful impact. Colin was nearly thrown out of his seat as the ship went into a wild spiral. After a moment, Diane regained control and flew the ship up into the open sky.

"That was one hell of a hit," Colin cried. "Kelly, any damage?"

"Our aft shields took a pounding. Shield strength is down to forty percent," Kelly stated.

"A few more shots like that will rip us apart," said Colin.

"What the hell was that thing?" Linda squealed.

Ava explained, "That has to be the Tritians' leader. Their queen, Vorloxa."

Kelly opened a message from a Protectorate ship. "Wenzer to Black Raven. We finished off most of those enemy fighters and managed to break away. Looks like you need some serious help here."

"You might say that," Colin called back to Wenzer.

"We've got incoming missiles," Kelly shouted.

Diane sent the Black Raven into a wild loop, then headed back down towards the city. Through the forward window was the sight of several oncoming Tritian missiles. Diane opened fire with the ship's plasma cannons. The rapid energy fire scored a succession of four hits, exploding the missiles in midair, but there were still several more that were posing an eminent threat. Diane dove the Black Raven down to avoid the missiles, but doing so put the ship on a direct course towards Vorloxa. With her wings flapping rapidly, she reached out with one of her scythe fore arms to take a slash at the Black Raven. With the exception of Diane, everyone in the cockpit screamed at this fearful sight. Diane put the ship in a sharp left turn, then pulled upward, just avoiding Vorloxa's strike. The Black Raven banked left, then dove down, heading straight for Vorloxa's back. Diane opened fire with the plasma cannons. Several of the crimson bolts tore into the monster's hide, causing fiery explosions. The Black Raven then headed straight, flying between Vorloxa's huge flapping wings.

After the Black Raven cleared away from the monster, it made a sharp dive and headed towards the four large oncoming Tritian ships below. Sclero's ship was flying in the forefront. Diane increased the Black Raven's speed and continued heading towards them.

Colin was frozen in his seat. His wide eyes were unblinking as he gazed at the scene through the forward window. "You know what you're doing, right?" he asked Diane.

Diane did not answer. She maintained the Black Raven's current course and speed towards the line of large ships. While it was making this wild charge, the Black Raven was shaken as it was struck multiple times by the Tritian's weaker ballistic firepower. Then the Black Raven flew in between two of the large ships. Along the way, Diane fired the plasma cannons, strafing the sides of both ships. The Black Raven passed from between the two ships, then made a sharp turn to head back towards them. Colin and the others watched as the group of missiles that were pursuing the Black Raven crashed into the sides of the two ships and exploded as they were trying to fly in between them. The few that did manage to safely fly through were quickly destroyed by the Black Raven's plasma fire.

With the threat of the missiles eliminated, Diane went on the offensive. She stopped the Black Raven and hovered behind the two Tritian ships. She targeted the one on the right. Its twin-engine ports, both glowing red, were exposed. Diane fired two fusion torpedoes that hit between both engine ports and exploded. The powerful twin blasts ripped apart large sections of the ship's hull. Both engine ports began to flicker, then remained dark. The damaged ship began to drift to the left towards the other, plowing into its side and shearing away large sections of its hull. Diane was about to continue her assault against both Tritian ships when Vorloxa suddenly swooped down from above them. She aimed her huge tail at the Black Raven and again shot out dozens of her long, deadly barbs. Diane jerked the control sticks to the left and right, weaving and bobbing the Black Raven around the oncoming projectiles, missing all of them. Diane now targeted Vorloxa. She opened fire with the plasma cannons. The rapidly fired crimson bolts burned across Vorloxa's thorax and head. The monster writhed under the damaging assault and let out a roar in pain.

Diane fired two torpedoes. They swiftly flew towards Vorloxa and scored direct hits in the middle of her thorax. The explosions knocked her back. The torpedo strikes left large flaming holes in the monster's thorax. Other sections of the monster's body that suffered the Black Raven's plasma attack were also left burning. Then several Protectorate fighters began to join the assault. They began to surround Vorloxa, flying circles around her while strafing her with plasma and laser fire. Desperately flapping her wings to stay aloft, Vorloxa writhed and let out a roar under the assault. Diane resumed her attack with the Black Raven's plasma cannons. Suddenly two thick, red beams of energy streaked across the front of the Black Raven and burned clear through the two Tritian ships. Under critical damage, both ships suffered from the explosion. Vorloxa was engulfed by the huge fireballs and swarms of flaming shrapnel. The third Tritian ship tried to veer off to the left but was also hit by two of the powerful beams. Its entire rear section exploded and then it made a quick descent to the ground. The only ship remaining now was Sclero's. Through the forward window, everyone saw that the powerful beam attack was coming from the large Protectorate ships, Medusa, Tsunami, and the Perseus. The trio of ships began to fire their main weapons at Sclero's ship. His already damaged vessel could not withstand the heavy assault. The combined Protectorate energy fire burned clear through his ship. Seconds later, a succession of explosions from the rear to the front tore the ship apart. During its destruction, the Black Raven received a final transmission from Viceroy Sclero in the form of his death screams.

Now the only Tritian target remaining was their monstrous queen. She was still reeling under the assault by the Black Raven and the Protectorate fighters. She frantically whipped her tail about, launching dozens of her huge barbs in all directions. The relentless fighter attack was taking a heavy toll on her. Her body was riddled with countless burning wounds. Her flapping wings were bearing several large holes. As a last-ditch effort, Vorloxa turned and began to fly head long towards the closest of the three Protectorate ships, the Tsunami. Vorloxa let out a final roar. In response, the Tsunami opened fire with its main plasma weapon. The massive and powerful beam hit Vorloxa head on. She stopped in mid-flight and was enveloped by a bright white flash. Then she exploded into a huge ball of fire and sparks. Three more explosions did the job of obliterating the last remnants of the monstrous Tritian queen.

In the Black Raven's cockpit there were more cheers. This time louder. Linda, not hiding her excitement, voiced her commentary in a rapid and high-pitched voice.

"This is Linda Jones. And what we've just watched was incredible. I hope that nobody at home missed this. We have just witnessed the destruction of the Tritian's leader. Their queen, Vorloxa." Linda hesitated for a few seconds, then continued. This time in a tearful voice. "We have just witnessed the total defeat of the Tritian forces on their home planet by the United Protectorate. The Tritians have been defeated. This could have a huge ripple effect back to our world. This could be a major step to finally driving these invaders off our world."

Colin turned to face Linda. "Hold on. Let's not get ahead of ourselves. It's not over yet. The Tritians still have swarms of fighters out there to throw against us."

Colin turned back to the forward window. He was expecting the Black Raven to resume the battle against the Tritian fighters. Instead, he was amazed to see many of them turning around and making a fast retreat. Even more amazing was that the ones who remained began to open fire and attack each other.

"What the hell is going on?" Colin asked.

The Black Raven received a message from Kozak. "Medusa to Black Raven. We're trying to figure out what's going on. Our fighter wings are reporting that a lot of these alien ships are starting to turn on each other. But beyond that, enemy resistance is now light."

"Then we can use that to our advantage," Colin replied. "Maybe they'll keep out of our way while we investigate that pyramid and see if they're holding any human prisoners."

"Understood Black Raven. And it appears that the fight isn't quite over yet. Those other alien ships that broke away from the others are heading your way."

That information greatly drew Colin's interest. "Sounds like Lieutenant Drake and his cronies are trying to get our attention. Stand down Medusa. We'll handle this. Black Raven out."

Colin stood up from his seat. "Hold position here," he told Diane.

Colin remained standing as he waited. After a few minutes, he saw the squadron of Guydrun ships in the distance. Flying in a close group, they were making a slow approach to the Black Raven. One large ship was flying in the forefront. This was the one that Colin assumed Drake would be aboard. He continued watching the Guydrun ships move in closer. Then they stopped and hovered just a few feet away from the Black Raven's nose.

Colin turned and raised a hand to Kelly. "Open a channel. I want to have a word with this asshole." Feeling emboldened, Colin spoke out in a loud, firm voice. "What are your intensions, Drake? Are you and your Guydrun force finally deciding to jump into this fight?"

Drake transmitted his response quickly. "Us fight you and your people? I think not. I hate to admit it, but we wouldn't stand much of a chance against you. You've already proven that against the Tritians. But do you have any idea what you've just done? You've destroyed their queen. Their supreme leader. Losing her will plunge the Tritians' entire society into complete chaos."

Colin was aware of the ramifications of Vorloxa's destruction. "I know. The Tritians are no better than any hive of insects when they lose their queen. And besides. We gave them every chance to avoid a conflict with us. We only wanted our people back. They chose to fight. Just like you chose to run."

"For now," Drake added. "As I've stated before. We know better than to get into a fight that's over our heads. But I can make you a promise, McKenzie. This isn't over. We will meet again."

Colin grinned. "No doubt about that. And the next time we do meet, I might not have the patience to avoid killing you on sight."

There were no further comments from Drake. The group of Guydrun ships slowly backed away from the Black Raven, then turned and flew off.

"I've got a feeling that we're going to regret not killing that guy," Diane told Colin.

"Maybe," replied Colin. "But right now, let's concentrate on finishing up here so that we can get off this hell hole planet."

"So, what's next?" Linda asked Colin. "We saved the transport ships with the prisoners."

"Those aren't the only prisoners," Kelly informed her. "The sensors are picking up a large concentration of humans inside that pyramid structure."

"Then we have to get them out, as well as free the prisoners aboard the transports," said Colin. "Contact Kozak and ask her to prepare some transports for the extra prisoners. We're going in there."

"I was afraid you'd say that," Kelly replied.

The Black Raven headed back towards the pyramid. After Kelly contacted the Medusa to inform Kozak of their next objective, they were given a squadron of seven wedge-shaped shuttles and six fighters as an escort. The Black Raven landed in a small field covered by brown grass near the pyramid. The other ships surrounded the Black Raven as they landed. Colin and the others exited the ship and stepped foot upon the planet Osidra. Colin was reluctant to allow Ava and Gaylie to accompany him, Diane, and Kelly, given the potential danger that they would be facing. He was especially doubtful of allowing reporters Linda and Al to come along and continue filming their story live, but everyone insisted on coming and there was little time to argue with them. So, Colin was forced to agree.

Accompanied by a large group of Protectorate troopers who emerged from the shuttles, the group approached the huge, circular entrance to the pyramid. Colin was expecting to face heavy resistance as they approached the alien structure that once housed the Tritian queen, but to his surprise there was no opposition. There were no guards or weapons emplacements protecting the entrance. As they drew closer to the dark, gaping entrance they were startled as several Tritians came flying out and soared high into the air and vanished behind a nearby tower.

As the group entered the pyramid, Kelly raised his left hand and created a bright, white sphere of glowing energy to provide light for the group. With his sensor pad in his right hand, he was leading the way. The group found themselves inside a wide corridor with dark walls that had a rough, jagged surface like stacks of thin, broken wooden boards. The floor was in the same condition and not too comfortable to walk on. The group was forced to proceed at a slow and careful pace. What was even more uncomfortable was the strong odor resembling vinegar inside the corridor.

The corridor began to slope upward, then split off into a two-way intersection. Following the readings on his sensor pad, Kelly directed the group to take the corridor at the right. They proceeded forward for several feet before they came across three Tritians that were crawling along the ceiling towards them. As the Tritians quickly moved towards the group they were met with a hail of laser fire from the accompanying troopers. The slain Tritians dropped to the floor.

Proceeding deeper into the pyramid, the corridor continued to slope up to a higher level. At the left and right they passed by the circular openings to dark rooms. Out of curiosity, Colin ventured inside one of these rooms and was horrified when he saw dozens of green, human-sized maggots nestled inside of round cells in the walls, floor, and ceiling. Each one of these creatures were pulsating with life. *Tritian grubs*, Colin's thought. *All waiting to mature into their adult stage so that they can add to the population.* He departed the room and resumed heading for their objective. The group came upon two more intersections. Then the next corridor leveled off. Taking a glance at his sensor pad, Kelly informed the group that their objective was just a few yards away.

Down the corridor, there was the sound of high-pitched screams up ahead.

"Did you hear that?" said Ava. "I heard voices. They sounded like they were human."

"They were human," said Colin. "Kelly, how much further?"

"Not far," Kelly told Colin. "Just a few more feet up ahead."

They proceeded deeper into the corridor, following Kelly's light. The corridor made a sharp left turn. The group traveled a few more feet and were met by six Tritians that were standing guard in front of a long wall of thick bars that were running along the left wall. Upon seeing the group, four of the Tritians spread out their huge bat wings and leaped into the air to attack. But their effort was in vain as the armed humans quickly cut them down. The two remaining Tritians turned and fled further down into the corridor, disappearing within the darkness.

With the threat of the Tritian guards removed, the

group had the opportunity to inspect the bars. They were composed of the same jagged wooden material as the walls and floor. Behind the bars was the source of the screams that they were hearing. Hundreds of human children confined in a huge cell. All of them huddled together in groups away from the bars. Several of them screamed out in fear when they saw Kelly's light.

Colin held up his hands. "Calm down. Take it easy. We're here to help."

Ava approached the bars to address the children. "Please don't be afraid. We mean you no harm. We're here to take you all home."

A few of the children, now being less apprehensive, approached the bars. A small girl wearing a tattered green dress, went over to Ava. She spoke in a trembling voice, displaying her fear. "The monsters. The monsters outside. Are they gone?"

Ava smiled. "Yes. My friends took care of the monsters. They won't hurt anyone else."

The girl turned and glanced back, then looked back at Ava. "But there are monsters in here too."

Monsters inside the cell? thought Colin. He pointed to the cell bars. "Let's get them out of there."

Diane stepped forward and grabbed a section of the bars. There was the sound of a loud snap as she pulled the bars away. Several of the children jumped to their feet when they saw that they now had an exit from their confinement. Ava urged the children to hurry out of their cell while Colin, Diane, and Kelly stepped inside to deal with any Tritians that they would find.

The large area inside the cell was filled with captive children who were beginning to rush outside the moment their freedom was at hand. But as Kelly's light burned through the darkness, there were no Tritians to be found. At the far left and right sides of the cell were long gates. The trio moved closer to the gate at the left to investigate what was behind its bars. They were horrified to see dozens of the large maggot creatures squirming among piles of soiled rags and scattered human bones. A few of the maggots were resting inside one of the numerous round cells in the floor. Diane, appalled by this sight, let out a gasp and covered her mouth with both hands. Colin, although shocked, had expected that this was the fate that had befallen the Tritians previous prisoners. Now after seeing the horror behind the gate, Colin had the perfect means to deal with it.

"Burn this place down," was Colin's frim order to Kelly. "Burn them all."

Colin and Diane stepped back as Kelly lowered his hand that was producing the light. A large burst of flame erupted from Kelly's hand and engulfed a group of maggots. The entire cage was illuminated by the bright light from Kelly's flame. The Maggots violently thrashed about as they burned, but they did not make a sound and produced a strong, sweet odor. Kelly used his fire to sweep the entire area behind the gate. Within minutes, all of the maggots were consumed by a huge wall of fire.

Kelly then went to the gate at the other side of the cell and incinerated the Tritian maggots there. Colin drew great satisfaction in seeing these creatures destroyed. But this action was symbolic without eliminating the entire brood that were occupying this building.

"Let's get out of here," Colin told Diane and Kelly. "We need to get out of here and then destroy this place."

Colin lead Diane and Kelly out of the cell. By now all of the captive children were already ushered outside and were being led back down the corridor by the troopers. Ava and Gaylie approached Colin.

"What happened in there?" Ava asked Colin. "I smell

something burning."

Colin frowned. "It was pretty bad. But we'll talk about it later. Right now, we need to get out of here and then destroy this place. Are all the children out?"

"The soldiers are leading the last of them outside now," Ava reported.

Relieved at this news Colin nodded, then approached one of the troopers that was standing guard in the corridor. "Trooper, we need to find a way to destroy this place and put an end to this horror story."

"We came equipped to do that," replied the trooper. "We can set up a couple of fusion charges and detonate them by remote."

This was the information that Colin wanted to hear. "Great. We'll let you guys handle it while we evacuate."

The trooper called over another man who quickly took three, one-foot wide disk-shaped devices out of a backpack that he was carrying. He sat the devices down onto the floor. Both devices had small keypads on top. The trooper pressed two keys on both keypads and they both took on a dim white glow. "Charges are set," the trooper said.

As the troopers began to place more of the fusion devices throughout the corridor, Colin and the others needed no urging to head down the corridor in order to exit the pyramid. Once outside, they saw that the last group of children were being loaded into the last four shuttles. Once their doors slid shut, the shuttles all rose into the air and then headed off towards the sky. Colin's group boarded the Black Raven and wasted no time joining the other ships as they flew from the area. As the Black Raven gained a safe distance, Diane turned the ship around so that its occupants could get a first-hand view of the pyramid's destruction. Detonated by remote control, the fusion charges that the troopers placed inside exploded. The entire pyramid became a bright white flash of light. Then, in an instant, the light was replaced by a gigantic ball of fire that rose up into the sky in the form of a mushroom cloud of flame. The area surrounding the pyramid was devastated by the power of the blast. Clouds of fire and burning debris quickly spread out while the towers in the vicinity began to topple. Within a few seconds, the Tritian pyramid, along with the queen that it housed, was totally destroyed.

CHAPTER THIRTEEN

When the Black Raven returned to the planet Sidra and landed on the resistance airfield in Zalakar, Colin was overwhelmed as he and the others were met by a huge cheering crowd that assembled to greet them. Word spread fast of their successful mission through Linda's live broadcast, transmitted to Markus through Kelly. Colin and the others, along with the United Protectorate forces, have become instant heroes. As he was looking through the sea of smiling faces, Colin found that their cheering was drowning out his own thoughts. Scores of people were pointing up at the three huge Protectorate task force ships that were hovering high above the base. Colin was concerned that the overt presence of the ships would be irresistible targets for the enemy forces on this planet, but then considered any hostile act against them to be foolish after their victory over the Tritians.

The children were all taken to hangars where they would be housed while given food, water, and medical examinations. The Protectorate troopers who accompanied them in the shuttles were mingling with the people. Linda was still giving her commentary as she was making her way through the crowd. Al, staying close to her, continued filming everything around them. As Linda and Al appeared to be enjoying the experience, Colin, Diane, and Kelly were finding it difficult to walk through the cheering crowd. Looking around the crowd, Colin lost track of Ava and Gaylie.

Colin turned to look back at Diane, who was using gentle force to push her way through the crowd. "So, this is what it's like to be a hero," Colin told her.

Diane smiled. "It's kind of noisy being a hero. I can do noisy. Just as long as nobody is shooting at us."

Among the crowd, Colin spotted a familiar face. A tall, middle aged man with a red beard and short hair, dressed in a black resistance uniform. It was the resistance leader Silas Johannon, husband to Ava and father to Gaylie. Upon seeing Ava, Silas rushed over to her and embraced her in a tight hug. Then their lips met in a long kiss. Then Gaylie went over and wrapped her arms around them both.

"You're safe," Silas exclaimed. His face beaming a bright smile. "Thank God you're both safe. I was watching Linda Jones' broadcast. I can't believe what you've been through." Silas turned around and looked at Colin, Diane, and Kelly. "Thank you for bringing them back alive."

Colin smiled at Silas. "It's good that we came back alive too."

"When I was watching the news footage, I thought you were all insane," Silas told Colin. "Invading the Tritians' home planet?"

Colin took a quick glance up to the Protectorate ships that were hovering overhead. "We couldn't have done it without the help of some friends."

Silas looked up at the three ships. "Those vessels are a marvel. They must be more powerful than anything we have if they can beat the Tritians on their home planet so easily."

"Don't let your guard down. The Tritians are still a threat," Colin warned. "And don't forget about Lieutenant Drake and the Guydruns. I'm also wondering how the Gatherers will react to an alien military presence on this planet."

"Since your return, we've received several curious reports from Markus," said Silas. "It seems that the Tritian forces are backing out from supporting their Guydrun allies. There have even been reports of the Tritians fighting the Guydruns. And even fighting among themselves."

"Infighting among the enemy?" Ava inquired.

"This is the possible fallout from the loss of their queen. Whatever the reason, this could work in our favor," Silas told her. "If there's disarray among the enemy forces, then that will make the war effort easier for us. And I don't see the Gatherers stepping in to lend the Guydruns their support unless they have something to gain by it. But Colin is right. We can't allow ourselves to let our guard down. This war is far from over."

"Now what will you do?" Gaylie asked Colin, Diane, and Kelly. "Now that you've found the missing task force ships, your mission is pretty much done."

Colin briefly pondered what would happen next. "That's hard to say. Our superiors could call us back home. Or they could order us to stay here for the time being and help maintain security for the task force. After all, their mission is to locate and establish contact with other human civilizations."

"Yeah and get them to help us with our own war," Kelly reminded Colin. "Not get in the middle of another."

Colin agreed. "Yeah. It seems that the war at home has followed us here too. I'd still like to know what the Brelac were doing here with the Tritians. Whatever it is, it can't be good."

"Well, however things turn out, I just hope that your people decide to stay for a while," said Silas. "Having their presence here makes me feel a lot more secure."

A faint chiming sound came from Kelly's pocket. He brought out his sensor pad. "It's a video from Kozak," he informed the others. Kelly tapped his sensor pad and held it up as Colin and Diane moved in closer to see the transmission.

On Kelly's sensor pad, the image of Captain Kozak appeared. A tall woman with short black hair, dressed in a grey fatigue uniform. Colin took note of the bright gold captain's bars on the arms of her fatigue shirt.

"Black Raven. I've got an urgent message for you from home. It's from Captain Melony Carter of the C.I.D. Please stand by."

Silas pointed at Kelly's sensor pad. "A message from home? I thought that your people are from a far-off quadrant. Yet you're able to communicate over such a vast distance of space through that little device?"

"During their voyage here, the task force set up a network of long-distance uplink units out in space," Kelly explained. "The uplinks intercept and boost our signals as they travel through space from one unit to the next. It's like having a direct pipeline between the two quadrants."

A few seconds later, Kozak's image was replaced by the face of Melony. She brushed the bangs of her short, cropped red hair away from her face and then began to speak.

"Colin, Diane, Kelly. I'm so glad to see that you're alive and well. And I saw Captain Kozak's report. Great job in locating and helping the task force. But unfortunately, we've got trouble here."

Trouble. The one word that Colin was not prepared to hear. "Trouble? What kind of trouble?"

"Eight hours ago, the city of Brookhaven on the planet Tacoma Three came under attack by an alien entity of unknown origin. We don't know how this creature was able to penetrate the planet's airspace, but at this point, that's unimportant. What matters is that she's caused massive destruction."

Colin felt his heart stop beating when he heard the word "she." *She? She? No way. It can't be.*

Melony continued. "We don't know if this creature is another Reploid like yourselves or something else. But either way, she's withstood everything that we've thrown against her and retaliated with a vengeance. She's unstoppable. Most of the city has been destroyed. Casualties are in the hundreds. And she seems to know you because she's been calling out your name. Here's some footage that was taken by a drone camera."

Melony's face blacked out. Then it was replaced by a video of a city street littered with rubble from damaged buildings. There were several destroyed cars strewn about, some of them burning. In the background, flames were shooting out from the windows of a tall building. Stepping out from around a burning car came a familiar dark-skinned female with long black hair, wearing black breast plate armor with overlapping scales. With a swift backhand blow of her fist she knocked the car aside, sending it rolling across the street. She then tilted her head back and raised her fist to the sky while shouting out a name in a loud voice. "McKenzie!"

"Deevor," gasped Kelly.

In the video, Deevor strode down the street towards the camera that was filming her. She scowled and pointed a finger. "McKenzie," Deevor shouted again. "Can you hear me, McKenzie? You and your two friends? Lytton and that bitchy girlfriend of yours, Christy. Can you see what I've done to your city and these puny vermin that used to live here? They don't deserve to exist in a universe where only the strongest can rule. I am here to wipe this city clean of these weak little people. And when I'm finished here, I'm going on to the next city. And I'll keep going until I've turned this entire planet into a funeral pyre. And there's nothing that your people can do to try to stop me. No one on this planet can stop me. Unless you decide to come out of hiding and try to stop me yourselves. Too bad the three of you are so far away."

Deevor raised her hand and a burst of red light flashed out from her palm. Then the picture went black. Seconds later, Melony's frowning face reappeared to continue her message.

"That's all we were able to record of her for now. She slaughters anyone she sees. So many have died. I know that you guys are so far away. But we need you. I'm hoping that you are the only ones that might have the power to stop this menace. Please come home. We need you."

Melony ended her transmission. Kelly's sensor pad turned black.

Colin felt his blood turn cold after watching the video. Kelly's wide-eyed face turning pale with fear and Diane's angered frown was a clear sign that they both shared his feelings. "Deevor on Tacoma Three. I can't believe it."

"Deevor?" Silas inquired. "What happened?"

"Deevor is on one of our planets back in our home quadrant," Colin told him. "While we were playing cat and mouse with her here, she's made her way to the United Protectorate. She's threatening to destroy an entire planet."

"I don't doubt that she can," Kelly's comment.

Gaylie stepped away from Silas and Ava. Colin noticed tears welling up in her eyes. "Her. She's the one enemy that we still have to run from. She's the one that still causes death and suffering. She's the one nightmare in this war that will never end."

Gaylie ran off from the group, ignoring Ava's calls for her to return. She blended in with the crowd and disappeared.

"Let her go. She just needs to be alone," Silas told Ava. "Zoe's death hit her harder than she wants to admit. And her helplessness to do anything doesn't make things any easier."

"I hope she'll be ok,' said Colin. "But in the meantime, we have to get home as fast as we can. We might be the only ones with the power to deal with Deevor."

Another video transmission from Kozak was coming in through Kelly's sensor pad. "That's it from Captain Carter. From what she described; the situation sounds pretty bad. I wish we could do something. And I'd like to offer you guys some help, but the task force has been ordered to stay here and establish a base of operations. We're to set up a safe zone for the planet's inhabitants during this war until further orders, so we'll pretty much have our hands full."

"I understand," Colin's reply. "My friends and I can handle things from here."

"Then I'll let you get to it. And good luck. Kozak out."

Kelly's sensor pad turned black as Kozak ended her transmission.

Colin looked at Diane and Kelly while holding in his mind the possibility that facing Deevor could be their last fight. "Let's go."

CHAPTER FOURTEEN

Sitting next to Diane in the Black Raven's cockpit, Colin could not remember the last time that he had gotten a good, restful sleep. The thought crossed his mind to try and take a quick nap during the trip back to the Poseidon quadrant, but he was feeling too tense to sleep. Diane, as well as Kelly, sitting at the computer station, were also deprived of sleep. But the urgency of their current situation prodded them to keep going.

The Black Raven has been flying at top speed for over three hours since leaving the planet Sidra. Diane sent the ship into two hyperspace jumps, both of them fifteen minutes apart from each other. Kelly informed Colin that they would have to give the hyperspace generator an hour to recharge after making two long distance jumps in such a short period of time. Colin understood the consequences of taxing the system to its limit, but with Deevor cutting a path of destruction through Tacoma Three, they had to return to Protectorate space in the shortest time possible. Kelly explained that by his estimate, with the Black Raven's current rate of speed and more extreme long ranged jumps, they will reach Tacoma Three in seven hours.

Providing that the ship's engines and the hyperspace generator will hold out.

Four more hours to go, Colin thought to himself. *How much of Tacoma Three will be left when we get there?* Colin turned his head, looking back at Kelly. "How much longer until we can make another jump?"

"Seventeen more minutes," said Kelly. "Let's hope nothing breaks down in mid-flight."

"You worry too much, kid. We'll get there," Diane told Kelly.

"Yeah, and that's the problem," said Kelly. "And when we do get there, have either of you given any thought as to how we're going to beat this bitch? The last times we've fought her weren't exactly cake walks."

"But we did beat her," Colin pointed out.

Kelly briefly laughed. "Yeah. We got lucky."

"When I kick somebody's ass, luck is never involved," Diane informed Kelly. "With me, it's all about skill and power."

"I just hope we've got the skill and power to take down somebody who can set off a nuke just by smacking her fists together," replied Kelly.

While he was still looking back at Kelly, Colin was taken by surprise when Gaylie walked into the cockpit. She stopped, standing behind Kelly and lifted her right hand to deliver a wave.

"Hi guys," Gaylie greeted in a faint voice.

Colin rose up from his seat. "Gaylie? What the hell? How did you get here?"

A weak smile appeared on Gaylie's face. "Before you left, I ran to the ship and hid in one of the rooms in the back. I'm surprised that you didn't find me."

"What the hell were you thinking?" Colin scolded. "You're light years from home. Your parents are going to wonder where you are. They'll be worried."

"I wrote them a note and told one of the soldiers to give it to them," Gaylie explained. "They'll know I'm okay since I'm with you. I hope."

Colin threw up his hands in frustration. "Okay? We're not okay! We're busting a gut trying to get back to our own quadrant while hoping that the ship holds up. And we're flying headlong into what might be the fight of our lives. I wouldn't exactly call that okay."

"Well, we've come too far to think about taking her back," Diane pointed out. "You might as well make yourself comfortable and enjoy the ride."

Gaylie moved closer to Colin. "Look. I'm sorry for sneaking aboard your ship like this. I didn't mean any harm. But you're going to fight Deevor. She murdered my sister. She's caused death and destruction across my planet. I need to see this thing through to the end."

Colin fully understood Gaylie's motivation for coming along. But that still did not lessen the danger in this upcoming mission. "The end, as you say, could turn out either good or bad. This fight is going to unleash all hell. There's no way we're letting you get mixed up in the middle of this once we get to Tacoma Three."

"I won't get in the way," Gaylie assured Colin. "I know I don't have the power to stand up against Deevor. But you do. That's why I'm here. I want to see you guys win. I know you're going to win."

Colin grinned. He turned his head to look at Diane. She was also grinning. He looked back at Gaylie. "You've got a hell of a lot of faith in us."

Gaylie nodded. A tear came from her right eye and rolled down her face. She replied in a quivering voice. "Yeah. I have a lot of faith in you guys. No matter how powerful that bitch thinks she is, you guys will win. You'll find a way to win."

There was silence in the cockpit as Colin and Gaylie looked at each other. Then he returned a nod. "Yeah. We can do this. We'll give you one hell of a story to take back to Sidra. Kelly, is the hyperspace generator ready?"

Kelly glanced at the computer monitor. "The generator is charged and ready."

"Finally," said Colin. He sat back down in his seat. "Diane, you have the next coordinates set?"

"Coordinates are set to go," Diane told Colin.

"Hit it," Colin ordered.

Diane tapped her finger on the touchpad controls before her. The next second, a bright white flash of light filled the forward window as the Black Raven executed its hyperspace jump.

CHAPTER FIFTEEN

Another hour had passed since the Black Raven's most recent hyperspace jump. Bringing the number to five. After the fourth jump, the Black Raven finally returned to the Poseidon Quadrant. Because the ship's hyperspace generator was set to execute jumps to a much greater distance than before, its recharge time was taking much longer. The last recharge took ninety minutes. This added an extra hour to Kelly's estimated seven-hour arrival time. Colin was relieved when Kelly informed him that they had arrived at the Tacoma star system. But he also feared what would be left of the planet Tacoma Three when they finally made planetfall.

Colin looked over at Diane, who was keeping her gaze as tightly locked on the forward window as her hands were gripped onto the flight control sticks. Like himself, she could not recall the last time she had gotten any sleep. The same as Kelly, who had not moved from his seat at the computer station since they left the planet Sidra. Gaylie, sitting in front of the communications console at Kelly's left, was keeping silent as she was gazing at the forward window.

"We're coming up to Tacoma Three," said Kelly.

"Sensors are picking up a large number of ships in orbit around the planet. It's like they've got the entire planet on lockdown."

"That's understandable. Considering what they're up against down there," Colin replied.

"I'm picking up a small group of ships heading our way. Six fighters," Kelly informed Colin.

"Stop and let's see what they want," Colin's order to Diane.

The Black Raven stopped and held their current position as the Protectorate fighters drew nearer. A few moments later, the view of six triangular fighters appeared through the forward window. Then Kelly patched through a message from one of the ships.

"Attention unidentified ship. You are currently in restricted space. The planet Tacoma Three is under quarantine. You are advised to either hold your position here or turn back."

Kelly radioed a reply. "This is the C.I.D ship Black Raven. I'm Kelly Lytton of the team, Silencers. We're here at the request of Captain Melony Carter of the C.I.D. I'm transmitting our identification code to you."

After Kelly transmitted the identification code, the response came seconds after.

"Your ID code checks out. So, you're Silencers. We've been given word that Captain Carter is down on the planet and expecting you. The situation is pretty bad down there. We'll escort you in."

Pretty Bad, thought Colin. He dreaded hearing such an assessment of the situation. He imagined that the picture would be much worse when they stepped foot onto the planet and saw things firsthand.

The Black Raven followed the group of fighters as they turned and headed back to the planet. After traveling for the next few minutes, the bright blue orb of Tacoma Three appeared in the distance. When

Black Raven and the fighters flew in closer to the planet, a line of fighters and battle cruisers came into view. They had formed a blockade to try to contain the menace on the planet below. Or to keep any new menaces from entering. Colin wondered if Deevor was aware of this show of force and what she was capable of doing to oppose it.

The Black Raven and the fighters flew below the blockade and continued on to the planet. It only took a few more minutes for them to penetrate the atmosphere and draw closer to the surface. Through the forward window, the scene of a city below came into view. In several areas among the city's tall, gleaming blue and silvery buildings were thick plumes of black smoke and flames. A closer view revealed that several buildings were reduced to rubble. Even more of them were on fire. As they pressed on further over the city, they passed a large area that was a sea of fire. Colin was correct in fearing that the damage below was worse after seeing it for himself.

"Dear God. It's hard to believe that one person is capable of causing all this destruction."

Colin agreed with Gaylie. "Yeah. And she's not going to stop. Not until one of us is dead."

A transmission came in from one of the escorting fighters. "Black Raven. We're coming up to the check point below. There's a huge force setting up a roadblock. Captain Carter is there. You're on your own at this point. Good luck down there."

The fighter escort scattered and soared out of view. Diane reduced the Black Raven's speed and took the ship lower to the street. Further up the street, they saw the roadblock that consisted of several hover tanks and dozens of armed troopers. Diane landed the Black Raven in the middle of the street. Minutes later, the group exited the ship, preparing to experience the worst.

"This is it. The fight of our lives," Colin mumbled.

He could not help experiencing the nauseated feeling in his stomach as he and the others were walking closer to the roadblock of hover tanks and troopers. Even the familiar sight of Melony Carter rushing towards them did not make him feel any better. Dressed in black knee-high boots and a grey camouflage uniform, Melony ran up to the group and then stopped just a few feet away. A smile appeared on her face.

"You're here," Melony exclaimed. "Thank God you're here."

"Hi," Colin simply greeted. "We tried to get back as fast as we could. How bad is it?"

"It's a war zone back there," Melony replied. "Whoever that monster is, she's cut a path of destruction through Brookhaven, then Malven, and now she's here in Givens. The death toll is in the hundreds. Brookhaven was caught totally off guard. But we were barely able to evacuate the other surrounding communities. So far, it's been quiet in there for the past hour. She murders anyone in sight. We can't even get our drones close enough to get her on video before she destroys them. So, we're keeping our distance and tracking her by scanners. She rants on like she knows you guys. Who or what the hell is she?"

Colin gathered his thoughts to try and give his best explanation. "Her name is Deevor. She comes from the other quadrant. She's possibly an alien version of a Reploid. We fought her before, so now she's feeling butt hurt and doing this to try to get back at us."

"She wants a rematch," Diane added. "So, we're more than happy to give her one."

"Well whatever she is, she's laughed off anything we could throw against her," Melony told Colin. "Lasers, plasma weapons, missiles. We couldn't put so much as a scratch on her. We even sent in three battle cruisers to deal with her, but she was too powerful. She managed to shoot down one of them and damaged the other two so badly that they were forced to withdraw. President Drennen is keeping a close eye on the situation. The military has advised her to authorize the use of nukes against her if the situation gets out of hand. We have to stop her."

Using nukes against one person. That is insane, thought Colin. But given Deevor's power, he knew such a drastic measure might be the only choice if he and the others were unable to stop her. "We'll stop her," Colin told Melony.

Melony looked past Colin to Gaylie. "Who is this young lady?"

"I'm Gaylie Johannon," she said as she stepped forward. "I'm from the planet Sidra. I've been helping Colin, Diane, and Kelly."

"And now her help ends here," Colin sternly added. "This is our fight now. You stay here with Melony. She'll keep you safe." Colin glanced at Diane and Kelly. "Let's go."

Colin, Diane, and Kelly strode down the street and passed through the the line of troopers and hover tanks. They advanced down the street, stepping over the twisted metal and broken masonry of the heavily damaged buildings at their left and right. Further down the street were dozens of vehicles that were overturned, ripped apart, and on fire. In the far distance, towers of black smoke were rising past the tall buildings. Beyond the buildings was the sight of the bright orange sun as it was beginning to set. But the most disturbing sight that they came upon were the numerous bodies that were scattered across the street. Unfortunate men and women laying dead under huge chunks of debris from the buildings. Some of them burned or dismembered. Colin could not help but wonder if he, Diane, or Kelly would also be laying among these people before this day was over.

As Colin, Diane, and Kelly continued moving deeper into the city, they passed by more heavily damaged and burning buildings at both sides. They were forced to step over more bodies in order to progress. Further ahead, they saw that the street was blocked by the rubble of a building that had collapsed. Looking at the top of this roadblock was more smoke and flames.

"What now?" asked Kelly.

Colin made a quick inspection of the rubble. "It's not that high. Maybe twenty feet. We should be able to climb over it."

"You want us to climb over that?" Kelly cried out.

Colin looked to his left and right. "The only alternative is to try and pass those burning buildings on both sides of the street. It's less appealing than making the climb over this."

Grabbing hold of a twisted bar of metal that was protruding from a mass of stone, Colin took the lead to begin the climb. As he predicted, scaling the mound of rubble was not too difficult. When they reached the top, they saw that there were countless abandoned and wrecked cars waiting for them at the bottom. To their right was the sight of a huge triangular battle cruiser that had smashed into the side of a collapsed building. There were several large holes ripped through its hull. Its rear section was burning.

"Are you guys seeing this?" Kelly asked Colin and Diane. "Did she actually have the power to shoot a battle cruiser out of the sky with just her bare hands?"

"Obviously," said Diane. "But the question is where the hell is she now? This is a big city. Or what's left of it. We could spend the rest of the day looking for her."

Colin agreed with Diane's assessment. "Then let's not spend too much time looking for her. She wanted us this badly, then we'll make her come to us."

"How are we going to do that?" Diane asked.

"Stand back," Colin warned.

Diane and Kelly stepped away from Colin. His right hand took on a bright white glow as he raised it high into the air. Then he discharged a massive bolt of lightning that streaked up to the sky. Colin maintained this electrical discharge for a full minute. Then he stopped and lowered his hand. "If she's close by, then she's got to see that."

Colin, Diane, and Kelly made a careful descent down to the street and passed through the collection of vehicles. They continued walking down the street for several more yards. Then Colin decided that they should wait before moving on.

As the minutes passed, Colin looked up to the sky and saw that the sun was setting lower behind the buildings. It was getting darker. Colin was starting to wonder if they should wait here longer or move further into the city. Then looking back down at the street up ahead he noticed a person in the distance moving in their direction. It was too far for him to get a clear view of this individual, but he knew that it could only be one person.

Kelly also saw the person approaching. "There's someone coming," he said, pointing a finger. "Is that her?"

"I doubt that anyone else is out here walking about," Colin's grim voiced reply. "Get ready. This is it."

The individual was casually walking down the middle of the street, getting closer until Colin could clearly make out their features. It was Deevor, coming to answer Colin's summons to battle. She stopped just a few yards away from Colin, Diane, and Kelly. But was just close enough for Colin to see the confident grin on her face.

"I came to see what caused that blast of energy," Deevor called out. "I suspected that it might be you, McKenzie. And I was right. So here you are. You decided to come out of hiding."

Colin crossed his arms against his chest. With unblinking eyes, he stared back at Deevor. "We saw that little message of yours. We couldn't resist the invitation to come kick your ass off our planet."

Deevor laughed at Colin's boast. "You must have rehearsed that line on your trip here. It's pretty tough talk from someone that's about to die. You don't know how many times I've dreamt about killing you, McKenzie. More ways than I have the time to describe. And your girlfriend here especially. Christy, I'm going to take such pleasure in tearing you apart. Small pieces at a time."

"And what about the kid here," said Diane. "How are you going to kill him?"

"Thanks for mentioning me. I didn't want to be left out," Kelly sarcastically replied to Diane.

Deevor began to walk forward. Her hands began to take on a red glow of energy. "Don't think that it simply ends here after I'm done with the three of you. As repayment for my inconvenience, I'm planning to wipe every city off the face of this pathetic world. This planet will become the galaxy's graveyard."

Deevor raised her hands. Kelly stepped out front and raised his hands to create a thick, blue wall of energy. Two large beams of crimson energy shot out from Deevor's hands, both merging into one as it struck Kelly's shield with a devastating effect. The shield wall exploded into dozens of shards that scattered about and quickly dissipated. The force of the explosion hurled Colin, Diane, and Kelly back several feet. Colin felt the pain of the impact as his body hit the hard pavement and then rolled until he stopped when he hit the side of a car. Colin felt his entire body aching. He looked over to his right to see that Diane and Kelly had also come to the same painful stop.

Colin looked back down the street to see that Deevor was quickly walking towards them. Kelly suddenly sat up and thrust his hands. In an instant, a thick wall of his blue energy appeared to block her way. Deevor bumped into the wall, then she let out a grunt as she reared her fist back and then thrust it through Kelly's wall. Her fist easily penetrated the wall of psionic energy, creating a large hole. She punched a second hole through the wall. Then a third. Each time the fragments of the wall flew out and vanished before they could touch the pavement. Deevor punched Kelly's wall a fourth time, causing it to shatter completely.

Now that the obstruction of Kelly's shield wall was removed, Deevor was free to proceed. But not without facing opposition from Diane. She jumped to her feet and bolted towards Deevor. She drew her fist back to deliver a fast punch. Diane thrust her fist towards Deevor's face, but she was surprised when Deevor reacted quickly enough to catch it. Deevor pulled Diane's fist towards her, and Diane along with it. She grabbed Diane by the back of her neck and hurled her backward. Diane went flying across the street and smashed through the windshield of an abandoned car. Deevor raised her hand. It took on a bright red glow, ready to fire a deadly blast of energy to destroy both the car and Diane. But not if Colin was able to prevent it.

Colin sprang up to a kneeling position and then fired massive electrical blasts at Deevor with both hands. He rose up while continuing to assault Deevor with his power, while keeping in mind her ability to absorb all energy-based attacks. Colin knew that his efforts were a mere distraction at best. But his real aim was to prevent Deevor from killing Diane. He accomplished that goal, but now she turned her attention from Diane to him. She smiled as her body took on a bright white glow while she was soaking up Colin's discharge of energy.

"You realize that this is a futile waste of time, McKenzie!" Deevor shouted.

Colin agreed. So, he decided to employ another tactic. While his left hand continued blazing its energy at Deevor, he lowered his right hand to the ground. His bolt of energy penetrated the pavement. Then a wide fissure began to open and quickly spread towards Deevor. She was taken by surprise and dropped down into the fissure. Colin discontinued his electrical attack against Deevor when he caught movement at the corner of his right eye. He turned and saw Diane, who had now climbed out of the car and was charging back into the fight. Deevor was just starting to climb out of the fissure and was unaware that Diane was racing towards her.

"This is another useless gesture, McKenzie!" Deevor shouted.

Deevor rose out from the fissure and stood back onto the pavement just in time to receive a solid punch to the side of her face by Diane. The impact from Diane's striking fist caused a faint boom. Deevor staggered backward for several steps but managed to remain on her feet. Diane quickly pressed her attack by charging forward and giving Deevor a second punch to her face. Deevor's head jerked back under the force of the blow. Diane gave Deevor a powerful left cross to her head, then she gave Deevor a punch directly to her chest that sent her flying backward for several feet until she slammed into the side of a car. The impact caused the car's windows to explode while the car itself was pushed back a few feet. Deevor once again quickly recovered from Diane's attack, springing to her feet and reaching down to pick up the car over her head, then hurling it towards Diane. Before Diane had the chance to react, Colin took action by raising his right hand and firing a bolt of energy at the vehicle. He had a unique tactic in mind when his electrical bolt hit the car. Utilizing his ferrokinetic ability, he caused the car to completely disassemble. The car's individual parts all spread out to form a swarm of debris that flew towards Colin. The debris stopped six feet away from Colin when he held out his hand towards Deevor. He then fired a continuous bolt of energy at Deevor while at the same time launching the cloud of debris at her. Deevor was simultaneously hit by the mass of car parts and Colin's electrical bolt, resulting in an explosion of fire and sparks.

Colin continued blazing away at Deevor with his electrical power, now using both hands. He increased his discharge of energy and began to hit her with a massive stream of energy. With the white flashes and sparks that were enshrouding her, Colin could barely make out the image of Deevor standing on her feet. At his far left, he spied Kelly aiming both hands towards Deevor and sending a massive burst of fire to engulf her. Between his power and Kelly's, Colin thought that Deevor's ability to absorb energy had to reach its limits. He was finding it difficult to conceieve that any living being could endure this amount of power, but Deevor was still standing without suffering any ill effects.

As he and Kelly continued their combined assault against Deevor, Colin was not surprised to hear her laughing through their best efforts. "This is futile, McKenzie. Futile," she shouted.

Colin knew that she was right. Not only was this attack ineffective, but he was now starting to feel his own power weakening. Colin's arms were beginning to grow numb while the rest of his body was tiring. His stream of energy against Deevor was growing smaller. He was now struggling to continue his attack. He was fearing that at any moment his power would completely fail.

Colin was startled by the sudden appearance of a huge object moving at his right. He turned his head and saw a large dump truck flying past him. A better view revealed that the truck was not flying on its own, but in fact hurled through the air by Diane. The truck flew headlong towards Deevor, who was so preoccupied by Colin and Kelly's attack that she did not see it coming in time to react. There was a loud boom as the truck bounced off the ground, then slammed into Deevor. Colin and Kelly both discontinued their attack as the truck rolled along on its wheels while dragging Deevor under its front end. It kept moving until it crashed through the wall of a nearby building.

Colin was barely able to contain his glee after witnessing this display of Diane's incredible strength. He felt like hugging her, but with Deevor down he thought that it would be unwise to lose their advantage. He looked to Kelly while pointing a finger at the building. It was a tall structure composed of ten floors. "Kelly. The top floor. Hit it," he quickly shouted.

Kelly aimed his hands at the building's upper floors. A blazing red fireball formed in front of him. In seconds, it grew from the size of a basketball to become larger than a car. While Kelly was creating his fireball, Colin aimed his hands at the building and sent twin bolts of energy at its base. He directed his electrical power to penetrate the building and surge through its support beams. It took little effort for Colin to use his power to cause every support beam in the building to disintegrate. Kelly sent his still growing fireball to fly out towards the building's top floors. The fireball exploded on impact against the side of the building. The blast ripping through an entire floor. This extensive damage, combined with the destroyed support beams, caused the top floors to collapse. Then the entire building began to implode in on itself. The air was filled with a loud thundering sound as tons of stone and metal collapsed to the ground. Colin, Diane, and Kelly stepped back to try to avoid the thick clouds of dust that was churning up and spreading across the street. After the building collapsed, they stood from a distance and stared at the rising clouds of dust that was obscuring the rubble.

Kelly inhaled and then exhaled a deep breath. "Do you think this is it? Do you think we got her?"

Colin frowned and shook his head. "I don't think so."

"Well then, what next?" asked Kelly.

The answer to Kelly's question came in the form of a powerful explosion from within the cloud of dust. Swarms of stone and metal debris were hurled in all directions. In the explosion's aftermath was a large blazing fire. A minute after the debris rained down upon the street, Colin was not surprised when he saw Deevor emerging from the fire. *I knew it,* he thought to himself. *I knew that wouldn't hold her for long.*

Deevor stood in front of the flames and held her arms out to her sides. Her right hand began to take on a bright red glow, then a basketball sized globe of energy began to form, while a glowing yellow globe of energy formed at her left hand. It was this moment that Colin knew that the situation was about to get worse.

"Run, go, move!" Colin shouted to Diane and Kelly.

Deevor raised her hands above her head to bring both globes of energy together. Colin spun around and started to run, as did Diane and Kelly. The next second, the sound of a thundering explosion filled Colin's ears while he was thrown from his feet by an irresistible force. Colin could not measure how far he went spinning through the air. Then his unpleasant flight came to a painful halt when he slammed through the windshield of a car. After that, Colin's only sensation was that of intense pain. His vision was black. After a few moments, Colin's vision began to clear. He found himself laying on the front seat of the car that he smashed into. He was covered by small shards of glass. He looked out through the broken windshield to see Deevor calmly walking towards the car. With Deevor approaching, he knew that this fight was far from over. But he was feeling too weak and in pain to try to stand against her.

Colin was starting to wonder where Diane and Kelly were. Or if they were even still alive. He heard a sound at his right. He turned and saw Diane running directly towards Deevor. She raised her fist to send a punch to Deevor's head, but Deevor quickly raised her forearm to block it. Diane hurled left and right punches at Deevor, but she also was able to block them. Diane changed tactics by giving Deevor a roundhouse kick to her stomach. Deevor folded over and stumbled back a few steps. As she straightened up, Diane charged forward and gave her a sharp right cross to her face. The impact of Diane's punch forced Deevor to take a step backward. Diane tried to hurl another punch, but Deevor easily swatted her arm away, then grabbed Diane by her hair and pulled her forward while thrusting her knee into Diane's stomach. Diane let out a grunt and folded over. Deevor released her hold on Diane's hair and allowed her to drop to the ground. Then Deevor gave Diane a kick that sent her flying through the air for several feet, then crashing through the glass doors of a nearby office building.

After witnessing the brief battle, Colin was not

certain if Diane was still alive. And so far, Kelly's location and condition were unknown. But now he was fearful of his own survival as Deevor was walking towards the car, and he was still feeling too weak and in pain to move.

Deevor stopped in front of the car to address Colin. "You and your friends put up a good effort, McKenzie. A good effort, but futile. I told you that from the start. Now this is your punishment for interfering with the Gatherers and trying to destroy our plans to bring back our great lord Kimdrack. I only wish that he could see how I've enforced his revenge."

Deevor walked over to the left side of the car and kneeled. The next moment, Colin felt the car shake. Then he saw that it was rising into the air. It was obvious to him that Deevor was lifting it. Then the car went flying forward, towards the building that Deevor had kicked Diane into. The car smashed through the remnants of the glass doors and bounced off the floor. Then it crashed into a large, circular receptionist desk, destroying it completely. The car stopped when its front end smashed into a wall. Colin felt more pain when his body was thrown onto the dashboard. His chest was aching. He felt as if several of his ribs were broken. Despite the current level of pain that he was feeling, he knew that he will be in far worse shape if he did not get out of this car.

Colin slid over to the driver's side door and shoved it open. He crawled out of the car and collapsed to the floor. As he painfully rose to his knees, he looked up to see Deevor walking towards the building. She was dragging Kelly behind her by his leg. She stopped in front of the broken glass doors and flung Kelly into the building. Kelly's body bounced off the floor and landed six feet in front of Colin. Colin, Diane, and Kelly were all together now, and in the direst situation of their lives.

"You dumped a building on me. Let's see how you

like it," Deevor shouted at Colin.

Deevor took several steps backward. Then she pointed her hands up and fired a massive burst of blazing red energy at the building. Colin heard an explosion going off in the building's upper floors. Deevor continued discharging her destructive power at the building for several seconds. Then she stopped and stepped away. Colin heard a loud rumbling coming from above. After Deevor's attack on the building, he knew what was going to happen next. The rumbling was growing louder. Long cracks began to form across the ceiling. A huge mass of metal and stone debris crashed through the ceiling and blocked the building's entrance. Colin's eyes were locked on the crumbling ceiling as the building was collapsing on top of him. Colin was able to form only one reaction to this situation.

"Oh shit!"

CHAPTER SIXTEEN

Colin opened his eyes in a sea of total darkness. After what he had just been through, he was grateful to be alive to open his eyes in the darkness or the light. The super powered alien psychopath, Deevor, had caused a building to collaspe on top of him. Seeing his impending death gave him a surge of adrenaline spurred by a desperate need to survive. As the ceiling was caving in and the exit from the building blocked, Colin saw only one direction to go in order to escape. Down. He quickly devised a plan to use his manipulative ability on the floor beneath him. Upon Colin's touch, the floor instantly disintegrated into a mass of fragments. He and the unconscious Kelly dropped down to the building's lower level. From there, Colin continued using his power on the floor of that level so that he and Kelly could drop down, then down to the next level. Then Colin used his power to disintegrate the floor, exposing the bare ground. He used his power to cause a wide area of the ground to quickly split apart and crumble, creating a shaft going deeper in order to escape the cave in from above. Colin stopped when he heard the rumble of the falling debris starting to subside. Then he began to wonder if he had actually escaped being crushed by the collapsing building. Or was his death simply postponed?

I'm still alive, he thought. *But for how long?* He felt along the floor, touching loose dirt and rocks. *It's too dark in here. I need light.* Colin raised his right hand and created a small electric arc between his fingers. This produced a light that was bright enough for him to see his surroundings. He was on his knees in a small grotto, surrounded by huge masses of broken masonry and metal girders. Dust began to drop down from the ceiling. Along with rocks dropping down around him. He heard a loud creaking sound. *How long is that going to hold up? I've got to get out of here.*

Kelly was laying on his back at Colin's right. Colin crawled over to him to see if he was still alive. Colin was apprehensive about checking Kelly's condition, fearing that he was as dead as he appeared. Then Colin worked up the nerve to grab Kelly's shoulder and give him a strong shake. To his great relief, Kelly moaned.

Thank God he's not dead, thought Colin. He shook Kelly again. "Kelly. Kelly, wake up."

Kelly moaned again. He moved his head. Colin shook him again.

"Kelly. Kelly, come on. Get up."

Kelly moaned again and opened his eyes. He raised his hand and rubbed his brow. He gasped for air.

"How are you feeling?" Colin asked.

"Bad. My head hurts," Kelly told Colin. He slowly sat up, then looked at his surroundings. "What happened? Are we underground?"

"Deevor dumped a building on us," Colin explained. "You slept through the whole thing. I did this to try to save our asses."

Colin again heard the creaking sound from above.

"I don't like the sound of that," said Kelly. "Is this place stable?"

Colin gazed up to the ceiling with its jumble of rocks and girders. "I don't know. But we're not going to stay here long enough to find out."

"Where's Diane?" asked Kelly.

Diane, Colin thought. "I have no idea where she is. I don't even know if she's alive or not." Colin did not want to accept the notion that Diane might be dead. Until he actually saw her lifeless body, he was still clinging to hope. "If we survived, then there's a chance that she might be alive too." Colin called out to her. "Diane!" He waited for a moment, then shouted again. "Diane!"

Colin stopped when he again heard the creaking sound above his head. Then he heard a response in the form of Diane's faint voice. It was a welcome sound. "Colin!"

"Diane! Where are you?"

"I'm over here. I'm coming your way. Stay where you are."

"There are not too many places I can go to right now," Colin's sarcastic reply.

Colin turned to his right when he heard metal grinding. Then a faint boom as if a heavy object had been dropped. Then more grinding metal. Colin was forced to glance up to the ceiling as he heard the creaking sound. More small rocks and dust came raining down. He looked back to his right and saw one of the huge fallen metal girders moving forward. Then it began to rise, revealing Diane kneeling under it. With one hand underneath the girder, she slowly stood upright while lifting it away. Colin smiled when he saw Diane. He even had to force himself to supress a laugh. He looked down at Kelly, who was also smiling at Diane's appearance. Her clothes, face, and hair were marred by dust. There was a bleeding cut running down her right cheek, but beyond that she was alive and well.

Diane pushed the girder aside and carefully set it down. Then she walked over to Colin and Kelly. She also smiled. "Guys. You're both alive."

"Just barely," replied Colin. "I'm glad you made it."

Diane looked around at the small shaft that they were in. "So, I'm taking that this is all you? I was out for a minute. Then when I came too, the ceiling of this building was coming down on me and then the floor started caving in."

The creaking up above was now louder. Colin looked up and saw that a girder and a huge mass of stone began to fall on top of him. Colin panicked. "Look out!"

Colin cringed as the two huge masses were falling. Kelly screamed. Diane rushed forward, putting herself underneath the girder and the stone, then holding up her hands to prevent them from falling. Dust and smaller rocks rained down around her, but for now the larger debris was held back.

Diane looked down at Colin and Kelly as they were both still cowering. "You big babies."

Colin stood up. "Thanks. But now we've got to get out of here."

"Yeah," said Kelly as he stood. "And we all know what's waiting for us up above."

Diane nodded. "Yeah. About that. Is it just me or did we get our asses kicked up there? I'm not too thrilled about that."

"Happens to the best of us," Colin jabbed. "But yeah, we pretty much got our asses kicked. Once we get out of here and she finds out we're still alive, she'll hunt us down. So, we've got no choice but to finish this. One way or the other. We took her down once."

Kelly agreed. "Yeah, but that was different. We

fought her in that temple of mirrors and her energy absorbing powers were cut off. We got lucky."

"Her powers were cut off because the temple couldn't take on any more energy that she was transferring," Colin replied. "That was her one weakness. There has to be a way that we can still use that."

"How?" Diane asked.

Colin explained, "Think about it. We're light years in a whole different quadrant, but she still has the ability to absorb our energy-based attacks. We hit her with enough power to reduce any human to ashes in a second, but she took it and was still standing. That means she must still be transmitting all that power. I'm thinking that she's doing so by some kind of subspace or hyperspace means. From what we've seen, the Gatherers are big on hyperspace tech. So, there has to be some way that we can block it."

"Makes sense," replied Kelly. "She's probably connected to some kind of hyperspace corridor or conduit."

"A hyperspace corridor?" Diane said. "Then maybe Kelly can use one of his energy deflecting shields to try and block it."

"My thoughts exactly," Colin told Diane. "So, what about it. Can you create a shield to block these energy transmissions?"

Kelly hesitated to ponder the possibility. "I probably could, but it would be tricky. It would probably take me a few hours to work out the right configuration between normal and hyperspace."

Given their situation, Colin had dire news for Kelly. "You've got about a half hour. Depending on how long it takes for us to dig our way out of here."

"Are you insane?" Kelly yelled out.

"You want to stay down here and practice?" Colin shouted back.

"I'm not standing here holding this ceiling up all day," Diane told them both.

"Then it's settled," Colin's stern answer. "Let's not waste any more time." Colin looked up at the unstable ceiling, then to Diane. "That passage where you came from. Was it stable?"

"I think so. Nothing the size of a car was falling on my head."

"Then that might be out best way out," Colin told her. "Let's get moving."

Colin and Kelly made their way to the passage that Diane emerged from. After they both passed, Diane carefully lowered the girder and the rock to the ground to try and avoid a bigger cave in with the rest of the debris from above. She quickly pulled herself away, allowing them both to drop to the ground. Colin crawled through the passage and entered a small chamber that was compacted by a cluster of large metal beams, girders, and huge fragments of stone. He was forced to remain kneeling as he looked up at the debris that were just five feet over his head. More beams and girders holding up masses of stone.

Diane and Kelly crawled over to join him as he examined the debris above. "All this looks pretty stable," he told them. "We should be able to dig ourselves out from here."

Colin reached up and touched one of the girders. Manipulating its electrically conductive form, he caused the girder to slowly bend and twist. Then it bent over to the right, away from a huge stone that it was supporting along with two other girders. Colin climbed up over several large fallen rocks to reach a second girder that was running diagonally. With the touch of his hand, Colin caused this girder to bend away from the rock. The third remaining girder was stable enough to support the stone. Colin climbed higher along the girders and rocks. Diane and Kelly also began to climb and stayed close to him. Colin used his power to easily move away any blocking girders while Diane held up and pushed aside any heavy debris that was blocking their way. Being cautious of causing any cave ins, their progression was slow but effective. During their climb, Colin wondered if he, Diane, and Kelly would be able to survive a second encounter with Deevor. They were lucky to have survived the first fight. He knew that their next battle would determine who walks away alive.

Colin lost track of how long it was taking for him, Diane, and Kelly to climb up out of the shaft. But then he used his power to disintegrate the last fallen girder while Diane shoved aside the last huge mass of stone. He felt like cheering when the cool, fresh air from the opening above blew into his face. Colin climbed up over a girder and emerged out into the open. Night had fallen. But the city was lit with the flames from countless burning buildings. *Deevor's handiwork*, he concluded. He gazed down and saw that he was standing on top of a mound of debris from the fallen building. He looked back at the glow of the fires. He was dreading what was coming next. But it was unavoidable. *Ok. We're out. Now comes the really hard part.*

Diane and Kelly joined him on the surface. Colin brushed the dust off his clothes and was the first to begin climbing down from the mound of debris. Once reaching the street Colin hesitated, wondering which direction they should take to try and find Deevor. The sudden sound of a loud explosion from the right gave him a blaring clue as to her current location.

Colin began walking down the street. "Kelly, how's that shield of yours coming?"

Colin turned his head to take a glance at Kelly. While walking, he was holding out his hands with a small, square panel of blue energy hovering between them. The panel was shifting from blue to black, then to a transparent state. "I'm working on it," said Kelly.

"So how are we going to do this, Sarge?" Diane asked Colin. "Fast and hard? Guns blazing?"

"The last time we did guns blazing, it blew up un our faces," came Colin's dour answer. "This time we have a better plan. We'll spread out. I'll take her on. Kelly will get behind her and put his shielding to work. Diane, you stay off to the side and take her on when you can get a good opening. But our plan is depending on whether Kelly's shield can work. How's it coming, Kelly?"

"The hell if I know. I can make this thing into different modulations. But I won't know if it's going to work until we test it under fire."

"We'll know soon enough," Colin grimly predicted.

They continued heading down the street, passing by overturned and mangled vehicles, and heavily damaged buildings. Many of which were on fire. As they were traveling, they heard three more explosions going off somewhere in the distance. By Colin's estimate, they continued traveling for a quarter of a mile. Two more explosions went off. These were louder than the previous blasts. They continued heading down the street for another quarter mile. The explosions were becoming much louder and more frequent. Colin knew that their quarry was dangerously close.

As they were proceeding down the street, they came to the next intersection and heard a loud explosion going off around the corner just a few yards away. Colin stopped. "This is it," he told Diane and Kelly. "Let's separate. I'll head down the street and get her attention. Kelly, you make your way behind her and get ready with your shielding. Diane, go around the next block and approach her from the side."

Colin was feeling nervous as he began to walk down the street and headed left at the intersection. Diane ran forward at the intersection while Kelly doubled back to try and approach Deevor from behind. Colin was walking down a street where all the buildings on both sides were demolished. It was obvious that Deevor was intent on continuing to destroy the city whether he, Diane, and Kelly were dead or alive. *This stops tonight,* he told himself.

Colin passed around a huge mound of rubble that was blocking the right half of the street. Just a few feet up ahead he saw his target, Deevor, standing with her back turned to him while sending a blast of energy from her hands to destroy a group of cars on the street in front of her. With a sucession of four powerful explosions, the vehicles were all transformed into burning wreckages. Colin's nervousness was now increasing to a point where his stomach was churning. He was again about to face the homicidal creature that he was powerless against. He looked about to spot any signs of Diane and Kelly. Neither of them was in sight, but still, he hoped that they were ready for their last battle with Deevor.

Colin took a deep breath and then bellowed out to Deevor, "Hey bitch! We're not done yet!"

Deevor turned to face Colin. The moment she saw him her eyes opened wide. Her mouth gaped open as well. "What?" she cried out. "You're still alive?"

"I guess you're slipping," Colin's taunt. "It's going to take more than dropping a few bricks on our heads to put us down for good."

Deevor gnashed her teeth in rage. "Where's the other two? Lytton and that bitch, Christy?"

Colin grinned. Evidently his sudden unexpected appearance left Deevor unsettled. "Don't worry about them. Just worry about me."

Looking past Deevor, Colin saw Kelly down the street. He was quietly moving up behind her. Colin was hoping that Deevor would not notice Kelly, also hoping that Kelly was prepared to put their plan into motion despite him having no time to properly prepare for his part.

Deevor began to walk towards Colin. Her hands began to take on a red glow. "If I didn't finish the job with you the first time, then I'll enjoy killing you again, McKenzie! And this time you won't come back!"

"Threats don't impress me," Colin shouted back at Deevor. His hands also began to glow. "Not unless you've got some real power to back it up."

Colin raised his hands at Deevor and discharged a massive bolt of energy to her. A bright white flash and a burst of sparks exploded against Deevor's body when she was hit by Colin's attack. At the same time, Kelly dashed closer to Deevor and stopped just a few feet behind her. He raised his hands and a panel of his red reflecting energy appeared behind her. Deevor stopped walking as Colin continued bombarding her with his power. Kelly's energy shield wall changed from a solid red color to a transparent state. Colin did not let up with his attack on Deevor, who still seemed to be absorbing every bit of it. Her entire body was now taking on a white glow. Colin was determined to keep up with his attack. Deevor was unaware of Kelly's shield wall behind her. As she stood there soaking in Colin's electrical energy attack, Kelly, with his hands still extended, caused his shield wall to change from a bright transparent red to a dark color. Then a large shower of sparks shot out from the shield wall. A white stream of energy jumped out from it and penetrated Deevor's back. Colin halted his attack and watched Deevor stagger forward after she absorbed this dose of energy from behind.

"That's it," he told himself. "We got her."

Deevor turned and glanced back at Kelly. Then she turned back to face Colin. "What the hell happened?" she exclaimed. "What was that?"

"That was your luck running out," Colin told her with a wide grin on his face. He sent a second massive blast of energy to Deevor. She again absorbed Colin's attack, and for the second time the charge was reflected from Kelly's transparent shield wall and directed back to her. She staggered forward, then spun around to threaten Kelly.

"You! This is your doing! I'll kill you!"

Before Deevor had the chance to make a move against Kelly, Colin pointed his hand to a blue car that was parked at his right across the street. The car's heavy fusion powered engine block was an easy object for Colin to manipulate. The entire engine block tore itself out of the car and went soaring towards Deevor. It slammed into Deevor's back and knocked her to the ground. With Deevor down, Colin took the opportunity to hit her with another powerful bolt of energy. A bright white flash and an explosion of sparks exploded over Deevor. Colin continued his attack and watched as streams of his energy shot out from Kelly's shield wall and went back to her.

Deevor struggled to rise to her feet. Her skin was radiating a bright white glow. While she was absorbing Colin's attack, he learned that she was still far from helpless. She spun around and fired a crimson bolt of energy from her hand at Colin. Closely watching her movements, Colin was able to duck down in time to avoid the blast. Even though her energy bolt missed him, Colin could still feel the searing heat of its power as it burned overhead. Deevor turned back to direct her rage upon Kelly. She lunged at him, but he jumped back while quickly shifting his shield wall from its transparent state to its normal solid blue form. Deevor slammed headlong into the wall, cut off from reaching Kelly. She screamed out in a rage and sent three swift punches to the wall, tearing gaping holes through it.

While Deevor was assaulting Kelly's shield wall, Colin looked over to his right and saw Diane, holding a large metal beam while sprinting towards her. While Deevor was concentrating on pounding Kelly's shield wall, Diane was able to approach her without being seen and swing the beam down on her head. Deevor dropped to one knee. Diane quickly raised the beam and clubbed Deevor over the head a second time. In spite of Diane's powerful attack, Deevor was still able to stand back up and raise her forearm to block Diane's next swing. The beam slammed down on Deevor's forearm and broke in half. Deevor quickly followed up by throwing a punch towards Diane's head. Diane's reflexes were acting on a hair trigger. She brought up the metal beam to block Deevor's punch. Diane then retaliated by returning a punch to Deevor's face. She pressed her attack by swinging the beam and striking Deevor on the left side of her face. She swung again, hitting her on the right side, then the left. Deevor growled and then sent a swift kick to Diane's chest. Diane dropped the metal beam and flew back through the air from the force of Deevor's kick. She traveled for several feet before bouncing off the ground and then rolling across the pavement.

Great. Diane is down again, Colin's thought. Taking this opportunity to strike while Deevor was distracted, Colin summoned up enough power to hit Deevor with a lightning bolt that was twice as massive than his previous ones. He glanced behind Deevor. Behind her, Kelly shifted his shield wall back to its transparent, dark red form. Deevor vanished from Colin's view as she was shrouded by the bright white flash and explosion of sparks from Colin's attack. The moment after she absorbed the energy that Colin was feeding her, it was reflected back onto her by Kelly's shield wall. The result was an even bigger flash and explosion than before. Colin disengaged his attack in order to see the results. And he was also starting to tire. It was starting to get difficult for him to summon and maintain this level of power. He needed a much-deserved rest but was determined to try and see the battle through now that they finally had Deevor on the ropes.

When the flash and sparks from Colin's attack subsided, Deevor was down on her knees. Her skin was still emitting the bright glow from the energy that she had absorbed. She struggled to stand to her feet. Then she staggered forward. Standing on unsteady legs, she turned to face Kelly. That was when Colin caught sight of the the strange, red, pulsating light running down along her back. It raised his curiosity. It was not like the glow that was radiating from the rest of her body. Colin quickly used another aspect of his power. The ability to telepathically read into any device that contains an electrical charge. In his mind he could see a long, thin metallic device running down along Deevor's back. With several thin filaments at its sides it resembled a centipede. It was pulsating with an alien power. A power that was connected to Deevor herself. It was easy enough for Colin to deduce the function of this alien device.

This is it, Colin's thoughts. *This the source of her energy absorbing power.* Colin looked over at Diane, who was just getting back to her feet. He pointed at Deevor and cried out, "I've seen the source of her power. Its some kind of device in her back. We take it out and she's finished."

"Is that all?" Diane cried back. She turned around and rushed over to a dark pickup truck that was parked behind her. With a swift, easy motion she picked the truck over her head and hurled it through the air at

Deevor. Deevor reacted by raising her hand and firing a bolt of crimson energy that caused the truck to explode in midair. Diane quickly picked up a small white car and threw it at Deevor, who dealt with it the same way as the first vehicle, firing a bolt of energy that destroyed it before it had the chance to reach her. Colin watched Diane sprint back down the street behind a building. Moments later, he was stunned at the sight of a fire engine swiftly floating a few feet above the ground. Taking a closer look, he saw that Diane was on the rear end of the massive vehicle, carrying it over her head while running towards Deevor.

"Where the hell did you get that?" Colin shouted to Diane. Again, Colin had to ask himself the question, *How powerful is Diane?*

Diane was running at full force at Deevor with the intention of using the fire engine as a battering ram. Deevor, spotting Diane and her huge weapon, was intent on stopping her. She raised a hand and fired a bolt of energy that exploded once it hit the front of the fire engine. Its entire front half was blown apart and set ablaze. But Diane did not break her stride. She smashed the flaming front end of the fire engine down on Deevor. Deevor raised her hands to try to hold back the vehicle but found herself being pushed back by Diane's strength. Diane used the fire engine to steadily push Deevor back for several feet. It churned up large chunks of the pavement along the way.

When the fire engine stopped scraping against the ground, Diane continued moving forward. She leaped on top of the fire engine and ran on top of it towards its flaming end. Undaunted, she ran through the flames and then jumped down on top of a surprised Deevor. Diane forced Deevor to the ground and immediately began pummeling her face with left and right fists. Deevor took six punches before she was able to retaliate by pushing Diane off her. Diane went flying halfway across the street but landed on her feet and went charging back towards Deevor. As Deevor stood up, she was met by Diane's fist ramming into her chest. The force of the punch sent her flying across the street. Her body bounced off the pavement and stopped when she slammed into the side of a white car, creating a huge dent on its side and causing its windows to explode. Deevor quickly rose to her feet but was again met by the charging Diane. Diane sent a punch to Deevor's face, causing her head to jerk back. Diane followed up her punch with a roundhouse kick to Deevor's stomach. Deevor took a step back and then threw a punch at Diane, who easily blocked it with her forearm. Diane gave Deevor another punch to her face, then leaped into the air to deliver a spinning kick to her head. Deevor staggered backwards, then spun around and dropped to her face.

Now that Deevor was down, Diane rushed over to her and thrust her fist down onto her back. Diane's fist penetrated the back of Deevor's armor. Deevor let out a piercing scream that made even Colin cringe. Diane then quickly pulled out a metallic object from Deevor's back, resembling a centipede with its long shape and thin filaments running along its sides. It was pulsating with a red glow. Diane also screamed and quickly dropped the device. Colin rushed in closer as Diane grasped her right hand that was covered with severe burns. Meanwhile, Deevor continued screaming in agony. She struggled to get back to her feet. She grasped the sides of her head and started to stagger about while bellowing a mad rant.

"No! What have you done? What have you done? You cut me off! I'm cut off! Kimdrack! I can't feel him! He's gone! No!"

Colin was not concerned about Deevor's frantic state of mind. He was worried about Diane's condition. She was still grasping her burned hand after touching the energized alien device. "Diane! Are you ok?" he called out to her.

Diane stood, staring at her hand. She began to flex her fingers while the burned skin began to peel away and reveal fresh, unblemished skin. "Give me a minute," she called back to Colin. She flexed her fingers again, then formed a fist, which she used to punch Deevor in her back. Deevor went sailing through the air. Her body ripped through and shredded the top of the white car that she previously crashed into. She landed several yards down the street, bouncing off the pavement and then rolling to a stop. Diane looked over to Colin. "I'm good."

In the heat of the battle, Colin forgot about Diane's ability to rapidly heal herself. That fact came as a relief. He turned his attention from Diane to the alien device that was laying on the ground in front of her. It was still pulsating with a red glow of energy. Colin extended his hand. His power to seize control over metallic objects easily worked on the device. In seconds, the device began to twist and contort, then its glow began to fade as it crumbled into a pile of metal shards.

Colin was not surprised to see that Deevor was still in her delirious state of mind as she struggled to rise to her knees. Then staggering on unsteady feet, she returned to the area, reaching out her hands to the destroyed device. "No! No! What have you done? You've destroyed it! You've destroyed everything!"

"Not everything!" Colin yelled at Deevor. He pointed to her and looked to Kelly, who was standing in the distance behind Deevor. "Get her!"

On Colin's command, Kelly raised his hands and sent a huge blast of flame down upon her. At the same time, Colin hit Deevor with a massive lightning-like bolt of electrical power. Deevor was engulfed by an explosion of fire, sparks and a bright white flash. During the twin assault, Colin could hear Deevor's anguished voice crying out. "Too much! Too much! Stop!"

Colin and Kelly had no intention of stopping their attack. They continued pouring their energy at Deevor. Colin stopped his lightning attack and took a step back as he created a glowing blue orb of energy. The orb began to rapidly grow until it was half the size of an automobile. Kelly, watching Colin's new tactic, followed suit by creating his own huge ball of blazing red energy. Colin launched his electrical energy ball at Deevor while Kelly sent his fireball flying. The two simultaneous attacks striking Deevor caused a powerful explosion. Colin instinctively turned his head away and raised his hands up to his face to defend himself from the blast.

The explosion's aftermath left a large flaming hole in the middle of the street. Colin was amazed to see Deevor kneeling in the middle of the fire. She slowly rose up to her feet and began to stagger out of the hole. *She still won't go down,* he thought. *What's it going to take to stop her for good?*

When Deevor stepped out from the flames, Colin received a shock when she revealed her new condition. Her skin was glowing brighter than before because of the massive amount of power that she absorbed. Her hair was now totally burned away. Through her unearthly glow, Colin saw that the skin of her face had now melted down to her skull. Her right eye had melted out of its socket. Even her breast plate armor was showing damage. It was now scorched black and torn. With a jerking movement, Deevor raised her hand and pointed at Colin. She shouted out in a slow, quivering voice, "You…haven't…won yet…McKenzie. I…can…still…see you…all…burn."

Deevor held her hands out at her sides. A red globe of energy began to form at her right hand, while a globe of energy formed at her left. Both globes of energy began to grow until they were as large as Deevor herself. Colin had felt the devastating effects of this attack before. And seeing the size of these two energy globes, he feared how destructive the effects would be when those two opposing energy charges touched together.

Colin considered hitting Deevor with an electrical bolt to try and force her to drop her two energy charges. Then Diane bolted towards Deevor and grabbed her wrists to prevent her from bringing her hands, and the energy charges, together. Deevor struggled to move her arms but was held back by Diane's strength. The test of strength lasted for several seconds. Deevor could not overcome Diane's power. But Colin noticed that Diane was beginning to suffer for her efforts. Being so close to the heat from Deevor's energized body was causing Diane's hair and clothes to smolder. Colin was fearing that at any moment Diane would burst into flames if she kept this up.

"Diane! Back off," Colin shouted at her.

Colin was not sure if Diane had heard him. She continued holding Deevor back while her hair and clothers were still smoldering. Her hands were also starting to burn. Then she finally decided to back off. "Screw this," she shouted. She released her hold on Deevor's left hand, At the same time, she managed to rip Deevor's right arm away from her body with a quick pull. Deevor howled out in agony. Her two energy charges from both her hands faded away. Deevor, still crying out in pain, staggered backward and then dropped down to her knees.

Colin now felt that after suffering this devastating damage, Deevor was finished. "It's over. You're done," he told her.

Holding her head down, Deevor was silent for a

moment. Then she raised her head and gave Colin her answer. "You...haven't...won anything, McKenzie. I still...have enough...power...to blow this entire...city...apart. Your...power. You...hit me with any...more...then I will turn this city...into an...inferno. And...it...will be your...fault."

"She has a point," Diane told Colin. "She already looks like she's going to blow. What are we going to do now?"

Colin looked at Deevor. Then he looked up to the night sky above the tops of the city's buildings. Then he glanced over at Diane. "We're going to do what we came here for. To put her name up in lights."

Colin pointed his hand to the ground and sent a large burst of energy into the pavement. Maintaining his mental control over his energy, he directed it to surge under the pavement and over to Deevor. Deevor was caught by a massive bolt of energy that lifted her body up into the air. Colin listened to her screaming for a final time as she was swiftly rose into the air. Establishing a telepathic link through his electrical power, Colin was able to follow Deevor's flight in his mind's eye. She was still screaming as Colin's energy bolt lifted her above the rooftops of the buildings. She continued flying upward for half a mile above the city before Colin mentally witnessed her glowing body finally exploding. The blast lit up the night sky with an expanding cloud of fire. Colin, Diane, and Kelly watched the fire spreading out like a brief sunrise. Then, after several minutes, it began to fade out, and with it a being who has caused countless death and destruction in her lifetime. Deevor the destroyer had finally met her end.

CHAPTER
SEVENTEEN

Sitting at the desk in their small office at C.I.D headquarters on the planet Maseklos Prime, Colin felt refreshed after getting some much needed sleep and a change into some fresh pair of blue jeans, brand new white sneakers, and a black T-shirt. Diane, sitting on the desk at his right, chose an attire with a more athletic look. Dark blue shorts with a matching tank top and sneakers. Leaning against the wall at Colin's left, Kelly decided to show up wearing his more casual look. A pair of cut off blue jean shorts, a green shirt, and flip flop sandals. Gaylie, standing next to Kelly, was still dressed in her black resistance uniform. After taking a night of well-deserved rest, they were all summoned here by Captain Melony Carter to discuss the current situation, as well as their plans for the future.

Wearing a black dress and high heel shoes, Melony entered the office and greeted Colin and the others with a smile. "Guys, it's great to see you all still alive and well. Thanks for coming. How are you all feeling?"

Colin grinned. "Much better after getting a good, long night's sleep and a hot breakfast."

Diane nodded in agreement with Colin. "We went through hell. After getting a rest, I'm good to go."

"Please tell me that you're not sending us out on another mission," Kelly whined.

Melony laughed. "In a way, yes. We are sending you guys off. It's a very special mission. It's called a two-week vacation."

A broad smile formed on Colin's face when he heard that news. Diane and Kelly's faces also brightened with smiles.

"A vacation? Now you're talking," Diane cheerfully exclaimed. "We can sure use one after everything that we've been through."

"I fully agree," said Melony. "Sending you guys on vacation is the least we can do. And this comes from the top. President Drennen herself."

"I hate to spoil the cheery mood, but how bad was the damage?" Colin asked Melony.

Melony's smile faded. "It was pretty extensive. Half of Brookhaven has been destroyed. The casualty rate is in the hundreds and counting. It could have been worse if we hadn't ordered an evacuation of the other cities that Deevor destroyed. I hope that these Gatherers you mentioned don't have any more monsters like her."

Colin cringed at that thought. "At this point, we really don't know what the Gatherers are capable of. They're using advanced alien technology. Most of what they do revolves around freeing their leader, Kimdrack, from his exile. Maybe with the loss of Deevor, they'll be shut down for good."

"Everything that you've told us, along with Captain Kozak's report, puts our whole exploratory mission into a different situation," Melony explained. "We sent out task force five to try to make human contact in order to get help for our war effort. Now after learning about the situation with Gaylie's people, we seem to have stumbled into a whole new war."

"I imagine that the war back on Sidra might go a little easier for the resistance now that the Tritians are reportedly turning against the Guydruns," Colin told Melony.

"Even so, President Drennen has ordered task force five to remain on Sidra to give the people there some help against the invading force," Melony told the group. "And I also hear that she's planning to send a second task force to bolster the existing force."

Gaylie smiled. "That's wonderful news. My parents were thrilled to have your people there. They felt that your support would give us a better chance to win the war, but this is better than any of us hoped. Thank you."

"We'll give your people whatever help we can," Melony assured Gaylie, "but it seems that the Guydruns and Tritians aren't the only threat that we have to be concerned with back in your quadrant. There's still the matter of the Brelac presense there. I'd like to know what they were doing there with these Tritians."

"Can't be anything good," Kelly's grim comment.

Colin agreed. "Yeah. Were they there on a mission of their own or just keeping the Protectorate's activities under surveillance? It's a big mystery."

Melony sighed. "Yes. A mystery. But one that we can't bother losing sleep over. Right now, your priority is to relax and enjoy yourselves for the next two weeks. No fighting. No blowing things up. And Gaylie is welcome to stay until the next task force ships out to her home quadrant." Melony turned and prepared to walk out of the office. Then she stopped and turned back. "And thanks for not screwing up."

If you only knew, was Colin's mental reply to Melony.

*****

Colin was getting an exhilarating feeling as he was riding along on a motorcycle at high speed along the long country road. Diane, sitting behind him, wrapped her arms tightly around him in order to hang on during the ride. At Colin's right, Kelly was riding a motorcycle of his own, with Gaylie holding on as his passenger. They were going against each other in a race away from the war and any threats that might be conspiring in the shadows. Their only interest was spending the next two weeks living as normal humans would. Engaging in fun, laughter, and the magic of their unique friendship.